FINGER LICKIN' FIFTEEN

JANET EVANOVICH

St. Martin's Paperbacks

This is a work of fiction. All of the characters, organizations, and events portrayed in this novel are either products of the author's imagination or are used fictitiously.

FINGER LICKIN' FIFTEEN

Copyright © 2009 by Evanovich, Inc.
Excerpt from *Sizzling Sixteen* copyright © 2010 by Evanovich, Inc.

For information address St. Martin's Press, 175 Fifth Avenue, New York, NY 10010.

Library of Congress Catalog Card Number: 2009018325

ISBN: 978-0-312-38329-9

Printed in the United States of America

St. Martin's Press hardcover edition / June 2009
St. Martin's Paperbacks edition / July 2010

St. Martin's Paperbacks are published by St. Martin's Press, 175 Fifth Avenue, New York, NY 10010

10 9 8 7 6 5 4 3 2

This book is dedicated to Lauren Tsai.

Thanks to Ann and Chris Duffy

for suggesting the title for this book.

ONE

When I was a kid, I was afraid of spiders and vegetables. As an adult, I've eliminated vegetables from my fright-o-meter, but I've added a whole bunch of other stuff. Homicidal maniacs, serial rapists, cellulite, Joe Morelli's Grandma Bella, rabid bats, and any form of organized exercise.

My name is Stephanie Plum, and I work as a bond enforcement officer for Vincent Plum Bail Bonds. It's not a great job, but it allows me to avoid organized exercise, and I hardly ever encounter rabid bats. The remaining fright-o-meter items lurk in the dark shadows of my daily life. Fortunately, there are also good things in those shadows. Joe Morelli without his Grandma Bella, fellow bounty hunter Ranger without his clothes, my crazy family, my hamster, Rex . . . and Lula. Lula actually fits somewhere between the rabid bats and the good stuff. She's a former 'ho, now working as the office file clerk and apprentice bounty hunter. Lula's got a plus-size personality and body, and a petite-size wardrobe. She's got brown skin, blond hair, and last week she had tiny rhinestones pasted onto her eyelids.

It was Monday morning. Connie, the office manager, and I were in the bonds office enjoying our morning coffee, and Lula slid her red Firebird to a stop at the curb. We watched Lula through the big plate-glass window in the front of the small office, and we did a joint grimace. Lula was in a state. She lurched out of the Firebird, beeped it locked, and burst into the office, her eyes wild, rolling around in their sockets, her hands waving in the air.

"I saw it all," she said. "It was terrible. It was horrible. I couldn't believe it was happening. And right in front of me." She looked around. "What do we got? Do we got doughnuts? 'Cause I need a doughnut. I need a whole bag. And maybe I need one of them breakfast sandwiches with the egg and cheese and bacon and grease. I got a big grease craving."

I knew it would be a huge mistake to ask Lula what she'd seen, but I couldn't stop myself.

"What was terrible and horrible?" I asked.

Connie leaned forward, elbows on her desk, already knowing the telling of the story would be a car crash. Connie is a couple years older than me, and while my heritage is half Hungarian and half Italian, Connie is Italian through and through. Her hair is jet black, her lipstick is fire-engine red, her body is *va-va-voom*.

Lula paced in front of Connie's desk. "First off, I hardly had time for anything this morning. I had a big date last night, and by the time I booted his butt out of my bed, I already missed a lot of my beauty sleep. Anyways, I got up late, and then I couldn't decide what to wear. One day it's hot out and next thing it's cold. And then I had to decide if I needed to wear shoes that kicked ass or were good for ass kicking, on account of there's a difference, you know."

"Jeez Louise," Connie said. "Could you get to it?"

"The point bein' I was late," Lula said. "I was tryin' to put makeup on and drive, and I missed a turn, and before I knew it I was someplace I didn't want to be. So I pulled over to look around and figure things out, and when I did that my makeup case rolled off the seat next to me, and everything went all over the floor. So I was bent over to get my makeup, and I guess it looked like there was no one in the car, because when I came back up there were two big hairy morons standing right in front of my Firebird, and they were removing a head from some guy's body."

"Excuse me?"

"This one moron had a giant meat cleaver. And the other moron had a hold of this man in a suit. And *whack*! No head. The head popped off its neck and bounced down the street."

"And then what happened?" Connie said.

"Then they saw me," Lula said. "They looked real surprised. And I know *I* looked real surprised. And then I laid down about two feet of rubber and took off."

"Do you know who they were?"

"No."

"Did you know the guy in the suit?"

"No, but it was a real nice suit. And he had a nice striped tie, too."

"Did you go to the police?" Connie asked.

"No. I came straight here. It's not like the police were gonna put Humpty Dumpty back together again," Lula said. "Didn't seem like there was a big rush, and I needed a doughnut. Holy cow. Holy shit. I really need a doughnut."

"You need to call the police," Connie told Lula.

"I hate the police. They give me the willies. Except for Stephanie's Morelli. He's a hottie."

Joe Morelli is a Trenton plainclothes cop, and Lula is right about Morelli being a hottie, but Lula is wrong about Morelli belonging to me. Morelli and I have had an off-and-on relationship for as long as I can remember, and we are currently off. Two weeks ago, we had a disagreement over peanut butter that turned into a disagreement over everything under the sun, and we haven't seen each other since.

Connie dialed into the police band, and we listened for a couple minutes to see if we could pick up anything to do with decapitation.

"Where did this happen?" Connie asked.

"The three hundred block of Ramsey Street. It was right in front of the Sunshine Hotel."

The Sunshine Hotel is a roach farm that rents rooms by the hour. No one coming or going from the Sunshine Hotel would ever report anything to anyone.

"I seen lots of stuff," Lula said, "but this was disgustin'. Blood shot out like one of them oil gushers. And when the head hit the ground, I swear the eyes were lookin' at me. I guess I need to tell the police, but I only want Morelli." Lula fixed on me. "You gotta call Morelli."

"No way. I'm not talking to him. *You* can call him."

"I don't know him like you know him."

"I don't know him that way anymore. I'm done with him. He's a jerk."

"All men are jerks," Lula said. "That don't mean they aren't good for some things. And Morelli's a *hot* jerk. He could be a movie star or a underwear model if he wasn't a cop. He got all that wavy black hair and dreamy brown bedroom eyes. He's kind of puny compared to some men I know, but he's hot all the same."

Morelli was actually six foot tall and solid muscle, but Lula used to be engaged to a guy who was a cross between an Army tank and Sasquatch, so I suppose by comparison Morelli might measure up short.

"I'll call Morelli," Connie said. "He's a cop, for crying out loud. You don't need a complicated relationship to call a cop."

I was halfway to the door. "I'm leaving. Things to do. And I don't want to see Morelli."

"Oh no," Lula said. "You get your boney ass back here. We're in this together. Through thick and through thin."

"Since when?"

"Since now. And before that, too. Remember when I rescued you from that big snake in the mobile home? And what about when we were lost in the Pine Barrens?"

"You ran screaming like a little girl when you *thought* you saw the snake. And Ranger found us in the Pine Barrens."

"Yeah, but if he hadn't found us, I would have got us out."

"You were up to your armpits in a cranberry bog."

"I don't never want to see another cranberry, neither," Lula said.

Twenty minutes later, Morelli sauntered in to the bonds office. He was dressed in jeans and running shoes, a blue button-down shirt that was open at the neck, and a navy blazer. He looked entirely edible and a little wary.

"What's up?" Morelli asked, eyes on me.

Okay, so I was no longer interested in Morelli. At least I was pretty sure I wasn't interested. Still,

I was wishing I'd spent more time on my hair and makeup this morning, so he'd feel really rotten about what he was missing. I have naturally curly shoulder-length brown hair that was currently pulled back into a ponytail. I have blue eyes that look a lot better when they have a swipe of liner and mascara, an okay mouth that so far hasn't needed artificial plumping, and a little nose that I consider my best feature. Morelli always thought my best feature was located considerably lower on my body.

"It was horrible! It was terrible!" Lula said. "I almost fainted."

Morelli shifted his attention to Lula. He didn't say anything, but he looked over at her and raised his eyebrows a little.

"I never saw nothin' like it," Lula told him. "One minute, I was having a day like any other, and then *whack* and this guy didn't have no head. And blood came out of him like he was a fountain. And when his head hit the ground, his eyes were lookin' at me. And I think the head might have smiled at me, too, but I'm not sure of that."

Morelli was back on his heels, thumbs hooked into his jeans pockets. "Is this for real?"

"Hell yeah," Lula said. "Who makes up shit like that? Don't I look traumatized? I'm practically turned white. I think my hand might even be shaking. Look at my hand. Is it shaking?"

Morelli's eyes cut back to me. "Were you with her?"

"Nope."

"Did anyone call 911?"

"Nope."

Lula was hands on hips, starting to look pissed. "We called *you*," she said to Morelli.

Morelli did a fast office scan. "You don't have the head here, do you?"

"So far as I know, the head and everything else is still in front of the Sunshine Hotel," Lula told him. "And I'm not sure I like your attitude. I'm not sure you're takin' this seriously."

Morelli stared down at his shoe. Hard to tell if he was trying hard not to laugh or if he was getting a migraine. After a five-count, he took out his cell phone, called dispatch, and sent a uniform to the Sunshine Hotel.

"Okay, ladies," Morelli said when he got off the phone. "Let's take a field trip."

I made a big show of looking at my watch. "Gee, I've got to run. Things to do."

"No way," Lula said. "I need someone with me in case I get faint or something."

"You'll have *him*," I said.

"He's a fine man, but he's the cop representative here, and I need someone from my posse, you see what I'm saying. I need a BFF."

"It's not gonna be me," Connie said. "Vinnie is

picking up a skip in Atlanta, and I have to run the office."

Morelli looked at me and gave his head a small shake, like he didn't believe any of this. Like I was a huge, unfathomable pain in the ass, and in fact maybe that was how he felt about women in general right now.

I understood Morelli's point of view because it was precisely my current feeling about men.

"Terrific," I said on a sigh. "Let's get on with it."

Lula and I followed Morelli in my ten-year-old Ford Escort that used to be blue. We didn't take the Escort because we liked riding in it. We took it because Lula thought she might be too overwrought to drive her Firebird, and she suspected she would need a bacon cheeseburger after visiting the scene of the crime and Morelli might not be inclined to find a drive-through for her.

There were already two cruisers angled into the curb in front of the Sunshine Hotel when Lula and I arrived. I parked, and Lula and I got out and stood next to Morelli and a couple uniforms. We all looked down at a red splotch that sprayed out over about a four-foot diameter. A couple smaller splotches trailed off the big splotch, and I assumed that was where the head had hit the pavement. I felt a wave of nausea slide through my stomach, and I started to sweat.

"This here's the spot," Lula said. "You can see it's just like I told you. There was a big gusher of blood when they whacked the head off. It was like Old Faithful going off, only it was blood. And then the head rolled down the sidewalk. It was like the head was a bowlin' ball with eyes. And the eyes were like big googly eyes kinda popping out of the head and lookin' at me. And I think I might have heard the head laughin', or maybe it was the guys who did the whackin' who were laughin'."

The uniforms all did a grimace, Morelli was impassive, and I threw up. Everyone jumped away from me, I gagged one last time and did some deep breathing.

"Sorry," I said.

"No problem," Morelli told me. "I feel like throwing up a lot on this job."

One of the uniforms brought me some paper towels and a bottle of water, and Lula stood a good distance away.

"You got lots of room for lunch now that you're empty," she yelled to me. "I could get a early start with one of them extra-crispy bird burgers they're servin' at Cluck-in-a-Bucket. Have you heard about them? They got some new secret sauce."

I wasn't interested in secret sauce. I wanted to go home and go to bed and not get up until it was a new day. I was done with this one.

"We got a couple footprints heading south," a uniform said. "One of these guys had real big feet. Looks like a size fourteen. And there's some skid marks where they dragged the body to the curb. Imagine they dumped it into a car and took off."

"You need to come downtown and give me some information," Morelli said to Lula.

"No way. Nuh-ah. I got a allergic reaction to police stations. I get irritable bowel and hives and the heebie-jeebies."

"You witnessed a murder."

"Yeah, but there's extenuating circumstances here. I got a medical condition. I got a extreme sensitivity to cops."

Morelli looked like he wanted to pull his gun out of its holster and shoot himself.

"I'll get you some cheeseburgers and a side of onion rings," he said to Lula.

Lula stood hands on hips. "You think I could be bought for some lame-ass burgers? What kinda woman you think I am?"

"I'll throw in a bucket of chicken and an ice cream cake from Carvel," Morelli said. "That's my final offer."

"Deal," Lula told him. "We goin' in your car?

On account of I'm not riding in a cop car, and I hate to say this, but Stephanie don't smell too good."

Twenty minutes later, I parked in the lot to my apartment building. My building straddles the line between Trenton proper and Trenton improper. It's a three-story utilitarian brick box filled with tenants who are struggling to make ends meet. Frequently, I have a gap between my ends, resulting in a lot of dinners mooched from my parents, who live ten minutes away in a blue-collar chunk of Trenton called The Burg.

My apartment is on the second floor and my windows look out at the parking lot. My only roommate is a hamster named Rex. I manage to keep a good supply of hamster food in my fridge and in my cupboards. People food is spotty. I own a fry pan and a pot. Perfectly adequate since I mostly eat peanut butter sandwiches. Peanut butter and banana, peanut butter and jelly, peanut butter and potato chips, peanut butter and olives, and peanut butter and marshmallow goo. So sue me, I like peanut butter. The rest of the apartment consists of dining alcove, living room with television, one bedroom, and bath.

I hustled from my car to my apartment, stripped, and jumped into the shower. I was approaching boiled lobster skin tone when I finally emerged and wrapped myself in a towel. I stepped out of the bathroom and spotted Ranger lounging in the club chair across from my bed. I gave a startled yelp and jumped back into the bathroom.

"Babe," Ranger said.

I stuck my head out and looked at him. "What are you doing here?"

"I need to talk to you."

"You could have called. Or how about ringing my doorbell?"

Ranger looked like he was thinking about smiling. His attention focused on the top of my towel and slowly moved to the bottom hem that hung a half-inch below my doodah. His brown eyes dilated black, and I took a stronger grip on my towel.

Ranger was the second biggest complication in my life, and now that Morelli was out of the picture, I supposed Ranger was elevated to numero uno. He's close to six foot, one way or the other, is Latino, with medium brown skin and dark brown hair cut short. His teeth are white and even, and he has a killer smile that is seen only on special occasions. He dresses in black, and today he was wearing a black T-shirt and black cargo pants. His given name is Carlos Manoso. His street name, Ranger, is a holdover from time spent in Special Forces. These days, he does the occasional high-risk bond enforcement job, and is the managing partner of a security firm located in a stealth building in center city.

I've seen him naked, and you can take it to the bank when I tell you he's all hard muscle and perfect in every possible way. And I mean *every* possible way.

Ranger and I have three things in common. We're the same age. We're both single. And we both were previously married for about ten seconds. That's where the common ground ends. I'm an open book with a lot of blank pages. His book is filled with life experience but written in disappearing ink. I have three locks on my front door, plus a sliding bolt, and I was sure they were all in place. Somehow, this never stops Ranger. He's a man of mysterious talents.

Ranger crooked his finger at me. "Come here."

"No way."

"Afraid?"

"Cautious."

"That's no fun," Ranger said.

"I didn't know you were interested in fun."

There was a very slight curve to the corners of his mouth. "I have my moments."

I had a big, cuddly pink robe in my closet, but I had to cross in front of Ranger to get to it. I wasn't worried Ranger would jump me. My fear was that if I got too close, I'd get sucked into his force field, and I'd jump *him*. And jumping Ranger was a dangerous deal. He'd made it clear that his emotional involvement would always have limitations. Plus, there was Morelli. Morelli was currently out of the picture, but he'd been out before, and he'd always slid back in. Getting naked with Ranger would make a reconciliation with Morelli much more difficult. Of course, that wasn't currently an issue, because I wasn't in a mood to reconcile anything.

"What did you want to talk to me about?" I asked him.

"Three of my clients have been robbed in the last two months. All three had state-of-the-art security systems. And in all three cases the systems were shut down for exactly fifteen minutes and then reactivated. My clients weren't home at the time. There was no sign of physical tampering."

"I see them using gizmos in the movies that can figure out codes."

"This isn't a movie. This is real life."

"Someone hacked into your system?"

"No."

"That leaves an unpleasant possibility," I said to Ranger.

"In theory, there are only a few people in my organization who have access to the codes, and I can't imagine any of those men being involved in this. For that matter, *everyone* I employ is rigorously screened. Plus, the entire building, with the exception of private living spaces, is monitored twenty-four hours."

"Have you changed the codes?"

"I changed them after each break-in."

"Wow."

"Yeah," Ranger said. "Someone on the inside is beating my system."

"Why are you telling this to me?"

"I need you to come in and snoop around without raising suspicion. I can't trust anyone already inside."

"Even Tank?"

"Even Tank."

Tank is exactly what his name would imply. He's big and solid inside and out. He's second in command at Rangeman, and he's the guy who watches Ranger's back.

"You've worked for me before doing computer searches, and that's where I'd like to put you again. Ramon has been doing the searches, but he'd like to get out of the cubby and back on the street. You'd be working on the fifth floor in the control room, but you'd have total access within the building. Every man in my organization knows you and understands that you're my personal property, so they're not going to talk freely when you're around, but they're also not going to think I hired you to snoop. They'll assume I gave you the job to have you close to me."

"Personal property?"

"Babe, you're the only one who would question it."

I narrowed my eyes at him. "I am *not* personal

property. A car is personal property. A shirt is personal property. A human being is not personal property."

"In my building, we share cars and shirts. We don't share women. In my building, you're my personal property. Deal with it."

At a later time, when I was alone and had given it some thought, I'd probably find the flaw in that reasoning, but oddly enough it made sense at the moment.

"What about my cases at the bonds office?" I asked him.

"I'll help you."

This was a really good deal, because I was a crappy bounty hunter and Ranger was the best. Not to mention I'd be drawing salary from Rangeman. All I had to do was keep my hands off Ranger and everything would be peachy.

"Okay," I said. "When do you want me to start?"

"Now. Do you have uniforms left from the last time you worked for me?"

"I have a couple T-shirts, and I have some black jeans."

"Good enough. I'll have Ella order some more."

Ella and her husband, Louis, serve as live-in property managers for Rangeman. They keep the building clean and running efficiently, and they keep the men fed and clothed. They're both in their early fifties, and Ella is dark-haired, and dark-eyed, and pretty in a no-nonsense kind of way.

"I assume you still have your key fob?" Ranger asked.

"Yep."

The key fob got me into the high-security Rangeman building, and it also got me into Ranger's private seventh-floor apartment. In the past, I'd used the apartment when I felt I was in danger. It wasn't a move I made lightly, because I had to weigh the danger at hand against the danger of living with Ranger.

Ranger's cell phone buzzed, and he looked at the screen. "I have to go," he said. "Tank and Ramon are expecting you. Ramon will bring you up to speed and then you should be able to take over. You know the drill." His eyes moved from my face to the towel and then back to my face. "Tempting," he said. And he left.

TWO

I dried my hair and put on makeup that stopped just short of slut. I dressed in black jeans and one of the black V-neck stretchy girl-type T-shirts I had left from my last stint at Rangeman. I topped the T-shirt with a black Rangeman hooded sweatshirt, grabbed my bag, and headed out.

I stopped at the bonds office on my way to Rangeman. Connie was alone when I walked in.

"Oh crap," Connie said, eyeballing my outfit. "You aren't quitting again, are you?"

"No. The Rangeman job is temporary."

"What about the stack of skips I gave you last week?"

"Ranger is going to help me."

"My lucky day," Connie said.

"Have you heard anything from Lula?"

"She called to say she was on her way back to the office, and she had a bucket of chicken."

That was worth the wait. I could get lunch at Rangeman, but it would be tuna salad on multi-grain bread, and it would be made with fat-free mayo. And for dessert, I could score an apple. Ranger encouraged healthy eating. Truth is, Ranger was a tyrant. If you worked at Rangeman, you had to be physically strong, mentally tough, loyal without question, and survive random drug tests. I was exempt from all those things, and that was a good deal, because the only one I could fly through was the drug test.

I saw Morelli's green SUV pull to the curb and make a Lula drop. Lula slammed the passenger-side door closed and waved Morelli off as best she could considering her arms were filled with fast-food buckets and bags and drink holders. She used her ass to push open the door to the bonds office and crossed to Connie's desk to dump her food.

"I got that done and over," Lula said. "And it wasn't so bad as I expected, on account of while I was there the head came in, so that speeded up a lot of stuff."

Connie leaned forward a little. "The head came in?"

"Yeah. One of the camera dudes at the television station went outside to smoke, and when he opened the back door, he saw a head sitting by the Dumpster. And here's the best part. This guy recognized the head right off. Turns out the head belongs to Stanley Chipotle."

"The celebrity chef?"

"Yep. He's on The Food Channel all the time. I don't know why I didn't recognize him. Guess I'm used to seeing him in his chef's clothes. You know how he wears that puffy chef hat, and lately, he's always got on the red apron advertising his barbecue sauce. Anyway, they brought the head in, and I identified it, and then Morelli said I could go home." Lula opened the bucket of chicken and dug in. "Help yourself," she said. "There's plenty."

Connie poked around in the bucket, looking for a recognizable chicken part. "What was Chipotle doing in Trenton? Did anyone know?"

"The camera dude said Chipotle was supposed to be in a big-deal national barbecue cookoff that's gonna be held at Gooser Park. He was gonna be talking about it on the station's cooking show this afternoon, but since only his head showed up, they got someone from Dawn Diner to make rice pudding instead."

"Chipotle's famous for his barbecue sauce," Connie said.

I polished off a mystery chicken part and selected another. I was out of the loop. I never watched The Food Channel, and I didn't do a lot of cooking. Mostly, I mooched food from my parents.

"What are you doing dressed up like Rangegirl?" Lula asked me.

"I'm temporarily filling in on a desk job." I

glanced at my watch. "I need to run. Ramon is waiting for me."

Rangeman is housed in a small office building on a side street in center city Trenton. The inside has been renovated into a high-tech, self-contained, secure corporate Batcave that operates 24/7. Ranger's private apartment occupies the top floor. Ella and Louis live on the sixth floor. The control room, dining area, and assorted offices are located on the fifth floor. And the remaining space is given over to efficiency apartments made available to some of the Rangeman employees, a gym, a gun range, meeting rooms, and more offices. The exterior façade of the building is nondescript, with only a small brass nameplate beside the front door to tell the world this is Rangeman.

I used my key fob to access the underground garage. I parked and fobbed my way into the elevator and up to the fifth floor. There were three uniformed men in the control room, watching monitors, and four men were in the kitchen area. All eyebrows raised when I stepped out of the elevator. I smiled and gave everyone a small wave and went directly to Ramon's cubicle.

"Hallelujah," Ramon said when he saw me. "I'm going back out into the land of the living. I hate this cubicle. The sun doesn't shine in here. There isn't even a window. After a half hour at this desk, I've got a cramp in my ass."

Ramon had dark hair, dark eyes, and dark skin, and eyelashes I'd kill for. He was a couple inches taller than me, and looked to be around my age. He had pierced ears but no earrings. Rangeman employees weren't allowed jewelry other than a watch when they were on the job.

"How did you get behind the computer in the first place? I thought you were a car guy."

"I got a speeding ticket, and Ranger stuck me here. This is like the dunce desk. I was lucky I didn't get fired."

Great. I was working the dunce desk.

"What did you do to deserve this?" Ramon asked me.

"I needed extra money, and this is what Ranger had available."

"Gotta pay the bills," Ramon said. "Let me show you what I've got on my desktop."

An hour later, I was on my own. A variety of searches passed through this position. There were background searches on employees and prospective clients, searches for outsourced services, plus security searches requested by clients.

Some of it was interesting, but after an hour of staring at the screen, it all grew monotonous. By five o'clock, I had a cramp in my ass. I put my computer to sleep and walked the short distance down the hall to Ranger's office.

"Knock, knock," I said.

Ranger looked up at me. "Babe."

"I have a cramp in my ass."

"I could kiss it and make it better."

"I was thinking more along the line of a new chair," I told him.

"Tell Louis. He'll get you whatever you want. Do you have plans for tonight?"

"No."

"Hang out for another hour. I want to talk to you, but I need to go through this paperwork first."

A little after six, Ranger ambled into my cubicle and collected me.

"Ella has dinner ready upstairs," he said. "We can eat and talk."

There was a time, not too long ago, when Ranger's address was a vacant lot. It turns out besides being a very tough guy, he's also a very smart businessman, and he now lives in an extremely upscale one-bedroom inner sanctum of civilized calm. The apartment was tastefully decorated by a professional, and is now maintained by Ella. The furniture is comfortable contemporary. Leather, chrome, dark woods, with earth-tone accents. It's clearly masculine but not overpowering. The apartment feels surprisingly warm in spite of the fact that there are no personal touches. No family photographs. No favorite books stacked at bedside. No clutter. I've spent a reasonable amount of time in Ranger's apartment, and I've always thought it was a place where he slept but didn't live. I've never been able to find the place he would call *home*. Maybe it doesn't exist. Maybe he carries it inside him. Or maybe it's a place he hasn't yet discovered.

We were silent in the elevator and small foyer that preceded Ranger's apartment. He fobbed his door open, and I stepped into the hall, with its subdued lighting and plush carpet. Ranger dropped his keys onto a small silver tray on the sideboard and followed me to the kitchen. His appliances were top-of-the-line stainless. His countertops were granite. Ella kept everything immaculate. I lifted the lid to the blue Le Creuset casserole dish on the stovetop. Chicken, rice, spicy sausage, and vegetables.

"This smells wonderful," I said to Ranger. "You're lucky to have Ella."

"If I can't stop these break-ins, I'm not going to have Ella or anyone else."

"What about security cameras? Weren't any of the thefts caught on tape?"

"All the burglaries were residential with no cameras in place." Ranger poured out two glasses of wine and handed one to me. "Without going into detail, I can tell you there are a lot of safeguards in the system to prevent this from happening."

"But it happened anyway."

"Three times."

"Is there anyone you especially want me to watch?"

"Martin Beam is the newest man in the building. He's been with me for seven months. Chester Rodriguez and Victor Zullick were on deck for all three break-ins. There are four men who rotate shifts monitoring the code computer. Beyond that, I have nothing."

"You've done recent background checks?"

"So far as I can tell, none of my men are in trouble, financial or otherwise."

I ladled the stew onto plates, Ranger cut into a loaf of bread set out on a breadboard, and we took our wine and plates of food to the table, where Ella had laid out placemats and silverware.

"Do you think this is someone needing money?" I asked Ranger. "Or do you think it's someone trying to ruin you?"

"Hard to tell, but if I had to choose, I'd go with trying to ruin me."

"That's ugly."

Ranger selected a slice of bread. "The men I hire aren't stupid. They have to know stealing the codes will end badly, and the items and cash taken can't compensate them for the risk. They'd be better off stealing from an ATM."

"Was there a pattern to the break-ins?"

Ranger refilled my wineglass. "Only that they all happened at night."

I've never known Ranger to have more than one glass of wine or beer. And usually, he didn't finish his first glass. Ranger never placed himself in a position of weakness. He sat with his back to the wall, and he was always sober. I, on the other hand, from time to time slipped into dangerous waters and counted on Ranger to scoop me out.

"So," I said to him. "If I drink this second glass of wine, will you drive me home?"

"Babe, you have no alcohol tolerance. If you drink a second glass of wine, you won't *want* to go home."

I blew out a sigh and pushed the glass away. He was right. "I have five open cases that need immediate attention," I told him. "You said you would help me."

"Do you have the files with you?"

I went to the kitchen and retrieved my bag from the counter, handed the five files over to Ranger, and returned to my place at the table.

Ranger paged through the files while he ate.

"You have two armed robberies, one exhibitionist, a mid-level drug dealer, and an arsonist," he said. "The dealer is a no-brainer. Kenny Hatcher. Better known as Marbles. I know where he works. He deals from the six hundred block of Stark Street."

"I've been checking. He isn't there."

"He's there. You just aren't seeing him."

I stared down at my dinner plate and wine-glass. Empty. Damn. "Someone drank my wine," I said to Ranger.

"That would be you."

I looked around. "Do we have dessert?"

"No."

Big surprise. Ranger *never* had dessert.

"Why can't I see my drug dealer?" I asked him.

Ranger leaned back in his chair and watched me. The lion assessing his prey. "He's using a runner," Ranger said. "If you want to find Hatcher, you have to follow the runner."

"How do I recognize the runner?"

"You pay attention."

"Okay, I'll give it another shot," I said, pushing away from the table, taking the files from Ranger. "I'm going to Stark Street."

I started to leave, and Ranger snagged me by the back of my shirt and dragged me up against him.

"Let me get this straight," he said. "You're going to Stark Street *now*?"

"Yeah."

"Alone?"

"Yeah."

"I don't think so."

"Why not?"

Ranger smiled down at me. I was amusing him.

"I can think of at least a half-dozen reasons," he said. "Not the least of which is you'll be the

only one on Stark Street not carrying a gun. It'll
be like open season on Plum pudding."

"I can take care of myself," I told him.

"Maybe, but I can take care of you better."

No argument there.

THREE

A half hour later, Ranger and I were parked on the six hundred block of Stark Street. Stark Street starts down by the river, cuts through the center of the city, and runs straight to hell. Storefronts are grimy, decorated with gang graffiti and the accumulated grit of day-to-day life in the breakdown lane. Hookers stake out corners, knots of kids going nowhere strut the street, men chain-smoke in doorways, and pushers work the sidewalks.

Ranger was behind the wheel of a shiny black Cadillac Escalade with tinted windows and fancy chrome wheel covers. No one could see us sitting in the SUV, and we were left unmolested as a sign of respect by the general population of Stark Street, who assumed the car belonged to contract killers, badass hip-hop gangsters, or high-level drug dealers.

The sun had set, but there was ambient light from streetlights and headlights and doors opening into bars. Enough light to determine that Marbles wasn't on the street.

"I don't see anyone who looks like a runner," I said to Ranger.

"The kid in the oversize sweatshirt, white T-shirt, and homeboy jeans."

"How do you know?"

"He's making deals."

"And?"

"And this block belongs to Marbles. The kid would be dead if he wasn't working for Marbles. Marbles isn't a charitable kind of guy."

"Maybe Marbles sold his real estate and left town."

"Not his style. He's in one of these buildings, conducting business. Besides owning drugs on the six hundred block, he also manages a couple hookers. Marbles read the memo on diversification. I ran into him two years ago, and he was operating an all-night dog-grooming and cock-fighting operation. The cockfighting didn't involve poultry."

It took me a couple beats to figure that out. And even then, how the heck did a guy go about it? Was it like thumb wrestling? I was debating asking about the rules and regulations of cock-fighting, but just then the kid in the sweatshirt ambled into a building halfway down the block.

"He's going back to the mother ship," Ranger said.

Mostly, Stark Street is filled with narrow red-brick town houses, two to four stories tall. Small businesses in varying degrees of failure occupy ground floors, and the upper floors are given over to cramped apartments and rented rooms. At odd intervals on the street, you might find a garage or a warehouse or a funeral home. The kid went into a four-story brick town house. All the windows had been painted black.

Ranger and I left the Escalade, crossed the street, and followed the kid into the building. The foyer was dimly lit by a bare bulb in an overhead fixture, the walls were entirely covered with graffiti. A door labeled HEAD MOTHERFUCKER opened off the foyer.

Ranger and I exchanged glances and went directly to the Head Motherfucker door. Ranger pushed the door open, and we looked inside at what at one time had probably been an efficiency apartment but was now a rat's nest office. The desk was piled high with papers, empty fast-food boxes, a laptop computer, a multiline phone, and two half-filled cups of coffee. There was a chair behind the desk and a two-seater leather couch against a wall. Nobody home.

We left the office, closing the door behind us. We returned to the foyer and took the stairs to the second floor, where a dull-eyed wannabe junior gangsta sat on a plastic lawn chair. He was hooked up to an MP3 player, and he had a small wooden table beside him. There was a cigar box and a roll of tickets on the table.

"Yuh?" he said. "You want a ticket for the night or just for a run-through?"

"Run-through," Ranger said.

"Twenty bucks each. Forty each, if you want a jumpsuit."

"Just the run-through ticket," Ranger said.

"You know the rules? You collect a ticket from the dude without no mess, and you get a kewpie doll. You're gonna be on the third floor."

Ranger and I climbed the stairs to the third floor and stood in the hallway.

"Do you have any idea what he was talking about?" I asked Ranger.

"No. Knowing Marbles, it could be most anything."

There were two doors that opened off the hallway. The doors were labeled PUSSY and MOTHERFUCKERS.

"I'm taking the Motherfucker door," I said to Ranger.

"No way. That's my door."

"Well, I'm sure as hell not taking the Pussy door."

"It's just a door, Babe."

"Great. Then *you* take it."

Ranger moved to the Pussy door and shoved it open. He walked through the front room and looked into two other rooms. "It's an apartment. Looks like it was decorated by someone on 'shrooms. No one home."

I opened the Motherfucker door and stepped inside. The door closed behind me, neon red, green, blue, and white strobe lights activated and flickered across the front room, and hip-hop boomed from overhead speakers. I opened a door. Closet. I opened another door and a crazy-eyed, woolly-haired, scrawny guy in too-big pants and too-big shoes shouldered a gun at me from across the room.

"Gonna put a cap up your pussy ass," he said. And *POW*.

I felt the bullet hit my shoulder, knock me back an inch or two, and something splattered out across my chest.

"What the?" I said.

"Run, Pussy!"

"What?"

"Run!"

And *POW*. I got shot again. *POW. POW.*

An arm wrapped around my waist, and I was lifted off my feet and whisked out of the room and back into the hall. Ranger kicked the door closed and set me down.

"What? Why?" I asked.

"Paintball. Are you okay?"

"No! It hurt. It's like getting hit with a rock. Why on earth do people do that? You'd have to be crazy."

"It's a game," Ranger said. "Usually. This version is more like shooting sitting ducks."

I checked myself out. I was completely splattered with blue, pink, and yellow paint. It was in my hair and on my shoes and everywhere in between. There was no paint on Ranger.

"You don't have a drop of paint on you," I said. "Why is that?"

Ranger smiled, liking that he hadn't gotten hit. "I guess they were hunting pussy."

"But I walked into the Motherfucker room."

"Yeah, but babe, you're clearly pussy."

"That is so sexist and *annoying*. These are my favorite sneakers, and now they're ruined. I'll never get this paint out."

"I'm sure it's water-based. Throw them in the washer."

"I don't have a washer."

Ranger took my hand and tugged me toward the stairs. "Then throw them in your mother's washer."

"You wouldn't be this cheery if *you* were covered in paint."

He pushed my back to the wall and leaned in to me. "Would you like me to take your mind off your sneakers?"

I bit into my lower lip.

"Well?" he asked, kissing me just below my ear, making the little man in the boat pay attention.

"I'm th-th-thinking."

Actually, I was thinking he'd have half my paint on him when he pried himself loose. And along with that I was thinking he felt great plastered against me. He was big and warm and strong.

A door banged open on the first floor and conversation carried up to us. Ranger listened for a moment and eased away. I followed him down the stairs and into the first-floor hall, where the kid in the white T-shirt and homeboy jeans stood talking to a stocky older man with wiry gray hair. Both guys looked up when we stepped into the hall. The kid froze in his tracks. The older guy spun around, ran to the office, and locked himself inside.

Ranger dismissed the kid and knocked on the locked office door. He waited a couple beats and knocked again. When there was no response to his second knock, he put his foot to the door and kicked it open.

"Jeez Louise," I said to Ranger, knowing he could have finessed the lock and opened the door.

Ranger smiled. "Making a statement."

The guy inside the office was behind his desk, waving his arms, his eyes rolling around in their sockets, popped out like marbles.

"This must be Marbles," I said to Ranger.

"Only one of them is real," Ranger said.

"You broke my door," Marbles said. "You're gonna pay. You think doors grow on trees?"

"Bond enforcement," Ranger said.

"That's bullshit. You owe me for a door. And she owes me for playing. Does she have a ticket? Where's her fuckin' ticket?"

Ranger never shows much emotion. I saw him walk into a room once, knowing he was going to get shot and maybe die, and he was perfectly composed. Only because I've spent a decent amount of time with him did I know the limit to his patience. So I took a step back and gave him some room, because I knew he was done talking.

"And another thing . . ." Marbles said, finger pointed at Ranger, eyes all googly-woogly.

Marbles never finished the sentence, because in a matter of moments, he was on the ground and cuffed. Ranger dragged Marbles to his feet and set him in his chair. Marbles opened his mouth to speak, Ranger looked at him, and Marbles clamped his mouth shut.

"You have a choice," Ranger said to me. "We can take him to the station and get him booked in, or I can have one of my men do it, and I can take you home so we can get you out of your clothes."

"*We* can get me out of my clothes? Are you planning on making it a group activity?"

"Figure of speech, Babe. I don't need help getting you undressed." He answered his cell phone, listened for a moment, and disconnected. "Change in plans," he said, yanking Marbles out of his chair. "There's been another break-in. We'll take Marbles with us and pass him off on site."

FOUR

The house was a big white colonial with black shutters and a massive mahogany front door. The grounds were professionally landscaped. A dusty and battered police cruiser and two gleaming black Rangeman SUVs were parked in the circular drive. Ranger parked behind one of the Rangeman SUVs, we got out, and Tank and Hal came forward to meet us.

I gave Hal my paperwork for Marbles, Hal got behind the wheel, backed the Escalade out of the drive and disappeared down the street.

"Same MO," Tank told Ranger. "The clients attended a political fund-raiser, came home, and found money and jewelry missing." He handed Ranger a list. "We interrogated the system and found it had been briefly disarmed and then reset."

"Anything missing besides the money and jewelry?"

"Some electronics. They're going through the house now, trying to make sure the list is complete."

"I want Stephanie to walk through the house and look at it from a woman's point of view. Make sure she has total access. Assure the owners her paint isn't wet."

Tank looked at my paint-splattered hair and clothes. He paused for a beat, but he didn't smile or frown or grimace. "Yessir," he said to Ranger.

I wandered around, checking out the kitchen with its professional-level appliances, marble countertops and splash plates, warming ovens and wine cooler. I thought it would be nice to have a kitchen like this, although most of it would go unused. All I actually needed was a butter knife, a loaf of white bread, and a jar of peanut butter. And can you fill a wine cooler with Bud Light?

The upstairs master bath had a crystal chandelier and a bidet. I knew the *purpose* for the bidet, because I had seen *Crocodile Dundee* about a hundred times, but I wasn't sure how one actually *used* a bidet. I mean, does it shoot water up your cooter or do you splash it around? And I thought I might have issues with the crystal chandelier. I wasn't sure I could do number two in a room with a crystal chandelier.

I'd looked at the list, so I knew what had been taken and what had been left. There was a safe in the master bedroom, but it hadn't been touched. Madame's jewelry had been easy access in a jewelry case on display in her walk-in closet. A couple thousand in twenties had been left on the dresser.

All this stuff was gone. Plus two laptop computers from the home office, and a Patek Philippe man's watch.

I wandered around in the house for a half hour while the police did their thing, and Ranger did his thing, and the burgled house owners, a conservatively dressed middle-aged couple, quietly sat in the living room, looking shell-shocked.

Ranger caught up with me in the front foyer. "Any ideas?" he asked me.

"The thieves only hit two rooms. The master bedroom and the home office. There was a woman's rose gold and diamond Cartier watch on the kitchen counter. And there were four icons that looked priceless in a display case in the living room. All untouched. Is this always the pattern?"

"Yes. They disable the alarm for precisely fifteen minutes, and they move directly to the master bedroom and office."

"Why fifteen minutes?"

Ranger did palms-up. "I don't know."

"No prints left on doorknobs?"

"None."

"And they only hit residential accounts?"

"So far."

"This house has two security keypads. Can you tell which was used?"

"They always enter and exit through the garage."

"The garage in this house opens into a short

hall that leads to the kitchen. That means they walked through the kitchen twice and didn't take the watch."

"Correct," Ranger said.

"Do you have anyone working for you who's OCD or superstitious?"

"Almost everyone. I'm going to have Tank take you back to Rangeman so you can get your car. I need to stay here for a while and then I have paperwork to complete."

"So I'm off the hook with the undressing thing?"

"Rain check," Ranger said.

I drove home and did my own undressing, lathering, and shampooing. When I flopped into bed, my hair was still multicolored.

I stopped at the bonds office on my way to Rangeman. It was a little before nine in the morning, and the air was warm, and the sky was almost blue. It was Indian summer in Jersey.

Connie and Lula looked over when I walked through the door.

"What the heck happened to you?" Lula wanted to know. "You got tutti-frutti hair. Is this some new fashion statement?"

"No, this is the result of a paintball encounter on Stark Street. The good news is I apprehended Kenny Hatcher."

"Your mother's going to have a cow when she

sees your hair," Connie said. "You try water? You try paint thinner?"

"I've tried everything."

"I like it," Lula said. "You should add some more pink. Pink's a good color on you. And by the way, have you been listening to the radio? There's a big reward being offered to anyone who brings in the guy who whacked Stanley Chipotle."

"How big?"

"A million dollars. It's from the barbecue sauce company he did all those advertisements for. Fire in the Hole Red Hot Barbecue Sauce. He was supposed to represent them in this cook-off coming up. And I'm gonna get that reward. I know what those guys look like. All I have to do is find them. So I thought I'd cut you and Connie in on it, and between us we could track them down and we'd each get a third of a million dollars."

"I'm so there," Connie said. "I could pay my mortgage off with that money."

"What would you do with the money?" Lula asked me.

I didn't know what I'd do. My mind was blank. The amount was incomprehensible to me. I could put a crystal chandelier in my crapper for that kind of money. I could buy a case of motor oil and feed it to my $700 car. I could download all the *3rd Rock from the Sun* episodes from iTunes. I could get the works on my pizza. I could buy new sneakers. I *really* needed new sneakers. I could probably buy a house, for crying out loud. Except I didn't actually *want* a house. I had a hard enough time keeping people out of my apartment. If I had a house, the weirdos would be coming in every door and window and down the chimney like Santa. Plus, I'd have to cut grass and paint the porch and caulk the tub.

"I think this is about barbecue sauce," Lula said. "Everyone knows it's dog-eat-dog out there in barbecue land. You wait and see, someone didn't want Stanley Chipotle in that barbecue contest. I looked into it, and he always wins those contests. He was the one who come up with Fire in the Hole Red Hot Barbecue Sauce. He invented that recipe, and when he's in a contest, he has a secret ingredient he puts in. I'm tellin' you, Stanley Chipotle's killer is a sauce freak. So I figure we just gotta bust into the barbecue circuit and we'll find the killer."

"Bust into the circuit?"

"All I gotta do is enter the contest as one of them chefs. I bet I could even win."

"You can't cook."

"That's true so far, but that could change. I'm real good at eatin'. I got a highly developed palate. Especially for barbecue. I just gotta take some of my eatin' talent and make it into cookin' talent. Anyways, I only gotta come up with sauce.

How hard could it be? I mean, you start out with ketchup and keep adding pepper until you feel it burnin' a hole in your stomach."

"I don't think it's that easy," Connie said. "I watch these contests on The Food Channel, and you have to use the sauce on ribs and chicken and stuff. Can you cook ribs or chicken?"

"Not yet," Lula said. "But I know I could be real good at it. Look at me. Don't I look like a woman who could cook the shit out of chicken? I'm like a combination of Paula Deen and Mario Whatshisname. I'm just around the corner from bein' the Mrs. Butterworth of barbecue sauce."

"The cook-off is in a week," Connie said. "Is there still time for you to enter? Do you have to qualify or something?"

"I don't have to do nothin' but sign up," Lula said. "I already looked into it, and the idiot who's runnin' the cook-off used to be a customer of mine back when I was a 'ho. He was what you call a drive-by. He'd pick me up on my corner, and two blocks later, we'd concluded our business."

"That's more information than I need," Connie said.

"Well, I'm just sayin' so you get the picture."

"I have to run," I told them. "I'm late for work."

"After we win the contest and capture the killer, none of us is gonna have to work," Lula said. "We're all gonna be ladies of leisure."

* * *

It was noon, and Ranger's men were moving around, breaking for lunch, so I left my cubicle and went to the kitchen area to mingle. Ella kept the large glass-fronted refrigerator filled with sandwiches, fruit, raw veggies, yogurt, low-fat milk, snack-size cheeses, a variety of fruit juices, plus individual cups of chicken salad and vegetable soup. Early in the morning, Ella supplemented this with a caldron of oatmeal and a chafing dish of scrambled eggs. The dinner offering was always some sort of Crock-Pot stew, plus a breadbasket.

Ranger almost always ate breakfast and dinner in his apartment. And lunch was usually a sandwich and piece of fruit from the common kitchen, taken back to his office. There were three small round tables set to one side of the kitchen. Each table held four chairs. Two men I didn't know were eating at one of the tables. Hal and Ramon were at another. The third table was empty. I selected a sandwich and joined Hal and Ramon. I've known Hal for a while now. Hal isn't the sharpest tack on the corkboard, but he tries hard. His nickname is Halosaurus, because there's a stegosaurus resemblance.

"You're my new favorite person," Ramon said. "You got me out of that cubicle. I was dying in that cubicle."

"It's not my favorite job, either," I said, "but I needed the money."

I unwrapped my sandwich and examined it. Multigrain bread, pretty ruffled green lettuce, thin-sliced chicken, a slice of tomato, slices of hard-cooked egg, and salad dressing that was for sure low fat. It looked good, but it would look even better with bacon.

"No bacon," I said, more to myself than to Hal and Ramon.

Hal grinned. "Ranger thinks bacon is the work of the devil."

"Sometimes I walk past Ella's apartment, and I smell bacon frying," Ramon said. "I think she makes it for Louis." He looked over at me. "Have you ever seen Ranger eat bacon?"

"No," I said. "Not that I can remember."

"I think sometimes he cheats and goes to eat with Louis," Ramon said.

"No way," Hal said. "Ranger's pure."

Both men looked at me.

"Forget it," I said. "I'm not commenting on that one."

Hal flushed red, and Ramon gave a bark of laughter.

I finished my sandwich and pushed back from the table. "I'm going for a walk around the building. Is there anyplace off-limits for us worker people?"

"Only the seventh floor. No one would mind if you went into the men's locker room, but there could be a lot of wood if you stayed too long. And then Ranger would probably fire us all," Ramon said.

"I don't want to get anyone fired."

"That's good," Hal said, "because everyone here wants to keep their job."

"Not everyone," Ramon said.

I cut my eyes to him.

"You were on the job last night," he said to me. "I'm sure you know the problem. *Everyone* in the building knows the problem."

"Then why isn't the problem solved?" I asked him.

Ramon did palms-up. "Good question. If I knew, I would tell immediately. And so would Hal. And before this happened, I would say every man in the building would tell and would lay down their life for Ranger."

"Maybe it's not in the building," I said to Ramon.

"I would like to believe that."

I glanced at Hal. "What do you think?"

Hal shook his head. "I don't know what to think. It used to be we were a team here, and now we're all pulled up inside ourselves. It's creepy working with people who are looking at you funny."

I stood and gathered my trash off the table.

"I'm sure Ranger has it under control. He doesn't seem overly worried."

"I saw Ranger jump off a bridge into the Delaware River in January once. He was going after a skip, and he didn't seem overly worried," Ramon said. "He handed me his gun, and he did about a sixty-foot free fall into black water."

"Did he get the skip?" I asked him.

"Yeah. He dragged the guy out and cuffed him."

"So he was right not to be worried."

"Anyone else would have fuckin' died. Excuse the language."

I wandered out of the kitchen, walked past my cubicle and down the hall to Ranger's office.

"Knock, knock," I said at his open door.

He looked up from his computer. "Babe."

"Do you have a minute?"

"I've got as much time as you need."

I knew he wasn't just talking about conversation, and there was a quality to his voice that gave me a rush. And then, for some inexplicable reason, I thought about Morelli. Morelli didn't flirt like Ranger. Morelli would say *sure* and then he'd look down my shirt to try to see some boob. It was actually very playful, and it felt affectionate when Morelli did it.

Ranger relaxed back in his chair. "I'm pretty sure I lost you for a couple beats."

"My mind wandered."

"As long as it always comes back."

I repeated my conversation with Hal and Ramon.

"This business runs on trust," Ranger said. "Ninety-five percent of the time, the work is mundane. When it rolls over into the other five percent, you need total confidence that the man watching your back is on the job. Knowing there's an unidentified weak link in the organization puts stress on everyone."

I left Ranger and walked through the building. I couldn't listen at doors or rifle through files, because I was always on camera. I peeked into the conference rooms and strolled halls. I stuck my head into the gym but stayed away from the locker room. The garage, the practice range, some high-security holding rooms were below ground, and I didn't go there. The men I encountered gave me a courteous nod and returned to work. No invitations to stay and chat.

I returned to Ranger. "You have a well-oiled machine," I told him. "Everything looks neat and clean and secure."

He almost raised an eyebrow. "That's it?"

"Yep."

"How much am I paying you?"

"Not enough."

"If you want more money, you're going to have to perform more services," he said.

"Are you flirting with me again?"

"No. I'm trying to bribe you."

"I'll think about it."

"Would you like to think about it over dinner?"

"No can do," I said. "I promised Lula I'd test-drive some barbecue sauce with her."

FIVE

I dropped into the office a little after five. Connie was shuffling papers around and Lula was nowhere to be seen.

"Where's Lula? I thought we were supposed to eat barbecue tonight?"

"Turns out, Lula only has a hot plate in her apartment, and she couldn't get the ribs to fit on it, so she had to find someplace else to cook."

"She could have used my kitchen."

"Yeah, she considered that, but we didn't have a key. And we thought you might not have a lot of equipment."

"I have a pot and a fry pan. Is she at your house?"

"Are you insane? No way would I let her into my kitchen. I won't even let her work the office coffeemaker."

"So where is she?"

"She's at your parents' house. She's been there all afternoon, cooking with your grandmother."

Oh boy. My father is Italian descent and my

mother is Hungarian. From the day I was born to this moment, I can't remember ever seeing anything remotely resembling barbecue sauce in my parents' house. My parents don't even have a grill. My mom *fries* hot dogs and what would pass for a hamburger.

"I guess I'll head over there and see how it's going," I said to Connie. "Do you want to come with me?"

"Not even a little."

My parents and my Grandma Mazur live in a narrow two-story house that shares a common wall with another narrow two-story house. The three-hundred-year-old woman living in the attached house painted her half lime green because the paint was on sale. My parents' half is painted mustard yellow and brown. It's been that way for as long as I can remember. Neither house is going to make *Architectural Digest*, but they feel right for the neighborhood and they look like home.

I parked at the curb, behind Lula's Firebird, and I let myself into the house. Ordinarily, my grandmother or mother would be waiting for me at the door, driven there by some mystical maternal instinct that alerts them to my approach. Today they were occupied in the kitchen.

My father was hunkered down in his favorite chair in front of the television. He's retired from the post office and now drives a cab part-time.

He picks up a few people early morning to take to the train station, but mostly the cab is parked in our driveway or at the lodge, where my father plays cards and shoots the baloney with other guys his age looking to get out of the house. I shouted *hello,* and he grunted a response.

I shoved through the swinging door that separated kitchen from dining room and sucked in some air. There were racks of ribs laid out on baking sheets on the counter, pots and bowls of red stuff, brown stuff, maroon stuff on the small kitchen table, shakers of cayenne, chili pepper, black pepper, plus bottles of various kinds of hot sauce, and a couple cookbooks turned to the barbecue section, also on the table. The cookbooks, Lula, and Grandma were dotted with multicolored sauce. My mother stood glassy-eyed in a corner, staring out at the car crash in her kitchen.

"Hey, girlfriend," Lula said. "Hope you're hungry, on account of we got whup-ass shit here."

Grandma and Lula looked like Jack Sprat and his wife. Lula was all swollen up and voluptuous, busting out of her clothes, and Grandma was more of a deflated balloon. Gravity hadn't been kind to Grandma, but what Grandma lacked in collagen she made up for with attitude and bright pink lipstick. She'd come to live with my parents when my Grandfather Mazur went in search of life everlasting at the all-you-can-eat heavenly breakfast buffet.

"This here's a humdinger dinner we got planned," Grandma said. "I never barbecued before, but I think we got the hang of it."

"Your granny's gonna be my assistant at the cook-off," Lula said to me. "And you could be my second assistant. Everybody's got to have two assistants."

"We're gonna get chef hats and coats so we look professional," Grandma said. "We're even gonna get our names stitched on. And I'm thinking of making this a new career. After I get the hat and the coat, I might go get a chef job in a restaurant."

"Not me," Lula said. "I'm not working in no restaurant. After I win the contest, I'm gonna get a television show."

"Maybe I could help you with that on my day off," Grandma said. "I always wanted to be on television."

I took a closer look at the ribs. "How did you cook these?"

"We baked them," Lula said. "We were supposed to grill them, but we haven't got no grill, so we just baked the crap out of them in the oven. I don't think it matters, anyways, after we get the sauce on them. That's what we're fixin' to do now."

"We got a bunch of different sauces we're trying out," Grandma said. "We bought them in the store and then we doctored them up."

"I don't think that's allowed," I said. "This is supposed to be your own sauce recipe."

Lula dumped some hot sauce and chili pepper into the bowl of red sauce. "Once it gets out of its bottle, it's my sauce. And besides, I just added my secret ingredients."

"What if they want to see your recipe?"

"Nuh-ah. No one gets to see Lula's recipe," Lula said, wagging her finger at me. "Everybody'll be stealing it. I give out my recipe, and next thing it's in the store with someone else's name on it. No sir, I'm no dummy. I'm gonna take the winning recipe to my deathbed."

"Should I start putting the sauce on these suckers?" Grandma asked Lula.

"Yeah. Make sure everybody gets all the different sauces. Since I'm the chef, I got the most refined taste buds, but we want to see what other people think, too."

Grandma slathered sauce on the ribs, and Lula eyeballed them.

"I might want to add some finishing touches," Lula said, pulling jars off my mother's spice rack, shaking out pumpkin pie spices. "These here ribs are gonna be my holiday ribs."

"I would never have thought of that," Grandma said.

"That's why I'm the chef and you're the helper," Lula said. "I got a creative flare."

"What are we eating besides ribs?" I asked.

Lula looked over at me. "Say what?"

"You can't just serve ribs to my father. He'll want vegetables and gravy and potatoes and dessert."

"Hunh," Lula said. "This is a special tasting night and all he's gettin' is ribs."

My mother made the sign of the cross.

"Gee," I said. "Look at the time. I'm going to have to run. I have work to do. Rex is waiting for me. I think I'm getting a cold."

My mother reached out and grabbed me by my T-shirt. "I was in labor twenty-six hours with you," she said. "You owe me. The least you could do is see this through to the end."

"Okay," Lula said. "Now we put these ribs back into the oven until they look like they been charcoaled."

Twenty minutes later, my father took his seat at the head of the table and stared down at his plate of ribs. "What the Sam Hill is this?" he said.

"Gourmet barbecue ribs," Grandma told him. "We made them special. They're gonna have us rolling in money."

"Why are they black? And where's the rest of the food?"

"They're black because they're supposed to look grilled. And this is all the food. This is a tasting menu."

My father mumbled something that sounded a lot like *taste, my ass*. He pushed his ribs around with his fork and squinted down at them. "I don't see any meat. All I see is bone."

"The meat's all in tasty morsels," Lula said. "These are more pickin'-up ribs instead of knife-and-fork ribs. And they're all different. We gotta figure out which we like best."

My mother nibbled on one of her ribs. "This tastes a little like Thanksgiving," she said.

My father had a rib in his hand. "I've got one of them, too," he said. "It tastes like Thanksgiving after the oven caught on fire and burned up all the meat."

What I had on my plate was charred beyond recognition. I loved Grandma and Lula a lot, but not enough to eat the ribs. "You might have cooked these a smidgeon too long," I said.

"You could be right," Lula said. "I expected them to be juicier. I think the problem is I bought grillin' ribs, and we had to make them into oven ribs." She turned to Grandma. "What's your opinion of the ribs? Did you try them all? Is there some you like better than others?"

"Hard to tell," Grandma said, "being that my tongue is on fire."

"Yeah," Lula said. "I made one of them real spicy 'cause that's the way I like my ribs and my men. Nice and hot."

My father was gnawing on a rib, trying to get something off it. He was making grinding, sucking sounds and really concentrating.

"You keep sucking like that, and you're gonna give yourself a hernia," Grandma said.

"It'd be less painful than eating these burned black, tastes like monkey shit, dry as an old maid's fart bones."

"Excuse me," Lula said. "Are you trash-talkin' my ribs? 'Cause I'm not gonna put up with slander on my ribs."

My father had a grip on his knife, and I thought the only thing stopping him from plunging it into someone's chest was he couldn't decide between Grandma and Lula.

"Are you really going to enter the competition?" I asked Lula.

"I already did. I filled out my form and gave it over to the organizer. He wanted me to do a favor for him, and I said *nuh-ah*. I said I don't do that no more. Not that I don't still have my skills, but I moved on with my life, you see what I'm sayin'."

"Did he take your form anyway?"

"Yeah. I got pictures of him from when he was a customer."

"You'd blackmail him?"

"I like to think of it as reminders of happy times," Lula said. "No need to negatize it. What happens is, he looks at the picture of himself and thinks bein' with me was better than a fork in the eye. And then he thinks it's special if that

shit stay between him and me and for instance
don't be seen on YouTube. And then he takes my
contest application and gives it the stamp of
approval."

"You got a way with people," Grandma said.

"It's a gift," Lula said.

"I'm making myself a peanut butter and olive
sandwich," I said. "Anyone else want one?"

"I got to go to the lodge," my father said, pushing away from the table.

I figured he might get there eventually, but
he'd stop at Cluck-in-a-Bucket on the way.

"I don't need a sandwich," Lula said. "But I'll
help clean the kitchen."

Lula, Grandma, my mother, and I all trooped
into the kitchen and set to work.

"I don't see any more barbecue sauce anywhere," Grandma finally said. "The floor's clean,
the counters are clean, the stove's clean, and the
dishes and pots are clean. Only thing dirty is me,
and I'm too pooped to get clean."

"I hear you," Lula said. "I'm goin' home, and
I'm goin' to bed."

I drove back to my apartment, changed into comfy
worn-out flannel pajamas, and was about to
settle in to watch television and *bang, bang, bang*.
Someone was hammering on my door. I looked
through the security peephole at Lula.

"I been shot at," she said when I let her in. "I'm lucky I'm not dead. I parked in front of my house, and I got out of my car, and just as I got to my front porch, these two guys jumped out of the bushes at me. It was the guys who whacked Stanley Chipotle, and the one had a meat cleaver, and the other tried to grab me."

"Are you serious?"

"Fuckin' A. Don't I look serious? I'm friggin' shakin'. Look at my hand. Don't it look shaky?"

We looked at her hand, but it wasn't shaking.

"Well, it used to be shakin'," she said. "Anyways, I hit the one asshole in the face with my pocketbook, and I kicked the other one in the nuts, and I turned and ran back to my car and took off. And one of them shot at me while I was driving away. He put bullet holes in my Firebird. I mean, I can stand for a lot of shit, but I don't tolerate bullet holes in my Firebird. What kind of a moron would do that, anyway? It's a Firebird, for crissake!"

"But you're okay?"

"Hell yeah, I'm okay. Don't I look okay? I'm just freakin' is all. I need a doughnut or something." She went to my kitchen and started going through cabinets. "You don't got nothin' in here. Where's your Pop-Tarts? Where's your Hostess Twinkies and shit? Where's your Tastykakes? I need sugar and lard and some fried crap."

"Did you call the police?"

"Yeah. I called them from my car. I told them I was coming here."

I got out my only fry pan, put a big glob of butter in it, slathered a lot of Marshmallow Fluff between two slices of worthless white bread, and fried it up for Lula.

"Oh yeah," Lula said when she bit into the bread and Fluff. "This is what I'm talkin' about. I feel better already. Another four or five of these, and I'm gonna be real calm."

There was a polite knock at the door, and I opened it to two uniforms. Carl Costanza and Big Dog. I made First Communion with Carl, and Big Dog had been his partner long enough that I felt like I made communion with him, too.

"What's up?" Carl said.

"I been shot at," Lula said. "That's what's up. And before that I almost got my head chopped off. It was terrifyin'."

Carl looked at me. "This isn't like the time she fell in the grave and thought the devil was after her, is it?"

"Your ass," Lula said to Carl.

"Just asking," Carl said.

"I got bullet damage to my Firebird," Lula told him. "It wasn't done by no devil, either. It was done by a certified killer."

Morelli appeared behind Carl. Morelli looked like he'd fallen asleep watching the ballgame, was jolted awake by dispatch, and reluctantly dragged his ass out to investigate. His black hair was overdue for a cut and curling along his neck in waves. His five o'clock shadow was way beyond shadow. He was wearing running shoes, jeans, and a faded navy blue sweatshirt with the sleeves pushed up to his elbows.

"I'll take it," he said to Carl and Big Dog.

"What are you doing here?" I asked him.

"I'm assigned to the Chipotle murder. Dispatch got a report of attempted murder by the same perps."

"That's right," Lula said. "I almost got my head chopped off. It was the same two idiots. And the one had a meat cleaver. Just like he used on Stanley Chipotle. Biggest meat cleaver I've ever seen. And this one with the meat cleaver was giggling. Not normal giggling, either. It was eerie. It was like horror movie giggling."

"Why didn't they chop your head off?" Morelli wanted to know.

"I kicked the one in the nuts and smashed my pocketbook in the other one's face."

"I guess that would slow them down," Morelli said. "Dispatch said this happened in front of your house?"

"Yeah. They were waiting for me. See, here's what happened. Stephanie and her granny and me were makin' ribs, only the ribs had to go in the oven, so they didn't cook right. Personally, I been thinking about it and I bet that oven was faulty."

Morelli blew out a sigh and went to my refrigerator. "There's no beer in here," he said.

"I need to go to the store."

Morelli closed the door and went back to Lula. "And?"

"And we had three special sauces, but it was hard to tell what was what since the ribs were all the same color when they come out of the oven."

"Has this got anything to do with Chipotle's murderers?"

"I'm gettin' to it," Lula said.

Morelli looked at his watch. "Could you get to it faster?"

"Boy, you're Mr. Cranky Pants tonight. What, do you got a date or something?"

I felt a small twinge of pain in the vicinity of my heart, and I narrowed my eyes at Morelli.

Morelli was hands on hips. "I haven't got a date. I just want to go home and see the end of the game."

"I guess there isn't much more to tell," Lula said. "They were waiting for me. They come at me with the mother of all cleavers. I kicked the guy in his nuts and got back in my car. And they shot at me when I drove away. And now my Firebird's full of bullet holes."

"I checked it on my way in," Morelli said. "I counted two in the right rear quarter panel and one in the back bumper. I don't suppose you noticed what kind of car these guys were driving?"

"I wasn't paying attention to that."

"Any distinguishing features? Anything you can add to your description of them?"

"One of them's got a broken nose and the other's walkin' funny."

"Did they say anything to you?"

"Nope. The one just was giggling."

"I'll send a uniform to check on your house, but it's unlikely your assailants are still there," Morelli told Lula.

"Okay, but I'm not going back there. I'm still freaked out. I'm staying here."

"Good luck with that one," Morelli said.

I cut my eyes to him. "What's that supposed to mean?"

He blew out another sigh. "Forget it."

I felt my eyes get squinchy and my lips compress. "*What?*"

"You're not exactly the easiest person to live with these days."

"Excuse me? I happen to be very easy to live with. You're the one who has issues."

"I don't want to get into this now," Morelli said. "Call me when you calm down."

"I'm *calm*!" I yelled at him.

He gave his head a shake and moved to the door. He turned, looked at me, and shook his head again. He murmured something I couldn't catch, and he left.

"He's hot," Lula said, "but he's a pig. All men are pigs."

"Do you really believe that?"

"No, but it's a point of view to keep in mind. You don't want to go around thinkin' shit is your fault. Next thing you know, they got you makin' pot roast and you're cutting up your MasterCard."

"I don't know how to make pot roast."

"Good for you," Lula said. "I don't suppose you got anything that would fit me. Like a big T-shirt. I'm all covered in barbecue sauce, and I'm beat."

I gave Lula an extra quilt and pillow and a worn-out T-shirt that belonged to Morelli. I said good night and I closed the door to my bedroom. I didn't especially want to see Lula in Morelli's T-shirt. Lula was a lot shorter than Morelli and a lot wider. Lula wearing Morelli's T-shirt wasn't going to be a pretty sight.

I woke up in a panic a little after midnight, thinking someone was sawing through my bedroom door. A couple seconds later, my head cleared, and I realized it was Lula snoring in my living room. I put my pillow over my head, but I could still hear Lula. Three hours later, I was thrashing around, plotting out ways to kill her. I got out of bed, marched into the living room, and yelled in her face.

"Wake up!"

Nothing.

"Wake up! Wake up! *WAKE UP!*"

Lula opened her eyes. "Huh?"

"You're snoring."

"You woke me up to tell me that?"

"Yes! My first choice was to suffocate you, but I don't have the energy to drag your lifeless body out to the Dumpster."

"Well, I happen to know I don't snore. You must have dreamed it."

"I didn't dream it. You snore loud enough to wake the dead. Roll over or something. I have to go to work in the morning. I need my sleep."

Brrrrrp. Lula let one go.

"Holy Toledo!" I said, backing away, fanning the air. "That's disgusting."

"I don't think it's so bad," Lula said. "It smells a little like ribs."

I drove to Rangeman in pouring rain. The temperature had dropped overnight, and the heater was broken on my car, so I was freezing my butt off. I parked in the underground garage, took the elevator to the fifth floor, and shuffled past the control desk to my cubicle. I turned my computer on, and next thing I knew, Ranger was standing over me.

"Rough night?" he asked.

"How did you know?"

"You were asleep at your desk. I was afraid

you were going to fall out of your chair and get a concussion."

I told him about Lula and the meat cleaver giggler, and the shooting, and the sleeping and snoring.

"Go to my apartment and take a nap," Ranger said. "I'll be out all morning on a job site. I'll catch up with you when I come back."

Ranger left and I finished a computer search I was doing on a job applicant. I took the elevator to the seventh floor and let myself into Ranger's apartment. It very faintly smelled like citrus, and everything was in perfect order. No thanks to Ranger. This was Ella's handiwork.

First thing in the morning Ella went through, polishing and straightening. Ranger's bed was made with fresh linens. His bathroom was gleaming clean, his towels neatly folded.

I kicked my shoes off, wriggled out of my jeans, slid under the covers, and thought this might be as close as I'd ever come to paradise. Ranger's three hundred thread count sheets were smooth and cool and heavenly soft. His pillows were just right. His mattress was just right. His feather quilt was just right. If Ranger were the marrying type, I'd marry him in a heartbeat just for his bed. There were other good reasons to hook up with Ranger, but the bed would be the clincher. Unfortunately, there were also some major reasons *not* to hook up with Ranger.

SIX

I opened my eyes and looked at my watch. It was almost one o'clock. I rolled out of bed, pulled my jeans on, and was tying my shoes when I heard the front door to Ranger's apartment open. Keys clinked onto the silver tray on the hall sideboard. A beat later, there was a heavy clunk, and I suspected this was his gun getting dropped onto the kitchen counter. Moments later, Ranger strode into the bedroom.

He was wearing a black ball cap, black windbreaker, black cargo pants, and black boots. He was soaking wet, and he didn't look happy.

"Still raining out?" I asked him.

It was a rhetorical question since I could hear the rain pounding on the bedroom window.

He bent to unlace his boots. "Everything I had to do this morning was outdoors. I'm soaking wet, and I'm late for a meeting." He kicked his boots off and moved to the bathroom. "Get me some dry clothes."

"What kind of clothes?"

"Any kind of clothes."

Ranger has a walk-in dressing room I would kill for. Shirts, slacks, blazers, T-shirts, sweatshirts, cargo pants, socks, underwear, gym clothes, shoes are all perfectly hung on hangers, stacked on shelves, or neatly placed in a drawer. Again, this is done by Ella.

It was easy for me to pick clothes for Ranger because everything he owns is black. The only question is dressy or casual. I went with casual and gathered together the same outfit he was wearing when he walked in.

There was a time a while ago when I searched for underwear in Ranger's dressing room and found just one pair of silky black boxers. Today, he had a drawer full of underwear. Boxers, bikini briefs, and boxer briefs. I closed my eyes and grabbed and came up with boxer briefs.

I brought the clothes to the open bathroom door in time to see Ranger strip off the last of his wet clothes.

"Sorry," I said. "I didn't mean to barge in on you."

"Babe, you've seen it all before."

"Yeah, but not lately."

"So far as I know, nothing has changed." He pulled the briefs on and arranged himself. "If I had more time, I'd let you figure that out for yourself." He removed his watch and tossed it to me. "Set this out to dry and get me a new one. Top drawer in the chest in my dressing room."

I brought him the exact duplicate of the watch he'd discarded, plus I handed him socks and shoes.

"On my desk in the den I have a list of items taken from all the break-ins. I'd like you to take a look at it. Plus, I have a map with the houses marked. I haven't been able to find anything significant, but maybe something will jump out at you." He finished lacing his shoes and stood. "I also have a list of every man in the building, his position, and his background. I'd like you to read through it."

I followed him to the door and watched him take his keys from the sideboard and pocket them. He pushed me to the wall, leaned in to me, and kissed me. "Later," he said, his lips brushing against mine. And he left.

It was a really great kiss, and if he'd said *now*, I might have been in trouble, but after a couple beats, when my heart had stopped jumping around in my chest and I wasn't pressed up against Ranger, I decided *later* was a scary idea.

I took the break-in and employee information down to the fifth floor, grabbed a sandwich from the kitchen, and went to my cubby. After a couple minutes, I realized my cubby didn't give me the privacy I needed, so I commandeered Ranger's office. The items taken were similar in all the houses. Jewelry, cash, iPods, laptop computers, handheld electronic games. The map showed the houses in three different neighborhoods. I saw nothing to tie them together. I was about a third of the way through the men's employment files when Ranger came in.

"I expected you'd stay in my apartment," Ranger said.

"I was worried about the *later* thing."

"And you think moving from my apartment to my office will save you?"

"I'm doing good so far."

Ranger slouched into a chair on the opposite side of the desk. "Is this move into my office permanent?"

"Is that a possibility?"

"No."

I looked around. "It's a really nice office. It has a window."

The corners of Ranger's mouth curved into the beginnings of a smile. "Would you like to negotiate for this office?"

"No, but I'd like to stay here until I finish reading. I have no privacy in my cubicle."

"Deal," Ranger said. "When you're done reading, I'd like you to find a way to talk to the four men who have access to the computer that holds the codes. Roger King, Martin Romeo, Chester Deuce, and Sybo Diaz. I don't want you to interrogate them. I just want you to make a fast character assessment. Chester Deuce is on the desk until six o'clock. Sybo Diaz will take the next six-hour shift. Romeo goes on at midnight. You should be able to catch him in the kitchen early afternoon. He occupies one of the Rangeman apartments and prefers Ella's cooking to his own."

"Okeydokey," I said. "I'm on it."

It was almost four when I finished reading. Ranger's men were a motley group, chosen for specific skills and strength of character over other more mundane attributes such as lack of a criminal record. From what I could tell, Ranger employed safecrackers, pickpockets, computer hackers, linebackers, and a bunch of vets who'd served overseas. He also had on his payroll a second-story burglar who the papers compared to Spider-Man, and a guy whose murder conviction was overturned on a technicality. I wouldn't want to be caught in a blind alley with any of these guys, but Ranger found something in each of them that inspired his trust. At least until a couple weeks ago.

I pulled two men out of the group for a closer look. One of them was Sybo Diaz, the evening monitor for the code computer. He was with Special Forces in Afghanistan and took a job as a rent-a-cop in a mall when he got out. His wife divorced him two months later. His wife's maiden name was Marion Manoso. She was Ranger's cousin. I didn't know the details of the divorce, but I thought there was the potential for some bad feelings. The other file I pulled was Vince Gomez. Vince wasn't one of the men with code computer access, but he caught my attention. He was a slim little guy with the flexibility of a Romanian acrobat. The inside joke was that he could crawl through a keyhole. He did system installation and troubleshooting for Ranger. I flagged him because he lived beyond his means. I'd seen him around, and I knew he drove an expensive car, and when he wasn't working he wore expensive jewelry and designer clothes. And he liked the ladies, a lot.

I left the paperwork in Ranger's office and returned to my desk. I worked at my computer for a half hour and wandered out to the kitchen. No one there, so I stopped in at the monitoring station and smiled at Chester Deuce.

"I've always wondered what you guys did out here," I said to him.

"There are always three of us on duty," he said. "Someone monitors the cars and responds to the men off-site. Someone watches the in-house video and is responsible for maintaining building integrity. And I watch the remote locations and respond to emergency calls and alarms."

"So if an alarm went off, what would you do?"

"I'd call the client and ask if they were okay, and then I'd ask for their password."

"How do you know if they give you the right password?"

"I have the information in an off-line computer."

I looked at the computer sitting to his right. "I guess it has to be off-line for security purposes."

He shrugged. "More that there's no reason for it to be on-line."

I returned to my desk and packed up. I had seven messages on my phone. All were from Lula, starting at three this afternoon. All the messages were pretty much the same.

"You gotta be on time for supper at your mama's house tonight," Lula said. "Your granny and me got a big surprise."

Thoughts of the big surprise had me rolling my eyes and grimacing.

Ranger appeared in my doorway. "Babe, you look like you want to jump off a bridge."

"I'm expected for dinner at my parents' house again. Grandma and Lula are taking another crack at barbecue."

"Has Lula had any more contact with the Chipotle hitmen?"

"I don't think so. She didn't mention anything in her messages."

"Keep your eyes open when you're with her."

My father was slouched in his chair in front of the television when I walked in.

"Hey," I said. "How's it going?"

He cut his eyes to me, murmured something that sounded like *just shoot me now*, and refocused on the screen.

My mother was alone in the kitchen, alternately pacing and chopping. Everywhere I looked there were pots of chopped-up green beans, carrots, celery, potatoes, turnips, yellow squash, and tomatoes. Usually when my mother was stressed, she ironed. Today she seemed to be chopping.

"Run out of ironing?" I asked her.

"I ironed everything yesterday. I have nothing left."

"Where's Lula and Grandma?"

"They're out back."

"What are they doing?"

"I don't know," my mother said. "I'm afraid to look."

I pushed through the back door and almost stepped on a tray of chicken parts.

"Hey, girlfriend," Lula said. "Look at us. Are we chefs, or what?"

Grandma and Lula were dressed in white chef's jackets. Grandma was wearing a black cap that made her look like a little old Chinese man, and Lula was wearing a puffy white chef's hat like the Pillsbury Doughboy. They were standing in front of a propane grill.

"Where'd you get the grill?" I asked.

"I borrowed it from Bobby Booker. He

brought it over in his truck on the promise he was gonna get some of our award-winning barbecue chicken someday. Now that we got this here grill, my barbecue is gonna turn out perfect. Only thing is, I can't get it to work. He said there was lots of propane in the tank. And my understanding is, all I have to do is turn the knob."

"I got some matches," Grandma said. "Maybe it's got one of them pilot lights that went out."

Lula took the matches, bent over the grill, and *Phunnf!* Flames shot four feet into the air and set her chef's hat on fire.

"That did it," Lula said, stepping back, hat blazing. "It's cookin' now."

Grandma and I had a split second of paralysis, mouths open, eyes bugged out, staring at the flaming hat.

"What?" Lula said.

"Your hat's on fire," Grandma told her. "You look like one of them cookout marshmallows."

Lula rolled her eyes upward and shrieked. "Yow! My hat's on fire! My hat's on fire!"

I tried to knock the hat off her head, but Lula was running around in a panic.

"Hold still!" I yelled. "Get the hat off your head!"

"Somebody do something!" she shouted, wild-eyed, arms waving. "Call the fire department!"

"Take the damn hat off," I said to her, lunging for her and missing.

"I'm on fire! I'm on fire!" Lula yelled, running into the grill, knocking it over. Her hat fell off her head onto the ground and ribbons of fire raced in all directions across my parents' yard.

Growing grass was never a priority for my father. His contention was if you grew the grass, you had to cut the grass. And what was the point to that? The result was that most of our backyard was dirt, with the occasional sad sprinkling of crab grass. In seconds, the fire burned up the crabgrass and played itself out, with the exception of a half-dead maple tree at the back of the yard. The tree went up like Vesuvius.

I could hear fire trucks whining in the distance. A car pulled into the driveway, a car door opened and closed, and Morelli strolled into the yard. Lula's hat was a lump of black ash on the ground. The tree was a torch in the dusky sky.

"I saw the fire on my way home from work," Morelli said. "I stopped by to help, but it looks like you have everything under control."

"Yep," I said. "We're just waiting for the tree to burn itself out."

He looked at the grill and the chicken. "Barbecuing tonight?"

A pack of dogs rounded the corner of the house, ran yapping up to the chicken, and carried it off.

"Not anymore," I said. "Want to go for pizza?"

"Sure," he said.

We each took our own cars, sneaking out between the fire trucks that were angling into the curb. I followed Morelli to Pino's, parked next to his SUV in Pino's lot, and we pushed through the restaurant's scarred oak front door into the heat and noise of dinner hour. At this time of day, the majority of tables were filled with families. At ten in the evening, Pino's would be crammed with nurses and cops unwinding off the second shift. We were able to snag a small table in the corner. We didn't have to read the menu. We knew it by heart. Pino's menu never changes.

Morelli ordered beer and a meatball sub. I got the same.

"Looks like you're working for Rangeman," Morelli said, taking in my black T-shirt and sweatshirt with the Rangeman logo on the left front. "What's that about?"

"It's temporary. He needed someone to fill in on the search desk, and I needed the money."

Back when we were a couple, Morelli hated when I associated with Ranger. He thought Ranger was a dangerous guy from multiple points of view, and of course Morelli was right. From the set of his jaw, I suspected he still hated that I was associating with Ranger.

"What have you got on your desk these days?" I asked him, thinking it best to get off the Ranger topic.

"A couple gang slayings and the Chipotle thing."

"Are you making any progress with Chipotle?"

We paused while the waitress set two glasses of beer on the table.

Morelli sipped his beer. "Originally, I thought it felt like a couple professionals had come in from out of town, but that didn't make sense after they went for Lula. These guys are afraid Lula will finger them."

"She gave you a description. Have you had any luck with that?"

"Lula's description fit half the men in this country. Average height, one shorter than the other, brown hair, average build, late forties to early fifties, she wasn't close enough to see eye color. No distinguishing features, and she said they dressed like white men. What the hell is that supposed to mean?"

"So you have nothing?"

"Worse than that, we have more than we can manage. The million-dollar reward brought out every crackpot in the state. We had to pull Margie Slater off traffic duty and sit her in a room with a phone so she could field the calls coming in. They were clogging the system."

"Lula's convinced Chipotle was killed over barbecue sauce, and she figures the killers will be at the cook-off. She's entered the contest so she'll have the inside track at identifying them."

"That'll make sense if she lives that long."

"Do you have someone watching her house?"

"That kind of surveillance only happens in the movies. We're so underbudgeted we're one step away from holding bake sales to pay for toilet paper."

"Have you considered the barbecue sauce connection?"

"I've considered a lot of connections. Chipotle had so much bad juju going it's a wonder he wasn't killed sooner. He has three ex-wives who hated him. Everyone on his television show hated him. His sister hated him. He was suing his manager. And the tenants in his New York co-op signed a petition to get him evicted."

"Who would have thought? He was all smiley on the jar of barbecue sauce."

"It's not that easy to slice off someone's head," Morelli said.

"The way Lula tells it, there wasn't any struggle."

"Yeah. That bothers me. Would you stand there and let someone decapitate you? And what about the guy who did it? Why would he choose decapitation? There are so many easier, cleaner ways to kill someone. And this was done in broad daylight in front of the Sunshine Hotel. It was almost like it wasn't planned."

"A spontaneous decapitation?"

Morelli grinned. "Yeah."

"And he just happened to be carrying a meat cleaver around with him?"

"Maybe he was a butcher."

"So all we have to do is look for an impulsive butcher."

Morelli signaled for another beer. "I'm having fun."

"Me, too."

"Do you want to go home and go to bed?"

"Jeez," I said. "Is that all you ever think about?"

"No, but I think about it a lot. Especially when I'm with you."

"I thought we were supposed to be mad at each other."

Morelli shrugged. "I don't feel mad anymore. I can't even remember what we were fighting about."

"Peanut butter."

"It was about more than peanut butter."

"So you *do* remember?"

"You called me an insensitive clod," Morelli said.

"And?"

"I'm not a clod."

"But you admit to being insensitive?"

"I'm a guy. I'm supposed to be insensitive. It's my birthright."

I was pretty sure he was kidding. But then, maybe not. "Okay," I said. "I'll take half of it back. You're not a clod."

The waitress brought our food and Morelli

took out his credit card. "We'll take the check now, and we'd like a to-go box."

"Since when?" I said.

"I thought we decided to go home."

"I can't go home. I have to go back to work."

"Doing what?"

"Doing what I do. I'm working at Rangeman."

"At night?"

"It's complicated," I said.

"I bet."

I felt my eyebrows squinch together. "What's that supposed to mean?"

"It means I don't trust him. He's a total loose cannon. And he looks at you like you're lunch."

"It's a job. I need the money."

"You could move in with me," Morelli said. "You wouldn't have to pay rent."

"Living with you doesn't work. Last time we tried to cohabitate, you threw my peanut butter away."

"It was disgusting. It had grape jelly and potato chips in it. And something green."

"Olives. It was just a little cross-contamination. Sometimes I'm in a hurry and stuff gets mixed into the peanut butter. Anyway, when did you get so fussy?"

"I'm not fussy," Morelli said. "I just try to avoid food poisoning."

"I have never poisoned you with my food."

"Only because you don't cook."

I blew out a sigh because he was right, and this was going to lead to another contentious topic. Cooking. I'm not sure why I don't cook. In my mind, I cooked a lot. I made whole mental turkey dinners, baked pies, roasted tenderloins, and whipped up rice pudding. I even owned a mental waffle maker. So to some extent, I understood Lula's delusional belief that she could barbecue. The difference between Lula and me being that I knew fact from fiction. I knew I was no kind of cook.

The waitress came back with a couple plastic take-out boxes and the check.

"Well?" Morelli asked me.

"Well what?"

"Are we eating here or are we taking these subs back to my house?"

"I'd rather eat here. I have to go back to work tonight, and this is closer to Rangeman."

"So you're choosing Ranger over me?"

"Rangeman. Not *Ranger*. I have a project I can only do in the evening. You should understand that. You choose your job over me all the time."

"I'm a cop."

"And?"

"And that's different," Morelli said. "*I'm* serving the public, investigating murders, and *you're* working for . . . Batman."

"Gotham City would have been a mess without Batman."

"Batman was a nutcase. He was a vigilante."

"Well, Ranger isn't a nutcase. He's a legitimate businessman."

"He's a loose cannon hiding behind a veneer of legitimacy."

We'd had this conversation about a hundred times before, and it never had a happy ending. Problem was, there was an element of truth to what Morelli said. Ranger played by his own rules.

"I don't want to get into a shouting match," I said to Morelli. "I'm going to pack up this sandwich and go back to work. We can try this again when I'm done working for Ranger."

The rhythm of Rangeman was always the same. As a security facility, it worked around the clock. The fifth-floor control room, the dining area, and most of the satellite offices were interior to the building and without windows. If you worked in these areas, it was difficult to tell if it was night or day.

The evening shift was in place when I came on the floor. Sybo Diaz was kicked back in his chair, watching several monitors. The code computer was to his right; the screen was blank. I'd never spoken to Diaz, but I'd seen him around. He wasn't the friendliest guy in the building. Mostly, he stayed to himself, eating alone, not making eye contact that would encourage conversation. According to his work profile, he was five foot nine inches tall and thirty-six years old. His complexion was dark. His face was scarred from acne he probably had as a teenager. He was built chunky, but he didn't look like he had an ounce of fat. He walked like his shorts were starched.

"Hey," I said to him, passing the desk on my way to my cubicle. "How's it going?"

This got me a polite nod. No smile.

I plunked myself into my chair and turned my computer on. I could see Diaz from where I sat. I watched him for twenty minutes, and he never moved or blinked or looked my way. I wanted to talk to him, but I didn't know how to go about it. The man was a robot. For lack of something better to do, I ran one of my assigned security checks. I printed the report and attempted to staple the pages, but the stapler was jammed. I pressed the button that was supposed to release the staples, I poked at it with my nail file, I banged it against the top of my desk. *Bang, bang, bang.* Nothing. I looked up and found Diaz staring at me.

"Stapler's jammed," I said to him.

His attention turned back to his monitors. No change in facial expression. Also no change in my stapler condition, so I hit it against my desktop some more. *Bang, bang, bang, bang, bang!*

Diaz swiveled his head in my direction, and I think he might have sighed a little.

I left my station and took my stapler over to Diaz. "I can't get it to work," I told him, handing him the stapler.

Diaz examined the stapler. By now the stapler had a bunch of dents, and the part that holds the staples was all bashed in. Diaz pushed the button that was supposed to release the staples, but of course nothing happened.

"It's dead," Diaz said. "You need a new stapler."

"How do I get a new stapler?"

"Storeroom on the second floor."

"Will it be open at this time of the night?" I asked him.

"It's always open."

This was like talking to a rock. "I don't suppose I could borrow your stapler?"

Diaz so looked like he wanted me to go away that I almost felt sorry for him.

"I don't have a stapler," he said.

"Would you like me to get one for you from the storeroom?"

"No. I don't need one. I haven't got anything to staple."

"Yeah, but what if suddenly you had to staple something and you didn't have a stapler? Then it would be a stapling emergency."

"Somebody put you up to this, right? Martin? Ramon?"

"No! Cross my heart and hope to die. I came in to catch up on my work, and I had this stapler issue."

Diaz looked at me. Not saying anything.

"Jeez," I said. And I went back to my cubicle.

I fiddled around for ten or fifteen minutes, drawing doodles in the margins of the report I'd just done, and Ranger called.

"This guy isn't human," I said to Ranger. "Does he ever talk to anyone?"

"No more than necessary to be a team member."

"I get the feeling he's been the brunt of some practical jokes."

"I'm not supposed to know, but I think there's a lottery going to see who's the first to get him to crack a smile."

"Why did your cousin divorce him?"

"She found someone she liked better."

"Gee, hard to believe there's someone better than Mr. Charming here."

"He's a good man," Ranger said. "He's steady."

"He's emotionally closed."

"There are worse things," Ranger said. And he disconnected.

Truth is, Ranger was every bit as silent and un-emotional as Diaz. Always in control. Always on guard. What made the difference was an animal intelligence and sexuality that made Ranger mysterious and compelling, while Diaz was simply annoying.

I ambled down to the second floor and prowled through the storeroom in search of a stapler. I finally found them and selected a small hand-held. I took it back to the fifth floor and showed it to Diaz on the way to my desk.

"Got my stapler," I said. "Thanks."

Diaz nodded and resumed staring at his collection of monitors. I walked around his desk and looked over his shoulder. He was watching multiple locations in the building. No activity at any of them.

"I thought for sure one of these would be tuned to the Cartoon Network," I said.

No response.

"What's this computer?" I asked, referring to the code computer. "Why isn't there anything on the screen?"

"I don't need it right now."

"What happens if you have to go to the bathroom?"

"One of the other men will cover. There's always an extra man in the control room."

I stood there for a while, watching Diaz ignore me.

"This is a little boring," I finally said to him.

"I like it," Diaz said. "It's quiet. It lets me think."

"What do you think about?"

"Nothing."

I found that easy to believe. I returned to my cubicle and my cell phone buzzed.

"Hey, girlfriend," Lula said. "Your granny needed a ride to a viewing at the funeral parlor tonight, so after the fire department hosed the tree down, I took her over here to pay respects to some old coot. Anyways, we were just about to leave and who do you think walked in? Junior Turley, your exhibitionist FTA. I didn't recognize him at first. It was your granny who spotted him. And she said she almost missed him, bein' he had all his clothes on. She said usually he's in her backyard waving his winkie at her when she's at the kitchen window. And she said she wouldn't mind seeing his winkie up close to make a positive identification, but I thought we should wait until you got here."

"Good call. I'm about fifteen minutes away."

I grabbed my purse and took the stairs, deciding they were faster than the elevator. I wanted to capture Turley, but even more I didn't want Grandma trying to make a citizen's arrest based on identification of Turley's winkie. I rolled out of the garage and called Ranger.

"Lula has one of my skips cornered," I told him. "I'll see you tomorrow."

"Babe," Ranger said. And he disconnected.

SEVEN

The funeral parlor is part renovated Victorian and part brick bunker. I found on-street parking and jogged to the front porch. Hours were almost over, but there were still a lot of mourners milling around. A group of men stood to one side on the wraparound porch. They were smoking and laughing, smelling faintly of whiskey. The funeral parlor had several viewing rooms. Two were presently occupied. Knowing Grandma, she probably visited both. Viewings were at the core of Grandma's social scene. On a slow week, Grandma would go to the viewing of a perfect stranger if nothing better popped up.

I found Grandma and Lula to the back of Slumber Room #3.

"He's up there at the casket," Lula said. "He looks like he knows the stiff's ol' lady."

"They're relations," Grandma said. "Nothin' anyone would want to admit to. That whole family is odd. I went to school with Mary Jane Dugan, the wife of the deceased. She was Mary

Jane Turley then. Up until fourth grade, she quacked like a duck. Never said a blessed word in school. Just quacked. And then one day she fell off the top of the sliding board in the park and hit her head and she started talking. Never quacked again. Not to this day. Junior's father, Harry, was Mary Jane's brother. He electrocuted himself trying to pry a broken plug out of a wall socket with a screwdriver. I remember when it happened. He blew out one of them transformer things, and four houses on that block didn't have electric for two days. I didn't see Harry after the accident, but Lorraine Shatz said she heard they had to put him in the meat locker to get him to stop smokin'."

"Stay here," I said to Lula. "I'm going to make my way up to the casket. You grab Junior if he bolts and tries to leave by this door."

"Don't you worry," Lula said. "Nobody's gonna get past me. I'm on the job. He come this way, and I'll shoot him."

"No! No shooting. Just grab him and sit on him."

"I guess I could do that, but shooting seems like the right thing to do."

"Shooting is the *wrong* thing to do. He's an exhibitionist, not a murderer. He's probably not even armed."

Grandma helped herself to a cookie set out on

a tray by the door. "You wouldn't be saying that if you saw him naked."

I eased my way along the wall, inching past knots of people who were more interested in socializing than in grieving. Not that this was a bad thing. Death in the Burg was like pot roast at six o'clock. An unavoidable and perfectly normal part of the fabric of life. You got born, you ate pot roast, and you died.

I came up behind Turley and snapped a cuff on his right wrist. "Bond enforcement," I whispered in his ear. "Come with me, and we don't have to make a big scene. We'll just quietly walk to the door."

Turley looked at me, and looked at the cuff on his wrist. "What?"

"You missed your court date. You need to reschedule."

"I'm not going to court. I didn't do anything wrong."

"You flashed Mrs. Zajak."

"It's my thing. Everybody knows I'm the flasher. I've been flashing for years."

"No kidding. This is the third time I've captured you for failing to appear. You should get a new hobby."

"It's not a hobby," Turley said. "It's a calling."

"Okay, it's a calling. You still have to reschedule your court date."

"You always say that, and then when I get to the courthouse with you, I get locked up in jail. You're a big fibber. Does your mother know you tell fibs?"

"Does your mother know you flash old ladies?"

Turley's attention switched to the door where Lula and Grandma were standing. "What are the police doing here?" he asked.

I turned to look, and he jumped away.

"Hah! Fooled you," he said. And he scuttled around to the other side of the casket.

I lunged and missed, bumping into Mary Jane Dugan. "Sorry about your loss," I said, shoving her aside.

"What's going on?" she wanted to know. "Stephanie Plum, is that you?"

Turley took off for the double doors at the front of the room, and I ran after him. He knocked some lady on her ass, and I tripped over her.

"Sorry," I said, scrambling to my feet in time to see Grandma do a flying tackle at Turley.

Turley wriggled away from Grandma and escaped into the ladies' room. Two women ran shrieking out, and Grandma, Lula, and I barged in.

Turley was trapped against the wall between the tampon dispenser and the sanitary hand dryer.

"You'll never take me alive," he said.

"Do you have a gun?" I asked him.

"No."

"Are you booby-trapped?"

"No."

"Then how are you going to die?"

"I don't know," Turley said. "I just always wanted to say that."

"Could we hurry this up?" Lula said. "I'm missing my Wednesday night television shows."

"I'll make a deal," Turley said. "I'll go with you if I can flash everyone on my way out of the ladies' room."

"No way," I told him.

"Eeuw," Lula said. "Ick."

Grandma slid her dentures around a little, thinking. "I wouldn't mind seeing that," she said.

Turley unzipped his pants and reached inside.

"Hold it right there," Lula said. "I got a stun gun here, and you pull anything out of your pants, I'll zap you."

Next thing there was a *zzzzt* from the stun gun and Junior Turley was on the floor with his tool hanging out.

"Whoa, Nellie," Lula said, staring down at Junior.

"Yep," Grandma said. "He's got a big one. All them Turleys is hung like horses. Not that I know firsthand, except for Junior. And maybe Junior's Uncle Runt. I saw him take a leak outside the Polish National Hall one time, and it was like he had hold of a fire hose. I tell you, for a little guy, he had a real good-size wanger."

"We need to get that thing back in his pants before we drag him out of here," I said.

"I'll do it," Grandma said.

"I think you done enough," Lula said. "You're the one encouraged him to take it out in the first place."

They looked over at me.

"No, no, no," I said. "Not me. No way, Jose. I'm not touching it."

"Maybe we could drag him out facedown," Lula said. "Then no one would see. All's we have to do is flip him over."

That seemed like an okay plan, so we rolled him over, and I finished cuffing him. Then Lula took a foot, and I took a foot, Grandma got the door, and we hauled him out of the ladies' room.

All conversation stopped when we dragged Junior through the lobby. It was like everyone inhaled at precisely the same time and the air all got sucked out of the room. Halfway across the oriental carpet, Junior's eyes popped open, his body went rigid, and he let out a shriek.

"Yow!" Junior yelled, flopping around like a fish out of water, wrangling himself over onto his back. He had a *huge* erection and a bad case of rug burn.

"I gotta tell you, I'm impressed," Lula said, checking out Junior's stiffy. "And I don't impress easy."

"It's a pip," Grandma said.

It was a pip and a half. I was going to have nightmares.

By now, the funeral director was hovering over Junior, hands clasped to his chest, face red enough to be in stroke range. "Do something," he pleaded. "Call the police. Call the paramedics. Get him out of here!"

"No problemo," I said. "Sorry about the disturbance."

Lula and I pulled Junior to his feet and muscled him to the door. We got him outside, onto the porch, and he kicked Lula.

"Hey," Lula said, bending over. "That hurts."

He gave Lula a shove, she grabbed me by my sweatshirt, and Lula and I went head-over-teakettle down the wide front stairs.

"Adios," Junior yelled. And he ran away into the night.

I was flat on my back on the sidewalk. My jeans had a tear in the knee, my arm was scraped and bleeding, and I was worried my ass was broken. I went to hands and knees and slowly dragged myself up to a semivertical position.

Lula crawled to her feet after me. "I'm surprised he could run with that monster boner," she said. "I swear, if it was two inches longer, it'd be draggin' on the ground."

I dropped Grandma off at my parents' house, drove to my building, parked, and limped to my apartment. I flipped the light on, locked the door behind me, and said hello to Rex. Rex was working up a sweat running on his wheel, beady black eyes blazing bright. I dropped a couple raisins into his cage and my phone rang.

"Myra Baronowski's daughter has a good job in the bank," my mother said. "And Margaret Beedle's daughter is an accountant. She works in an office like a normal human being. Why do I have a daughter who drags aroused men through funeral parlors? I had fourteen phone calls before your grandmother even got home."

The Burg has a news pipeline that makes CNN look like chump change.

"I think it must have happened when he got rug burn," I told my mother. "He didn't have an erection when I cuffed him in the ladies' room."

"I'm going to have to move to Arizona. I read about this place, Lake Havasu. No one would know me there."

I disconnected, and Morelli called me.

"Are you okay?" he asked. "I heard you dragged a naked guy through the funeral parlor, and then shots were fired, and you fell down the stairs."

"Who told you that?"

"My mother. Loretta Manetti called her."

"He wasn't naked, and no shots were fired. He kicked Lula, and Lula took me down the stairs with her."

"Just checking," Morelli said. And he hung up.

I dropped my clothes on the bathroom floor

and washed the blood away in the shower. I pulled on my old flannel pajamas and went to bed. Tomorrow would be a better day, I thought. I'd get a good night's sleep in my nice soft jammies and wake up to sunshine.

My phone rang at 5:20 A.M. I reached for it in the dark and brought it to my ear.

"Who died?" I asked.

"No one died," Ranger said. "I'm coming into your apartment, and I didn't want you to freak."

I heard my front door open and close, and moments later, Ranger was in my bedroom. He flipped the light on and looked down at me.

"I'd like to crawl in next to you, but there was another break-in tonight. This time it was a commercial account. I want you to take a look at it with me."

"Now? Can't it wait?"

Ranger grabbed jeans from my closet and tossed them at me. The jeans were followed by a sweatshirt and socks. "I want to go through the building before people arrive for work."

"It's the middle of the night!"

"Not nearly," Ranger said. He looked at his watch. "You have thirty seconds to get dressed, or you're going in your pajamas."

"Honestly," I said, rolling out of bed, scooping my clothes up into my arms. "You are such a *jerk*."

"*Twenty* seconds."

I stomped off into the bathroom and slammed the door closed. I got dressed and was about to brush my hair when the door opened and Ranger pulled me out of the bathroom.

"Time's up," Ranger said.

"I didn't even have time to fix my hair!"

Ranger was dressed in a black Rangeman T-shirt, cargo pants, windbreaker, and ball cap. He took the ball cap off his head and put it on mine.

"Problem solved," he said, taking my hand, towing me out of my apartment.

The building that had gotten hit was just four blocks from my apartment. Police cars and Rangeman cars were angled into the curb, lights flashing, and lights were on inside the building. Ranger ushered me into the lobby and one of his men brought me a cup of coffee.

"This building is owned by a local insurance company," Ranger said. As you can see, the first floor is mostly lobby, with a front desk and satellite glass-fronted offices. Executive offices, a boardroom, a small employee kitchenette, and a storeroom are on the second floor. It's not a high-security account. They have an alarm system. No cameras. For the most part, there's nothing of value in this building. The computers are antiquated. There are no cash transactions. The only thing of value was a small collection of Fabergé eggs in the company president's office. And that's what was taken."

"Was the routine the same?"

"The thief entered through a back door that had a numerical code lock. He deactivated the alarm, went directly to the second-floor office, took the eggs, reset the alarm, and left. The alarm was off for fifteen minutes."

"He had to be moving to get all that done in fifteen minutes."

"I had one of my men run through it. It's possible."

"Was the president's office locked?"

"The office door was locked, but it wasn't a complicated lock, and the thief was able to open it. He didn't bother to close the door or relock it when he left."

"How much were the eggs worth?"

"There were three eggs. One was especially valuable. Collectively, he probably lost a quarter of a million."

"Is this guy going to have a hard time fencing the eggs?"

"I imagine they'll go out of country."

I looked around. There was one uniform left in the building and one plainclothes guy from Trenton P.D. I didn't know either of them. Ranger had four men on site. Two were at the front door, and two were at the elevator.

"How was this discovered?" I asked Ranger. "Is there a night watchman or something?"

"The company president likes to get an early start. He's here at five every morning."

Morelli was awake at five. Ranger was awake at five. And now here was another moron at work at five. As far as I was concerned, five was the middle of the night.

"What am I supposed to do?" I asked Ranger.

"Look around."

I went to the back door and looked outside. From what I could see, there was an alley, a small blacktop parking lot with six designated spaces. No light. There should be a light. I stepped outside and looked up at the building. The light had been smashed. There were some glass shards on the ground under the light.

I went back inside and looked for the alarm pad. On the wall to my right. Exactly where I would have put it. I walked to the stairs, imagining the thief doing this in the dark. Probably had a penlight and knew exactly where he was going. And he was in a hurry, so he would take the stairs rather than the elevator.

I prowled through the second floor, peeking into offices, the kitchen, the storeroom. It all looked pretty normal. The president's office was nice but not extravagant. Corner office with windows. Executive desk and fancy leather chair. Couple smaller chairs in front of the desk. Built-in bookcase behind the desk with an empty shelf. I guessed that was where the eggs used to be.

I sat in the fancy leather chair and swiveled a little, checking out the pictures on the desk. Balding, overweight guy with a cheesy mustache, posing with a preppy dark-haired woman and two little boys. The corporate family photo display placed next to the corporate pen-and-pencil set that some decorator probably requisitioned and the guy never used. Matching leather blotter. And alongside the desk was the matching corporate wastebasket. A single Snickers wrapper was in the wastebasket.

I called Ranger on my cell phone. "Where are you?" I asked.

"Downstairs with Gene Boran, the president of the company."

"How did the thief know about the eggs?"

"The Trenton paper ran a feature on them two weeks ago."

"Perfect."

"Anything else?" Ranger asked.

"It looks like the cleaning crew came through here last night."

"They left at eleven-thirty."

"There's a Snickers wrapper in the wastebasket."

There was some discussion at the other end, and Ranger came back on. "Gene said he saw it on the floor, so he put it in the wastebasket."

"It could be a clue," I said to Ranger.

Ranger disconnected.

I ambled downstairs and slouched into a man-size chair in the lobby. The police had cleared out, and there were only two Rangeman employees left. Ranger spoke to the company president for another five minutes, they shook hands, and Ranger crossed the room to where I was sitting.

"I'm leaving Sal and Raphael here until the building opens for business," Ranger said. "We can go back to Rangeman."

"It isn't even seven A.M.! Normal people are still asleep."

"Is this going somewhere?" Ranger asked.

"Yes. It's going to . . . *take Stephanie home so she can go back to bed.*"

"Babe, I'd be happy to take you back to bed."

Unh. Mental head slap.

It was almost noon when I left my apartment for the second time that morning. I'd run out of Rangeman clothes, so I was dressed in jeans and a stretchy red V-neck T-shirt. My hair was freshly washed and fluffed. My eyes were enhanced with liner and mascara. My lips were comfy in Burt's Bees lip balm.

I stopped at the bonds office on my way to Rangeman.

"Just in time for lunch," Lula said when I walked in the door. "Me and Connie are feeling like we should try the chicken at the new barbecue place by the hospital."

"That's sacrilege. You always get your chicken at Cluck-in-a-Bucket."

"Yeah, but we gotta do barbecue research. I don't have my just-right gourmet barbecue sauce yet. I might have had it on the chicken last night, but the dogs run off with it. Anyways, I thought it wouldn't hurt to shop around. And I hear the guy who owns the barbecue place is gonna be in the contest."

"Sorry, no can do. I'm late for work."

"Just tell Ranger you needed barbecue," Lula said. "Everybody understands when the barbecue urge comes over you. And besides, there's no place to park by that barbecue place. I need a ride up there. It'll take you a minute, and it's the least you can do since I rescued you from that embarrassing experience last night."

"You didn't rescue me! You pulled me down the stairs and let Junior escape."

"Yeah, but people was watching me go ass-over-elbows down the stairs, and they hardly noticed you at all."

That could be true. "Okay, I'll give you a ride, but then I have to go to work."

Lula hiked her purse onto her shoulder. "We got it all planned out what me and Connie want to eat. All's I gotta do is run in and out."

Lula and I stepped out of the office onto the

sidewalk and stood for a moment squinting into the sun.

"This here's a beautiful day," Lula said. "I got a real good feeling about today."

A black Mercedes with tinted windows pulled out of a parking space half a block away and cruised up to the bonds office. It slowed, the side window slid down, a gun barrel appeared, there was maniacal giggling, and four rounds were fired off.

I heard a bullet whistle past my ear, the plate-glass window behind me cracked, and Lula and I hit the ground. Connie kicked the bonds office door open and aimed a Glock at the Mercedes, but the car was already too far away.

"That asshole took out my computer," Connie said.

Lula hauled herself up off the sidewalk and pulled her lime green spandex miniskirt down over her butt. "Someone call the police. Call the National Guard. Those guys are out to get me. That was one of those Chipotle killers behind that gun. I saw his idiot face. And I heard that crazy-ass giggling. Did someone get that license plate?"

Vinnie appeared in the doorway and cautiously peeked outside. "What's going on?"

Vinnie was my rodent cousin. Good bail bondsman. Scary human being. Slicked-back hair, face like a ferret, dressed like Tony Soprano, had a body like Pee-wee Herman.

"Someone's trying to kill Lula," Connie said.

Vinnie put his hand to his heart. "That's a relief. I thought they were after me."

"It's no relief to me," Lula said. "I'm a nervous wreck. And stress like this is bad for your immune system. I read about it. I could get shingles or something."

People from nearby businesses migrated onto the sidewalk, looked around, and realized it was just the bonds office getting shot at. Their faces registered that this was no big whoopity-do, and they drifted back into their buildings.

Lights flashed in the distance on Hamilton, and a fire truck and an EMS truck rumbled to a stop in front of the office.

"Hey!" I yelled to the fire truck. "You're blocking me in. I have to go to work. We don't need you."

"Of course we need them," Lula said. "Do you see that big beautiful man drivin' that fire truck? I think I saw him on one of them Fire Truck Hunks calendars." Lula stood on tiptoes in her spike heels and waved to him. "Yoohoo, sweetie! Here I am. I been shot at," she called. "I might be faint. I might need some of that mouth-to-mouth."

Ten minutes later, I was still waiting for the fire truck to take off, and Morelli strolled over.

"Now what?" he said.

"A guy in a black Mercedes shot at Lula. She said it was one of the Chipotle killers."

Morelli cut his eyes to Lula. "Guess they didn't tag her."

"No, but they got Connie's computer."

"Anyone see the license plate?"

"Nope."

"I like this red shirt you're wearing," Morelli said, tracing along the neckline with his fingertip. "Did you get fired from your new job already?"

"No. I ran out of black clothes."

"What happens if you don't dress in black? Do you have to go to detention? Do you get fined?"

I did an eye roll.

"I'm serious," Morelli said, laugh lines crinkling the corners of his eyes. "Are all the towels in the building black? Is there black toilet paper?"

I did a five-count of deep breathing as an alternative to kicking him in the knee.

"If you could get that fire truck to move, I could go to work," I finally said.

Morelli was still smiling. "You would owe me."

"What did you have in mind?"

"A night of wild gorilla sex."

"Good grief."

"How bad do you want to go to work?" he asked.

"Wild gorilla sex isn't going to happen. I'm not interested. I'm done with men."

"Too bad," he said. "I learned some new moves."

"We are no longer a couple," I told him. "And

you better not have learned those moves from Joyce Barnhardt."

Morelli and I went to school with Joyce Barnhardt, and she'd always had a thing for Morelli. For as long as I can remember, Joyce Barnhardt has been like a needle in my eye. I severely disliked Joyce Barnhardt.

It was close to two o'clock when I walked through the fifth-floor control room and settled myself in my cubicle.

My intercom buzzed and Ranger came on. "My office," he said.

I walked the short distance to his office and looked in at him. "What?"

"Come in and close the door."

I closed the door and sat in a chair opposite him. He was at his desk, and I was struck by the same thought I had every time I came into his office. Ranger always looked at ease, but he never actually looked like he belonged behind a desk. He looked like he should be scaling a wall, or jumping out of a helicopter, or kicking the crap out of some bad guy.

"Do you like doing this?" I asked him. "Do you like running this security firm?"

"I don't love it," he said. "But I don't hate it, either. It's a phase in my life. It's not so different from being a company commander in the military. Better work conditions. Less sand."

I wondered if my job was also just a phase in my life. Truth is, I felt a little stalled.

"Do you have any new thoughts on my problem?" he asked.

"Nothing big. Sybo Diaz gets the prize for most suspicious guy so far, but he doesn't fit into the puzzle right. He's like trying to ram a square peg into a round hole. Diaz was on duty when two of the break-ins occurred, so he'd have to be working with someone else. Problem is, I don't see Diaz having a partner in this kind of operation. He's totally closed. He'd have to do it all himself.

"The computer with the security codes is actually available to a lot of people. Four men have primary responsibility, but a bunch of other guys fill in for them when they take a break. And all the other men who are watching other monitors have the ability to see the screen on the code computer. You already knew this.

"The thing is, the longer I'm here, the less likely I'm inclined to believe this is an inside job. Everyone is watching everyone now. And the code computer is under constant scrutiny. And yet there was a new break-in. I think you have to look at outside possibilities. Maybe a rival security firm. Or a techno freak you fired or didn't hire. Or maybe someone not associated with you at all who's doing it for the rush."

"This isn't a large firm," Ranger said. "We offer quality personal service to a select group of clients. If I remove all clients with video surveillance, I cut the list in half. If I only look at residential accounts, the list gets much smaller. I was able to increase the number of cars I have patrolling video-free, residential accounts during hours when the break-ins occurred. If I have to enlarge that list to include commercial accounts spread over a two-shift period, I'm short manpower."

"Maybe you can get more accounts to use video."

"That's like announcing my system is corrupted. I'm trying to keep this quiet." He handed me a list of names. "These are non-video clients, both residential and commercial. The clients that have been hit by this guy are printed in red. I'd like you to ride around and see if anything jumps out at you."

EIGHT

I took the list back to my apartment, made myself a peanut butter sandwich, and marked Ranger's at-risk accounts on a map of Trenton. Commercial accounts in green Magic Marker. Residential accounts in pink Magic Marker. Accounts already hit in red.

Grandma called on my cell phone. "Guess who's standing in the backyard waving his winkie at me?"

"I'll be right there."

I called Ranger and told him I needed help with an FTA who was currently in my mom's backyard. I shoved the map and the client list into my purse and ran out of my apartment, down the stairs, and across the lot to my car. If I had luck with traffic, I could make my parents' house in five minutes. It would take Ranger ten to twenty minutes.

I called my grandmother when I was two minutes away. "Is he still there?"

"He's making his way through backyards. I

can see him from the upstairs window. I think he's going to Betty Garvey's house. She gives him cookies."

I went straight to Betty Garvey. I parked at the curb in front of her house and walked around back. I didn't see Junior Turley, but Betty was at her kitchen door.

"Have you seen Junior?" I asked her.

"Yes. He just left. I gave him an oatmeal raisin cookie, and he thanked me and went on with his walk. He's such a nice, polite man."

"Which way did he go?"

"He was walking toward Broome Street."

I jogged through the next two yards, crossed the street, and saw Junior at the end of the block. He was eating his cookie with one hand and shaking his wanger at Mrs. Barbera with the other. He looked my way and shrieked and took off running.

I chased Junior for half a block and lost him when he cut through Andy Kowalski's driveway. I stopped a moment to catch my breath and answer my phone.

"Babe," Ranger said.

"I lost him at the corner of Green and Broome. I think he's doubling back toward my parents' house. You can't miss him. He's eating a cookie, and he's got his barn door open."

I looked between houses and saw Ranger's black Porsche Turbo glide down the street. I stood perfectly still and listened for footsteps. A dog barked on the next block, and I ran in that direction. I crossed the street, hopped a fence, bushwhacked through a jungle of out-of-control forsythia, and spotted Junior Turley displaying his wares to old Mrs. Gritch.

I bolted out of the bushes and tackled Turley. We both went down to the ground, where we wrestled around, Turley trying to get away and me holding on.

"Stop that this instant," Mrs. Gritch said. "You're going to roll over my mums." And she turned the hose on us.

A black boot came into my line of vision, the water stopped, and Ranger lifted Turley off me and held him out at arm's length, Turley's feet not touching the ground, his pride and joy hanging limp against his drenched pants like a giant slug.

"I'm guessing this is the flasher," Ranger said.

I got to my feet and pushed my wet hair back from my face. "Yep. Junior Turley. And he owes me cuffs."

"I left them with your granny," Junior said.

I was soaked to the skin and getting cold. "I need to get out of these wet clothes," I said to Ranger.

"Go home and change. I'll have one of my men drop Mr. Turley at the police station."

"Thanks. I'll start riding around, checking things out for you, as soon as I get dry clothes."

* * *

I took a shower, put on clean jeans and my last clean sweater, and carted my overflowing laundry basket out to my car. The plan was to ride around and do a fast look at the Rangeman accounts that were between my house and my parents' house. This included Hamilton Avenue. Then I would mooch dinner from my mom and do my laundry at her house. There were machines in the basement laundry room of my apartment building, but I was pretty sure the place was inhabited by trolls, and I'd eat dirt before I'd go down there.

I drove by two houses and three businesses. The third business was the insurance company that had already been robbed. I didn't see anything suspicious at any of the locations. No one skulking in the shadows, casing the joint. No one throwing Snickers wrappers on the ground. The two houses were large, set in the middle of large landscaped lots. Easy to burgle if you didn't have to worry about the alarm system. The two remaining businesses were on Hamilton and would be more difficult to break into. They were both in high-visibility areas with poor back access. In both cases, the rear entrance opened to a chain-link-fenced lot that was gated at night.

I motored over to my parents' house and was surprised not to find Lula's car parked at the curb. I thought for sure this would be another barbecue night.

My mom and dad and Grandma Mazur were already seated when I walked in. I told them not to get up, but my mother and grandmother jumped to their feet and set a place for me. My father kept eating.

"Leave the laundry," my mother said. "I'll do the laundry later."

I sat at the table and filled my plate with pot roast, potatoes, gravy, and green beans.

"Where's Lula?" I asked Grandma Mazur. "I'm surprised you aren't barbecuing again tonight."

"She had a date with some hot fireman," Grandma said. "She said she was gonna give him brown sugar, and I said that was okay so long as she had some left for the barbecue sauce."

The phone rang and my mother and grandmother looked at each other and sat firm.

"Aren't you going to answer the phone?" I asked.

"It's been ringing off the hook," Grandma said. "I don't want to talk to any more grumpy women. Who'd think this would make such a stink? I help my granddaughter do her job, and next thing, we're all in the doghouse."

"It's about Junior Turley," my mother said to me. "Some of the women in the neighborhood are upset because you put him in jail."

"He exposed himself," I said. "Men aren't supposed to go around exposing themselves at unsuspecting women."

"Well, technically none of us was unsuspecting," Grandma said. "We wait for him to show up. I guess it's one of them generation things. You get to an age and you look forward to seeing a winkie at four in the afternoon when you're peeling potatoes for supper. The thing about Junior and his winkie is, you don't have to do anything about it. You just take a look and he moves on."

I poured more gravy over my potatoes. "Mrs. Zajak filed a complaint against him."

"She was in a snit because he skipped her that day," Grandma said. "It was starting to rain and he cut his circuit short. Everybody's mad at her, too."

"He won't be in jail forever," I said. "I'm sure Vinnie will bail him out again in the morning."

"Yeah, but I think his winkie-waggin' days are over," Grandma said.

It was dark when I left my parents' house. Clouds had rolled in and a light drizzle was falling. I did a sweep past the accounts I'd checked out earlier, and I went on to Broad Street and the area around the arena. Traffic was relatively heavy, and I was only able to catch glimpses of Ranger's buildings. The drizzle turned to rain, and I decided to quit for the night and start over in the morning.

An hour later, I was changed into my pajamas, watching television, and Lula showed up.

"I swear I don't know what things are coming to," Lula said, bustling through my front door and heading straight for the refrigerator. "What have you got in here? Did you eat at your mama's house tonight? Do you got leftovers? I need something to calm my stomach. This keeps up, and I'm gonna get a ulcer or diarrhea or something." She by-passed the pot roast and mashed potatoes and went straight for the pineapple upside-down cake. "You don't mind if I eat this, do you?"

"Knock yourself out."

Lula found a fork and dug into the cake. "First off, I got myself a date with that hot-lookin' fireman. You remember the one. The big brute with muscles bulgin' out everywhere. So he came over, and we did some talkin'. And then one thing led to another, and he said would I mind if he go into my bedroom. And I told him he was sittin' on my bedroom on account of I had to turn the bedroom into a closet. I mean, where's a girl supposed to put her shoes and her dress-up clothes? Anyways, I supposed he had things to do with himself, so I pulled out my sleep sofa, and I wasn't paying much attention to him, and next thing he's all dressed up in one of my cocktail dresses from the Dolly Parton collection."

"Get out."

"Swear to God. And he didn't look good in it, either. It was all wrong for him. He sees me lookin' at him and he says, *I hope you don't mind I'm wearing your dress.* And I say, hell yeah, I mind. You don't fit in that dress. You're bustin' out of it. You're gonna ruin it, and it's one of my favorites."

"And then what?"

"Then he gets all huffy, saying he thought he looked pretty darn good in the dress, and I shouldn't be talkin' about bustin' out of stuff. So I ask him exactly what that's supposed to mean, and he says, *figure it out, fatso.*"

I sucked in some air on that one. Calling Lula fatso was like asking to die.

"It got ugly after that," Lula said. "I don't want to go into the depressin' details, but he got his ass out of my apartment, and he wasn't wearin' my dress when he exited, either." She looked down at the empty cake plate. "What happened to the cake?"

"You ate it."

"Hunh," Lula said. "I didn't notice."

"Easy come, easy go," I said.

"That's so true. It's true about cake and men."

"Doesn't sound traumatic enough to give you an ulcer," I said.

"That wasn't the traumatic part. The traumatic part came after I booted him out. I was putting my gown away, and I heard someone knockin' at my door. I figured it was the moron fireman coming back to get his clothes. . . ."

"He left without his clothes?"

"He was in a hurry after I got my gun. The thing is, I already threw his clothes out my window. You know I live on the second floor of the house, so the clothes kind of floated down and landed in some bushes, and maybe he didn't notice. So I'm thinkin' it's just this loser again, and I open the door, and it's the Chipotle killers, and the one's got the big-ass meat cleaver and the other's got a gun."

"Omigosh."

"Yeah, that's what I said. I jumped back real quick and slammed the door shut, and *bang, bang, bang*, there was three bullets shot through my door. Can you imagine the nerve of them defacing my door? And it's not even like I own the door. This here's a rental property. And I don't see where I should be held responsible to pay for that door."

"What happened next?"

"I got *my* gun and *I* shot a whole bunch more holes in the door while they were trying to kick it in."

"Did you hit anyone?"

"I don't know. I emptied about half a clip in the door, and when I stopped shooting, there weren't any sounds coming from the other side. So I waited a minute, and then I peeked out, and I didn't see no decapitators. And there wasn't any blood all splattered around, either, although hard to believe I missed them, on account of they had their foot to the door when I started shooting."

It was easy for me to believe. Lula was the worst shot ever. Lula couldn't hit the side of a barn if she was three feet away from it.

"So that's why I'm here," Lula said, retrieving a big black garbage bag she'd left in the outside hall. "I brought some clothes and stuff with me because I figure I could stay with you while my door is getting fixed. It looks like Swiss cheese, and the lock's broke from those assholes kickin' at it." Lula closed my door behind her and took a look at it. "You got a real good door here. It's one of them metal fire doors. I only had a wimp-ass wood one."

I was speechless. Lula's a good friend, but having her as a roommate would be like getting locked in a closet with a rhinoceros in full attention deficit disorder mode.

"You don't have Morelli coming over or nothin', do you?" she asked. "I don't want to interfere. And I'll be gone as soon as they get my new door put up. Don't seem to me there's much to it. You get a new door and you put it up on those hinges, right?"

I nodded. "Yuh," I said.

"Are you okay?" Lula asked. "You look all glassy-eyed. Good thing I'm here. You might be coming down with something." She settled into my couch and focused on the TV screen. "This is one of my favorite shows. I watch this every Thursday."

I joined her on the couch and tried to relax. It'll be fine, I told myself. It's just for tonight. Tomorrow she'll get the door fixed, and I'll have my apartment back. And Lula's a good person. This is the least I could do.

Three minutes after sitting down, Lula's head dropped forward, and she was asleep, softly snoring. The snoring got louder and louder, until finally it was drowning out the sound from the television and I was sitting on my hands to keep from choking her.

"Hey!" I yelled in her ear.

"What?"

"You're snoring."

"No way. I was watching television. Look at me. Do I look like I'm asleep?"

"I'm going to bed," I said.

"You sure you don't want to see the end of this? This is a real good show."

"I'll catch it on reruns."

I closed the door to my bedroom, crawled into bed, and shut my light off. I took a couple deep breaths and willed myself to go to sleep. Relax, I told myself. Calm down. Life is good. Think of a gentle breeze. Think of the moon in a dark sky. Hear the ocean. My eyes snapped open. I wasn't hearing the ocean. I was hearing Lula snoring. I put my pillow over my head and went back to talking myself into sleep. Hear the ocean. Hear the wind in the trees. *Shit!* It wasn't working. All I could hear was Lula.

Okay, I had a choice. I could kick her out of my apartment. I could hit her in the head with a hammer until she was dead. Or I could leave.

I parked in the Rangeman garage and fobbed myself into the elevator and up to the seventh floor. I knew all eyes were on me in the control room. I waved at the Minicam hidden in the far corner of the elevator and tried to look nonchalant. I was wearing sneakers, flannel pajamas, and a sweatshirt. I'd called Ranger on the way across town and told him I needed a room. He said he was out on surveillance, and the only room available was his bedroom . . . so that was where I was headed.

I walked through his apartment in the dark and debated sleeping on the couch, but in the end Ranger's bed was too alluring. He was working a double shift, doing drive-bys on accounts he felt were at highest risk for break-in. That meant he wouldn't be back until six A.M. All I had to do was set the alarm so I'd be out of his bed before he rolled in.

The next morning, I was still in my pajamas and was standing in Ranger's kitchen when he got home. I wasn't entirely with the program, needing at least another two hours of sleep and a lot of hot coffee. Ranger had been up for more than twenty-four hours and looked annoyingly alert.

He wrapped an arm around me and kissed me just above my ear. "There's something wrong with this picture," Ranger said. "You're in my bed a lot, but never with me."

"It was nice of you to let me stay here. Lula has taken over my apartment."

"Nice has nothing to do with it," Ranger said.

"How was your night?"

"Long. And uneventful. I need to get some sleep. Are you coming back to bed with me?"

"No. I'm up for the day. Gotta get to work and solve all your problems."

"If you call Ella, she'll bring breakfast. Or you can get dressed and have breakfast on the fifth floor."

"I haven't got any clothes."

"Ella has clothes for you."

He took a bottle of water from the refrigerator, kissed me on the forehead, and left the kitchen. I called Ella, told her I was in Ranger's apartment, and ten minutes later, Ella was at the door with a breakfast tray and a shopping bag filled with Rangeman gear.

Ella wore Rangeman black just like everyone else in the building. Today she was in a girl-style V-neck T-shirt and black jeans.

I took the bag and tray from her at the door and thanked her.

"Let me know if the clothes don't fit," she said. "I saw you in the building yesterday, and I took a guess at the size. I didn't think you'd changed from the last time you worked here."

"I didn't see you," I said. "I never see you! Food just mysteriously appears and disappears in the fifth-floor kitchen."

"I try to stay invisible and not disrupt the men's routine."

Ella left, and I ate a bagel with cream cheese, drank a couple cups of coffee, and picked at some fresh fruit. My eyes were pretty much open, but I wasn't sure my heart was beating fast enough to propel me through the day. I collapsed on Ranger's couch and woke up a little before eight A.M. I picked some clothes out of the shopping bag, tiptoed past Ranger, and quietly closed the bathroom door.

I took a shower, brushed my teeth, dressed in my new clothes, and emerged from the bathroom feeling like a functioning human being. I was awake. I was clean. The caffeine had kicked in and my heart was racing. Okay, maybe it wasn't the caffeine. Maybe it was the sight of Ranger with a day-old beard, sleeping in the bed I'd recently vacated.

I left the apartment and took the elevator to the fifth floor. Roger King was monitoring the station that included the code computer. I paused in front of him to watch him work. He was on the phone with an account that had accidentally tripped their alarm. He was polite and professional. The conversation was short. The account gave King their password, King verified the password and ended the call.

"That's the first time I've seen someone verify a password," I said to King.

King was a nice-looking guy with a voice like velvet. I knew from his human resources file that he was twenty-seven years old and had a degree in criminal justice from a community college. He'd worked as a cop in a small town in Pennsylvania but quit to take the job with Rangeman.

"If you work this shift, you get a lot of bogus alarms," King said. "People get up in the morning and forget the alarm is on. By the time Chet takes over, this desk is like a graveyard."

When Chet showed up for his shift, I ventured out of my cubicle again and attempted small talk. Chet was polite but not stimulating, and I was feeling like I was contributing to the graveyard syndrome, so I moseyed on back to work, starting a computer search on a deadbeat client.

Louis had made good on the new chair, and my ass no longer cramped after a half hour. I was wearing black slacks that had some stretch, and a short-sleeved V-neck knit shirt with *Rangeman* stitched on it and my name stitched below the *Rangeman*. Ella had also given me cargo pants and matching button-down-collared shirts with roll-up sleeves, a couple stretchy little skirts, black running shoes, black socks, a black zippered sweatshirt, and a black windbreaker. I was on my own for underwear.

A little before noon, I sensed a shift in the climate and looked up to find Ranger on deck. He spoke briefly to each of the men at the monitoring stations, grabbed a sandwich from the kitchen, and stopped at my cubicle on his way to his office. He was freshly showered and shaved and perfectly pressed in black dress slacks and shirt.

"I have a client meeting in the boardroom in fifteen minutes," he said. "After that, I need to catch up on paperwork, and then I'll take another surveillance shift at six. How far did you get on the accounts list yesterday?"

"Not that far. I was getting ready to pack up here and spend the afternoon riding around."

"Do you need a company car?"

"No. I'm okay in the Escort."

I stuffed myself into my new Rangeman sweatshirt, hiked my purse onto my shoulder, and went to the kitchen to load up on free food. Ella had set out vegetable soup and crackers, assorted sandwiches, a salad bar, and a large display of fresh fruit. I looked it all over and blew out a sigh.

Ramon was behind me, and he burst out laughing. "Let me guess what that sigh was about. You want a hot dog, fries, and a brownie with ice cream."

"I'd kill for a meatball sub and a hunk of birthday cake, but this is better for me," I said, selecting a barbecue chicken sandwich.

"Yeah, I keep telling myself that. If I get shot dead on the job, there won't be an ounce of fat on me."

"Do you worry about that?"

"Getting shot dead? No. I don't do a lot of worrying, but the reality is most of this job is routine, with the occasional potential for really bad shit."

I dropped the sandwich into my purse, along with an apple and an organic granola bar. "Gotta go," I said. "Things to do."

"Knock yourself out."

I took the elevator to the garage, wrenched open the rusted door on my p.o.s. Escort, and motored out to the street. Probably it was stupid to refuse Ranger's offer of a company car, but it seemed like the right thing to do at the time. I had lousy car karma, and I always felt crappy when I used Ranger's Porsche and it got stolen or crushed by a garbage truck.

I had my map on the seat beside me, and I drove from one account to the next according to neighborhood. By four o'clock, I'd gone through all the accounts and had checked off a handful that I thought had the potential for a future break-in. I'd gone full circle around the city and ended on lower Hamilton, a half mile from the bonds office.

Lula hadn't called about the door, but I felt confident the door had been replaced and everything was cool. I drove up Hamilton to talk to Connie and Lula and found Connie was manning the office all by herself.

"Where is everyone?" I asked Connie.

"Vinnie is writing bond for someone, and Lula is at your apartment. She said she lives there now."

"I let her stay last night because her door was broken."

"I guess her door is still broken," Connie said.

"That's ridiculous. How long does it take to replace a door? You go to Home Depot, buy a door, and hang it on those doohickey hinge things."

"Something about it being a crime scene. The door can't be replaced until the lab checks it out."

"Who said that?"

"Morelli. He stopped by the office to talk to her after she reported the shooting."

Unh! Mental head slap.

I dialed Morelli and did some anti-hyper-ventilation exercises while I waited for him to pick up.

"What?" Morelli said.

"Did you tell Lula she couldn't replace her door?"

"Yeah."

"That's stupid. She has to replace her door. How can she live in her apartment without a door?"

"It's a crime scene that's part of an ongoing murder investigation, and we couldn't schedule evidence collection today. I'll have a guy out there tomorrow, and then she can replace her door."

"You don't understand. She's camped out in my apartment."

"And?"

"I can't live with her! She rumbles around. She takes up space. *Lots of space!* And she snores!!"

"Listen," Morelli said. "I have my own prob-lems."

"Such as?"

"You don't want to know."

A woman's voice called out in the background. "Get off the phone. I need help with my zipper."

My heart felt like it had stopped dead in my chest. "Is that who I think it is?" I asked Morelli.

"Yeah, and I can't get rid of her. Thank God

her zipper's stuck. I'm moving in with my brother."

For a moment, my entire field of vision went red. Undoubtedly due to a sudden, violent rise in blood pressure once my heart started beating again. It was Joyce Barnhardt. I hated Joyce Barnhardt. She was a sneaky, mean little kid when we were in school together. She spread rumors, stole boyfriends, alienated girlfriends, cheated on tests, and looked under stall doors in the girls' bathroom. And now that she was all grown up, she wasn't much different. She stole husbands, boyfriends, and jobs, cheating in any way possible. Her very presence in Morelli's house sent me into the irrationally enraged nutso zone.

I sucked in some air and pretended I was calm. "You're a big strong guy," I said, my voice mostly steady, well below the screaming level. "You could get rid of her if you wanted."

"It's not that easy. She walked right into my house. I'm going to have to start locking my doors. And she came in with a tray of lasagna. I'm afraid to touch it. She's probably got it laced with roofies."

Okay, get a grip here. She walked into Morelli's house. She wasn't invited. It could be worse, right?

"Why is she suddenly bringing you food?" I asked him.

"She's been up my ass ever since you broke up with me."

"Hey, stud," Joyce yelled to Morelli. "Get over here."

"Shit," Morelli said. "Maybe I should just shoot her and get it done with."

I had a bunch of bitchy comments rolling through my head, but I clamped my mouth shut to keep the comments from spewing out into the phone. I mean, honestly, how hard is it to shove a woman out your back door? What am I supposed to be thinking here?

"I have to go," Morelli said. "I don't like the way she's looking at my olive oil."

I made a sticking-my-finger-down-my-throat gagging motion and hung up.

"What was that about?" Connie wanted to know.

"Barnhardt is trying to feed her lasagna to Morelli."

"She's fungus," Connie said.

"I'm not too happy with Morelli, either."

"He's a man," Connie said. As if that explained it all.

"I suppose I should go home and see what Lula is doing."

"I know what she's doing," Connie said. "She's brewing barbecue sauce with your grandmother."

"In my apartment?"

"That was the plan."

Eek! Okay, so I know my apartment isn't going to get a full-page spread in *Home Beautiful*, but it's all I've got. Bad enough I have Lula in it. Lula and Grandma together are total facaca.

"Gotta go," I said to Connie. "See you tomorrow."

Vinnie stuck his head out of his office. "Where are you going? Why are you dressed up in Rangeman stuff? Christ, you're not moonlighting, are you? You aren't any good when you're working for me full-time. Now I'm sharing you with Ranger?"

"I brought two skips in this week."

"Big deal. What about all the others still in the wind? This isn't a goddamn charity. I'm not buying these idiots out of jail for my health. And it's not like you're the only bounty hunter out there," Vinnie said. "You could be replaced."

"Lucille's been talking redecorating again," Connie said to me. "Vinnie needs money."

Lucille was Vinnie's wife. She tortured Vinnie by constantly redecorating their house and by spending his money faster than he could make it. We figured this was retribution for Vinnie boinking anything that moved. The good part of the deal was that all Vinnie could do was pedal twice as fast, since Lucille's father, Harry the Hammer, financed the bonds office. If Vinnie left Lucille, not only would he be unemployed, there was a good chance he'd be dining with Stanley Chipotle.

"She's killing me," Vinnie said. "I haven't got money to buy a hot dog for lunch. My bookie took me off his iPhone."

Actually, it wasn't a good thing when Vinnie got this broke, because instead of buying favors from professionals on Stark Street, we suspected Vinnie was forced to chase down ducks at the park.

NINE

I left the bonds office, drove a couple blocks on Hamilton, and took a right into Morelli's neighborhood. Best not to examine my motives too closely. I was telling myself morbid curiosity was the driving force, but my heart was beating pretty hard for something that benign. I left-turned onto Morelli's street, cruised half a block, and stopped in front of his house. His SUV was gone, and there was no sign of Joyce's car. No lights on in the house. No sign of activity. I turned at the next corner and headed for the Burg. I drove past Morelli's brother's house. No SUV there, either.

Okay, get a grip, I told myself. No reason to get crazy. Morelli is a free man. He can do whatever the heck he wants. If he wants to act like a jerk and get friendly with Barnhardt, it's his problem. Anyway, I have to expect that he'll be seeing other women. That's what happens when people break up . . . they spend time with other people, right? Just because I don't want to spend time with other people doesn't mean Morelli has to feel that way. I'm one of those people who needs space between relationships. I don't just jump into stuff. And I don't do one-night stands. Usually. There was that time with Ranger, but you couldn't really categorize it as a one-night stand. It was more like a onetime-only ticket to WOW.

I turned out of the Burg onto Hamilton, and five minutes later, I pulled into my parking lot. I parked next to Lula's Firebird and looked up at my windows. No smoke. No sign of fire. No one running screaming out of the building. That was good. Maybe I wasn't too late. Maybe they hadn't started cooking yet. Maybe they'd discovered I only had one pot and decided to watch television.

I jogged across the lot, up the stairs, and down the hall to my apartment, reminding myself to stay calm. Lula and Grandma were in my kitchen and my counters were filled with bottles of barbecue sauce, dry rub, vinegar, cooking sherry, a half-empty bottle of rum, lemons, onions, oranges, a keg of ketchup, and a ten-pound can of tomato sauce. Grandma and Lula were in their chef's clothes, except Lula was missing her hat. My sink was filled with dirty measuring cups, assorted utensils, bowls, and measuring spoons. There was a large pot hissing on the stove.

"What the heck is that?" I asked Lula.

"I got my pressure cooker goin' here," Lula

said. "I saw it advertised on QVC. It cuts cookin' time in half. Maybe more. And it preserves all the goodness of the food. It was real expensive on television, but I got this one off of Lenny Skulnik. It's good quality, too, because it was made in China."

Lenny Skulnik sold knockoff handbags and kitchen appliances out of the trunk of his car. I went to school with Lenny. He was totally without scruples, and one of the more successful graduates.

"Are you sure it's supposed to make those noises?" I asked Lula. "And what about all that steam?"

"It's supposed to steam," Lula said. "It's why you call it a pressure cooker. And if you look close, you could see the pressure indicator is all red. That's the sign of good pressure cookin'. You wouldn't want no green shit on a pressure-cookin' indicator."

"Are you sure? Did you read the instructions?"

"This one didn't come with no instructions. This was the economy model."

I kept Rex's cage on the kitchen counter. It was lost behind the bottles and cans, but I could see Rex running on his wheel for all he was worth, every now and then sneaking a peek at the pot on the stove.

The pot had gone beyond hissing and was now whistling a high keening wail. *We-e-e-e-*

e-e-e. Red sauce was sputtering out of the steam hole and the pot was vibrating.

"Don't worry," Lula said. "It's just workin' itself up to maximum pressurizin'."

"It's a modern miracle," Grandma said.

I had a bad feeling in the pit of my stomach. I always worried when the little bulb at the top of anything went red. And I recognized the sound the pot was making. I felt like that sometimes, and it never ended well.

"Maybe you should turn the heat down a little," I said to Lula.

"I guess I could do that," Lula said. "It must almost be done. We've been cooking it for over an hour."

Lula reached for the knob on the stove and at that exact moment there was a *popping* sound and the two latches flew off the lid.

"Holy cats," Lula said.

"She's gonna blow!" Grandma yelled. "Run for your life!"

Rex darted into his soup can. Lula and Grandma and I turned tail and bolted. And the lid exploded off the pot. *BANG!* The lid hit the ceiling like it had been launched from a rocket, and barbecue sauce was thrown onto every exposed surface. There was a hole in the ceiling where the lid had impacted, and sauce dripped from the ceiling and slimed down cabinets.

"Guess we aren't having barbecue for dinner

tonight," Grandma said, creeping back to the stove to look in the pot.

Lula swiped at some of the sauce on the counter and tasted it. "Not exactly right yet, anyways."

A splotch of sauce dripped off the ceiling onto Grandma's head, and she retreated out of the kitchen.

"I feel like getting some of that Cluck-in-a-Bucket chicken," Grandma said. "I wouldn't mind the Clucky Dinner Tray with the extra-crispy chicken and mashed potatoes."

"That's a good idea," Lula said. "I could use some chicken, and I got a coupon for the Clucky Dinner Tray."

"What about my kitchen?" I asked Lula.

"What about it?"

"It's a mess!"

Lula glanced at the kitchen. "Yeah, it don't look too good. You're gonna have to use one of them degreasers on it."

"I'm not cleaning this kitchen."

"Well, somebody gotta do it," Lula said.

I narrowed my eyes at her. "That would be you."

"Hunh," Lula said. "In my opinion, that pot manufacturer should be responsible for the cleanup. I got a faulty pot."

"The manufacturer in China?" I asked her.

"Yeah. That's the one. I'm gonna tell Lenny Skulnik he needs to get in touch with them."

"And you think they're going to send someone from China to clean my kitchen?"

"I see your point," Lula said. "I guess I could do some cleaning, but I'd need a stepladder. Or else I'd need a big strong fireman to help me out."

"I thought you pulled a gun on him."

"Yeah, but he might be persuaded to overlook that if I let him wear my dress again."

Twenty minutes later, Lula rolled her Firebird into the Cluck-in-a-Bucket parking lot. Cluck-in-a-Bucket is a fast-food hot spot in Trenton. The food is surprisingly good, if you like nice greasy chicken, heavily salted gelatinous potatoes, and gravy so thick you could walk across a vat of it. Lula, Grandma, and I gave it five stars. And the very best part of Cluck-in-a Bucket is the giant red, yellow, and white chicken impaled on a thirty-foot candy-striped pole that rotates high above the red-roofed building 24/7. Paris has the Eiffel Tower, New York has the Empire State Building, and Trenton has the revolving chicken.

On weekends and during the dinner rush, there was always some poor sap dressed up in a Mister Clucky chicken suit. He clucked at kids, and he danced around and annoyed the heck out of everyone. The guy who owned Cluck-in-a-Bucket thought the dancing chicken was great, but the truth was everyone would have been happy to pay more for the chicken if Mister Clucky never clucked again.

Lula was one of three people out of ten thousand who liked Mr. Clucky.

"Lookit here," Lula said. "It's the dancin' chicken. I love that chicken. I like his red hat and his big chicken feet. I bet there's a real cute guy inside that chicken suit. You'd have to be cute to get a job as Mister Clucky."

I was betting there was a scrawny kid with a bad complexion inside the suit.

Lula got out of the car and went up to Mister Clucky. "You're a big Mister Clucky," Lula said. "You must be new. I got a bet with my friend that you're a real cutie-pie. How'd you like to give us a look?"

"How'd you like my beak up your ass?"

"Excuse me?"

"You heard me. Fuck off, fatso."

"Fatso? Did I hear you call me fatso? Because I better be mistaken."

"Fatso. Fatso. Fatty fatty fatso."

Lula took a closer look at Mister Clucky. "Hold on here. I recognize your voice."

"No you don't," Mister Clucky said.

"Larry? Is that you?"

"Maybe."

Lula turned to Grandma and me. "This is Larry, the fireman I was telling you about."

"The one who wears dresses?" Grandma asked.

"Yep. That's the one," Lula said.

"Lots of men wear dresses," Mister Clucky said. "It's not against the law."

"That's real true," Lula said. "And I've been reviewing our unfortunate date, and I decided you didn't look all that bad in that turquoise cocktail dress. Now that I'm thinking about it, that gown might have brought out the color of your eyes."

"Do you really think so?"

"Yeah. That gown was made for you," Lula said. "In fact, if you want to let bygones be bygones I might let you try it on again."

"I saw you had a beaded sweater that looked like it might match," Mister Clucky said.

"Yeah, you can wear the sweater, too."

He adjusted his clucky head and hiked up his privates. "I have to work until nine."

"That's fine," Lula said. "Only thing is, I'm staying someplace else. I'll get my food and come back with my new address."

We put our orders in and moved to the pickup station.

"He seemed like a real nice chicken," Grandma said.

"Yeah," Lula said. "I guess he's not so bad. And he's a real good dancer in his chicken suit. And on top of that, I bet he could get me a discount on chicken. He just took me by surprise the other night, causing me to overreact about the dress."

We all had the Clucky Dinner Tray, plus Lula supplemented hers with a side of biscuits and a bucket of barbecue chicken, which she said was research. She wrote my address on a napkin and handed it to Mister Clucky when we left.

"It must be fun to be Mister Clucky," Lula said to him.

"Yeah, the suit is pretty cool, and I get to dance around. Mostly, I do it for spending money, though. I do okay as a fireman, but nice handbags don't come cheap."

We all piled into the Firebird, and Lula drove a couple blocks to the supermarket.

"I'll be right back," Lula said. "I just gotta get some cleaning products."

"I'll go with you," Grandma said. "We could take another look at the barbecue aids."

I stayed in the car and called Ranger. "Just checking in," I said. "Anything interesting going on?"

"Nada. And you?"

"Lula and Grandma exploded a pot of barbecue sauce in my kitchen, Lula has a date later tonight with Mister Clucky, and it looks like I'll be spending the night in your apartment again."

"Something to look forward to," Ranger said. "Do you have any thoughts on my accounts?"

"Yes. I picked out several that I think have break-in potential." I gave him the addresses and told him Vinnie was having a cow over my open files. "I'm going to need some time off tomorrow to look for one of these guys," I said.

"Done," Ranger said. And he disconnected.

Lula swung her ass out of the supermarket and Grandma trotted behind her. They hustled across the lot to the car, Lula rammed herself behind the wheel, and in moments we were back on the road.

"Next stop is my house," Lula said. "I gotta get clothes for Larry."

Grandma leaned forward from the backseat. "What if the killers are waiting for you?"

"That would be good luck," Lula said. "We could take them down and get the reward. I'd shoot the heck out of them, and then we'd drag their carcasses to the police station."

"We'd kick their asses," Grandma said.

"Damn skippy," Lula said.

Lula eased the Firebird to the curb in front of her house, and we all piled out. Lula lived in an emerging neighborhood of hardworking people. Homes were small, yards were postage stamp size, and aspirations were modest. Lula rented half of the second floor of a two-story Victorian house that had been painted lavender with pink gingerbread trim. It was possibly the most inappropriate house in the entire universe for Lula. It was too small, too dainty, and too lavender. Every time I saw her walk through the front door, I had the feeling she was going through a portal into another dimension . . . like Harry Potter at the train station.

We got to the top of the stairs and gaped at Lula's bullet-hole-riddled door. Yellow-and-black crime scene tape had been plastered over the door, but it hadn't been applied in such a way that it prevented the door from being used.

"Cheap-ass plywood hollow-core door," Lula said. "Bird shot would go through this crap-ass door."

Grandma and I followed Lula into the one-room apartment and waited by the door while she went to her giant closet.

"This won't take long," Lula said. "I got everything organized in here by collection, so depending who I want to be, it's easy to find."

Lula opened her closet door and two men jumped out at her.

One had a gun and the other had a cleaver, and they were both wearing gorilla masks.

"It's the killers! *It's the killers!*" Lula shrieked.

"Grab her," the cleaver guy said. "Hold her still so I can chop off her head." And then he giggled and all the hair stood up on my arms.

His partner was trying to sight his gun on

Lula. "For crying out loud, get out of the way and let me shoot her. Big deal, you're a butcher. Get over it."

The guy with the cleaver swung out at Lula, giggling the whole time. Lula ducked, and the cleaver got stuck in the wall.

Lula scrambled hands and knees under a table, around an overstuffed chair, out her door, and thundered down the stairs.

The killers ran after Lula, not even noticing Grandma and me standing with our eyes bugged out and our mouths open.

"Don't that beat all," Grandma said.

She hauled her .45 long-barrel out of her big black patent-leather purse, stepped into the hall, planted her feet, and squeezed off a couple shots at the two guys running down the stairs.

The gorilla guys disappeared out the front door, into the night. There was the sound of car doors opening and slamming shut. An engine caught, and I heard the car drive away. A moment later, Lula appeared at the front door. She had a bunch of leaves stuck in her hair and a big dirt smudge on her wraparound blouse.

"What happened?" she said. "I don't hardly remember anything except I fell in a big bush."

"It was the killers," Grandma said. "We kicked their asses."

"Oh yeah. Now it's all coming back to me." Lula climbed the stairs and sleepwalked through her door. "It's a nightmare," she said. "It's a friggin' nightmare."

Grandma rooted through Lula's cabinets in the little kitchenette area of the room and came up with a bottle of Jack Daniel's. She took a pull from the bottle and handed it over to Lula. "This'll fix you up," Grandma said. "Take a snort of this."

Lula chugged some Jack Daniel's and looked a little better. "This is bullshit," she said. "This gotta end."

TEN

I took Grandma home, and then I drove to my apartment building and walked Lula into the apartment.

"Smells like barbecue in here," Lula said.

It *looked* like barbecue.

"Are you going to be okay?" I asked Lula.

"Yeah, I'm fine. I'm gonna hang my Dolly Parton dress and sweater up and get to work. I want to be working when Larry gets here."

"You should call Morelli."

"I guess, but I don't see where it does any good."

"He's working on finding these guys, and it gives him a more complete picture." And most important, it probably annoys the hell out of him and interrupts whatever he's doing.

"What's with you two?" Lula said. "Are you really calling it quits?"

"Hard to say. Every time we see each other we get into an argument. We don't agree on anything."

"Sounds to me like you're talkin' about the wrong things. Why don't you talk about other things? Like you could make a list of things you won't fight over and then you only talk about those things."

"I think he might be seeing Joyce Barnhardt."

"What?" Lula's eyes almost popped out of her head. "I hate Joyce Barnhardt. She's Devil Woman. And she's a skank. Men have relations with her and their dicks fall off. If I was you, and I found out Morelli was foolin' around with Joyce Barnhardt, I'd drop-kick his ass clear across the state."

I wrapped my arms around the hamster cage. "I'm taking Rex to Rangeman while you clean the kitchen."

"That's a good idea," Lula said. "We don't want to traumatize him with cleaning fumes. And he might not want to see a giant hairy man in a turquoise cocktail dress. I'm not sure I even want to see it."

I set Rex's cage on the counter in Ranger's kitchen and scrubbed the barbecue sauce off the glass sides.

"This is temporary," I said to Rex. "Don't get attached to Ranger. I know he's strong and sexy. And I know he smells nice, and he has good food, and his apartment is always the right temperature. Problem is, he's got secrets. And he's not in the market for a wife. Okay, so the wife thing might not be a deal breaker since I'm having commitment issues anyway, but the secrets he carries are troublesome."

I gave Rex fresh water and a chunk of bread, and I poured myself a glass of red wine. I took the wine into Ranger's small den, got comfy on the couch, and clicked the television on. I watched an hour-long show on Spain on the Travel Channel, and after that I couldn't find anything of interest. I dropped one of Ranger's T-shirts over my head by way of pajamas, crawled between his orgasmic sheets, and couldn't decide if I wanted him to come home early or stay away until morning.

I came awake with a start, not knowing where I was for a moment, and then remembering. Ranger's bed. I looked at the clock. 6:20 A.M. The light was on in the bathroom. Ranger emerged, still dressed in Rangeman tactical gear. He came to his side of the bed and kicked his shoes off.

"Either get out of the bed or else take your clothes off," he said. "I'm not in a mood to compromise."

"You've been working for eighteen hours. You're supposed to be tired."

"I'm not *that* tired." He removed his watch and set it on the bedside chest. "I saw Rex in the kitchen. Is this going to be an extended stay?"

"Would that be a problem?"

"We'd have to negotiate terms."

"Rent?"

"Sex and closet space," Ranger said.

I heaved myself out of bed. "If you sleep on my side, it's already warm."

I took a shower, dried my hair, and tiptoed past Ranger. He looked dangerous even in sleep, with a beard that was eight hours past five o'clock shadow and a shock of silky brown hair falling across his forehead. I dressed in Rangeman black, grabbed a sweatshirt, and went to the kitchen to say hello to Rex.

"Remember what I said about Ranger," I told Rex, but I'm not sure Rex cared. Rex was asleep in his soup can.

I pocketed my Rangeman key fob, hung my bag on my shoulder, and took the stairs to the fifth floor. Hal and Ramon were sitting at a table in the kitchen. Ramon looked fresh as a daisy. Hal looked like he'd just come off a shift. I got coffee and a bagel and joined them.

"What's going on?" I asked them.

"Same ol', same ol'," Ramon said.

Hal didn't say anything. Hal looked like he was asleep, with a spoon in his hand.

"Earth to Hal," I said.

Ramon cut his eyes to Hal. "Hal's working a double shift in the car."

"It's killing me," Hal said. "I don't know if it's morning or night anymore."

"Big guys like Hal need sleep," Ramon said. "Wiry little guys like me can do with less. And people who aren't exactly human, like Ranger, hardly need sleep at all."

"When we find out who's doing these break-ins, I'm going to personally beat the crap out of him," Hal said. "Then I'm going to sleep for a week."

I ate my bagel, and when Hal and Ramon left for parts unknown, I took a second cup of coffee to my desk. Aside from a couple men looking a little bedraggled from double shifts, everything was business as usual. I ran employee background checks for a start-up company in Whitehorse for almost three hours. My ass didn't cramp in my new chair, but my mind went numb from the tedium of staring at the screen. At ten o'clock, I stopped working for Rangeman and pulled Vinnie's remaining three current files from my bag.

Ernie Dell was wanted for setting fire to several abandoned buildings at the bombed-out end of Stark Street. This strip of Stark was so bleak and devoid of anything resembling civilized society that only a whacked-out crazy person like Ernie Dell would set foot there. Ernie was my age, and for as long as I've known him, which is pretty much my whole life, Ernie has been handicapped with a shape like a butternut squash. Narrow, gourd-like head, narrow shoulders, huge butt.

The second guy on my list was Myron Kaplan. Myron was seventy-eight years old, and for reasons not given in my file, Myron had robbed his dentist at gunpoint. At first glance, this would seem like an easy apprehension, but my experience with old people is that they don't go gently into the night.

That left Cameron Manfred. If I asked Ranger to help me with an apprehension, this is the one I'd choose. Manfred didn't look like a nice guy. He was twenty-six years old, and this was his third arrest for armed robbery. He'd been charged with rape two years ago, but the charge didn't stick. He'd also been accused of assault with a deadly weapon. The victim, who was a rival gang member, lost his hearing and right eye and had almost every bone in his body broken but refused to testify, and the charges were dropped for insufficient evidence. Manfred lived in the projects and worked for a trucking company. His booking photo showed two teardrops tattooed onto his face. Gang members were known to tattoo a teardrop below their eye when they killed someone.

I left a text message for Ranger that I'd be away from Rangeman. I stuffed myself into my sweatshirt, swiped a couple granola bars from the kitchen, and took the elevator to the garage. Traffic was light at mid-morning. Gray sky. The temperature was in the fifties. It felt cold for September.

I parked in front of the bonds office behind a truck that was repairing the front window. Connie was inside, and Lula was nowhere to be seen.

"She called a couple minutes ago," Connie said. "She said she was having a wardrobe issue, but she'd solved it, and she was coming in to work."

The door banged open, and Lula waddled in dressed in a flak vest and riot helmet. "Is it all safe in here?" she asked. "You checked the back room and all, right? I'm not taking no chances until those Chipotle killers are caught."

"Did you drive here dressed like that?" I asked her.

"Yeah. And it wasn't easy. I'm sweating like a pig in this. And this helmet is gonna ruin my hairdo, but it's better than having my head ventilated with bullet holes."

"Did you talk to Morelli this morning?"

"I did. Jeez Louise, he was in a mood. That man needs to get some. He was cranky."

I tried not to look too happy about that. "Have they made any progress finding the killers?"

"He said they had an out-of-town lead."

"Are you going to take that helmet off, or are you wearing it all day?" Connie asked.

"I guess I could take it off in here."

"I'm looking for Ernie Dell today," I said to Lula. "Do you want to ride shotgun?"

"Is he the firebug?"

"Yep."

"I'm in."

"I don't mind if you wear the flak vest," I told her, "but I'm not riding around with you in the helmet. You look like Darth Vader."

"Okay, but I'm gonna hold you responsible if I get killed."

Ernie lived alone in a large house on State Street. No one knew how he got the house, since no one could ever remember Ernie having a job. Ernie alternately claimed to be a movie producer, a stockbroker, a racecar driver, and an alien. I thought alien was a good possibility.

I idled in front of his house, and Lula and I craned our necks and gaped up at it. It was on about a half acre, on a hill high above the street. Shingles had blown off the roof and lay sprinkled across the yard. Window frames were down to bare wood and were splintered and split. The clapboard siding was charcoal gray. I wasn't sure if it was water stain, battleship paint, or mold.

"Holy crap," Lula said. "Are you shitting me? Someone lives in that? It's falling apart. And there must be a hundred steps to get up the hill. I'll get shin splints climbing those steps."

"There's an alley behind the house. And there's a back driveway and a two-car garage."

I drove around the block, took the alley, and parked in Ernie's driveway.

"What's the deal with this guy?" Lula asked. "Has he always set fires?"

I thought back to Ernie as a kid. "I can't remember him setting fires, but he did a lot of weird things. One time, he entered a talent show and tried to burp "The Star-Spangled Banner," but he was hauled off the stage halfway through. And then he went through a period where he was sure he could make it rain, and he'd start chanting strange things in the middle of arithmetic. *Oowah doowah moo moo hooha.*"

"Did it rain?"

"Sometimes."

"What else did he do? I'm starting to like this guy."

"He took a goat to the prom. Dressed it up in a pink ballerina outfit. And he went through a fireworks stage. You'd wake up at two in the morning and fireworks would be going off in your front yard."

We got out of the Escort, and I transferred cuffs from my purse to my back pocket for easier access.

"We don't want to spook him if he's home," I said to Lula. "We're just going to walk to the back door and be calm and friendly. Let me do the talking."

"Why do you get to do the talking?"

"I'm the apprehension agent."

"What am I then?"

"You're my assistant."

"Maybe I don't want to be the assistant. Maybe I want to be the apprehension agent."

"You have to talk to Vinnie about that. Your name has to be on the documentation."

"We could write me in. I got a pen."

"Good grief."

"How about if I just say *hello*."

"Fine. Terrific. Say *hello*."

I knocked on the back door, and Ernie answered in his underwear.

"Hello," Lula said.

Ernie looked like he'd just rolled out of bed. His thinning sandy blond hair was every which way on his head. "What's up?" he asked.

"You missed your court date," I said. "You need to go downtown with me and reschedule."

"Sure," he said. "Wait in the front room while I get dressed."

We followed him through the kitchen that was circa 1942, down a hall with peeling, faded wallpaper, and into the living room. The living room floor was bare, scarred wood. The furniture was minimal. A lumpy secondhand couch. Two folding chairs with the funeral home's name engraved on the back. A rickety end table had been placed between the two folding chairs. No lamps. No television.

"I'll be right back," Ernie said, heading for the stairs. "Make yourself comfortable."

Lula looked around. "How are we supposed to get comfortable?"

"You could sit down," I told her.

Lula sat on one of the folding chairs, and it collapsed under her weight.

"Fuck," she said, spread-eagle on the floor with the chair smashed under her. "I bet I broke a bone."

"Which bone did you break?"

"I don't know. Pick one. They all feel broke."

Lula struggled to her feet and felt around, testing out her bones. Ernie was still upstairs, getting dressed, but I didn't hear him walking overhead.

I went to the bottom of the stairs and called. "Ernie?"

Nothing. I climbed the stairs and called his name again. Silence. Four rooms, plus a bathroom, led off the center hall. One room was empty. One room was filled with bizarre junk. Store mannequins with broken arms, gallon cans of cooking oil, stacks of bundled newspapers, boxes of firecrackers and rockets, gallon cans of red paint, a wooden crate of rusted nails, a birdcage, a bike that looked like it had been run over by a truck, and God only knows what else. The third room housed a sixty-inch plasma television, an elaborate computer station, and a movie house popcorn machine. A new leather La-Z-Boy re-cliner sat in the middle of the room and faced the television. The fourth room was his bedroom. A sleeping bag and pillow had been thrown onto the floor of the fourth room. Clothes were scattered around in no special order. Some looked clean and some looked like they'd been worn a lot.

The window was open in the bedroom, and two large hooks wrapped over the windowsill. I crossed the room to the window and looked down. Rope ladder. The sort you might stash in a room as a fire precaution.

I ran downstairs and headed for the kitchen. "He's gone."

Lula and I reached the back door just as an engine caught in the garage, and a baby diarrhea green VW bug chugged out to the alley. We ran for the Escort, jumped in, and took off. I could see the bug two blocks away. Ernie turned right and I floored it, bouncing along the pot-holed service road. I turned right and caught a flash of green a block away. I was gaining on him.

"Do you smell something?" Lula asked.

"Like what?"

"I don't know, but it's not good."

I was concentrating on driving and not on smelling. Ernie was going in circles. He was driving a four-block grid.

"It's like a cat was burning," Lula said. "I never actually smelled a cat burning, but if I did, it would smell like this. And do you think it's getting smokey in here?"

"Smokey?"

"*Yow!*" Lula said. "Your backseat is on fire. I mean, it's a inferno. Let me out of this car. Pull over. I wasn't meant to be extra crispy."

I screeched to a stop, and Lula and I scrambled out of the car. The fire raced along the upholstery and shot out the windows. Flames licked from the undercarriage and *Vrooosh!* The car was a fireball. I looked up the street and saw the pea green VW lurking at the corner. The car idled for a few moments and sedately drove away.

"How long do you think it's gonna take the fire trucks to get here?" Lula wanted to know.

"Not long. I hear sirens."

"This is gonna be embarrassing. This is the second thing we burned up this week."

I dialed Ranger. "Did I wake you?" I asked.

"No. I'm up and functioning. I just got a report that the GPS unit we attached to your car stopped working."

"You know how when you toast a marshmallow it catches fire and gets all black and melted?"

"Yeah."

"That would be my car."

"Are you okay?"

"Yes, but I'm stranded," I told him.

"I'll send Tank."

* * *

I watched the fire truck disappear down the street, followed by the last remaining cop car. What was left of my Escort was on a flatbed.

"Where do you want me to take this?" the flatbed guy asked me.

"Dump it in the river."

"You got it," he said. And he climbed into the cab and rumbled away.

"Guess you gotta be careful when you're going after someone who likes fire," Lula said.

I had a shiny new black Porsche Cayenne waiting for me. Tank had dropped it off, made sure I didn't need help, and returned to Rangeman. The car was one of several in Ranger's personal fleet. It was immaculate inside, with no trace of Ranger other than a secret drawer under the driver's seat. The drawer held a loaded gun. All cars in Ranger's personal fleet had guns hidden under the seat.

I remoted the car open, and Lula and I got in.

"Now what?" Lula said.

"Lunch."

"I like that idea. And I think we should take something to Larry on account of he's still working on your kitchen."

"It sounds like things went okay last night."

"One thing you learn when you're a 'ho is there's all kinds in this world. Bein' a 'ho is a broadening experience. It's not just all hand jobs, you know. It's listenin' to people sometimes and tryin' to figure out how to make them happy. That's why I was a good 'ho. I didn't charge by the hour."

"And Larry fits in there somewhere."

"Yeah. He's a real interesting person. He was a professional wrestler. His professional name was Lady Death, but he was one of them niche market wrestlers, and his feelings got hurt when the fans didn't like him in his pink outfits. So he quit, and he got a job as a fireman. Turns out he's a hottie, too. He likes wearing ladies' clothes, but he isn't gay."

We decided Larry was probably tired of chicken, so we got ham and cheese and hot pepper subs and brought them back to my apartment.

"Boy, that's great of you to bring me lunch," Larry said. "I'm starving."

He was still wearing the Dolly Parton number. It had a fitted bodice with spaghetti straps and a swirly chiffon skirt, and there was a lot of chest hair and back hair sticking out of the top of the dress. There was also a lot of armpit hair, leg hair, and knuckle hair. He'd accessorized the dress with heels and rubber gloves.

"I know this looks funny," he said, "but I like to feel pretty when I clean."

"Go for it," I told him. And I meant it. I didn't care what he was wearing as long as I was getting barbecue sauce removed from my walls.

My cell phone buzzed, and I recognized Morelli's number.

"I'm trying to find Lula," he said. "I called the office, and they said she was with you."

"Why didn't you just call her cell?"

"She's not answering her cell."

"Do you want to talk to her?"

"I need to show her a photograph. Where are you?"

"We're in my apartment."

"Stay there. I'm a couple minutes away."

"That was Morelli," I said to Lula. "He's coming here with a photograph he wants you to look at. He said you're not answering your cell phone."

"It's out of juice. I forgot to plug it in."

Five minutes later, I opened my door to Morelli. He looked at me in my Rangeman clothes, and the line of his mouth tightened. "Why don't I just lie down in the parking lot and let you run over me a couple times. It would be less painful."

"Been there, done that," I said.

The bright red splotches in my kitchen caught his attention. "Remodeling?" he asked.

"Pressure cooker full of barbecue sauce."

That got a smile. "Where's Lula?"

"Eating lunch in the dining room."

The smile widened when Morelli walked into the dining room and eyeballed Lula in her flak vest and Larry in his cocktail dress.

"This here's Larry," Lula said to Morelli. "He's Mister Clucky."

"I'm a fireman full-time," Larry said. "Being Mister Clucky is my part-time job."

Morelli extended his hand. "Joe Morelli. Isn't it early in the day for a cocktail dress?"

"I guess," Larry said, "but I stayed over, and this was all I had to wear."

Morelli cut his eyes to me. "He stayed over?"

"It's complicated."

"I bet."

"Are those pictures you're holding for me?" Lula asked. "You need to be figuring this out, because I'm gettin' tired of this *kill Lula* bullshit."

Morelli gave her the photos, and Lula flipped through them.

"This one," Lula said. "This guy with the bad haircut and a nose like Captain Hook. He's one of the killers. He's the one with the meat cleaver."

"That's Marco the Maniac," Morelli said.

"Oh shit," Lula said. "I got a killer named Maniac. Where's my helmet? I need my helmet. I think I left it at the office."

"His profile finally popped out of the system," Morelli said. "He's from Chicago. Works as a butcher, but he makes spare change by chopping off fingers and toes of people who annoy the Chicago Mob. Mostly gets off on insufficient evidence, but did some time a couple years ago. I don't know how he's connected to Chipotle. I'm assuming it was a contract hit, but we don't really know."

"You're gonna arrest him, right?" Lula said.

"As soon as we find him."

"Well, what are you doing standing here!" Lula said. "You gotta mobilize or something. Put out one of them APB things. I need all my fingers and toes. I got some Via Spiga sandals that aren't gonna look right if I only got nine toes. And what about the guy with the gun? Why don't you got a picture of him?"

"We're working on it," Morelli said.

"Working on it, my ass," Lula said. "I'm gettin' the runs. I need a doughnut."

Morelli grabbed my wrist and tugged me to the door. "I need to talk to you alone," he said, moving me into the hall and down toward the elevator.

"I don't want to argue about Rangeman," I told him.

"I don't care about Rangeman," Morelli said, his voice cracking with laughter. "I want to know about the guy in the dress. What the heck is that about?"

"Lula exploded the barbecue sauce in my kitchen and didn't want to clean it up, so she told this cross-dresser he could wear her dress if he scrubbed the sauce off the walls and ceiling."

"And he spent the night?"

"Lula's guest."

"The crime lab got to her apartment first thing this morning. She can change out that door anytime she wants."

"I'm not sure she'll go back there. She's really freaked."

"From what I can tell, Marco is an animal with a very small brain. He's dangerous and disgusting but not smart. At the risk of sounding insensitive, Lula is a large target, and anyone else would have killed her by now."

"So you think she shouldn't be worried?"

"I think she should be terrified. If this goes on long enough, Marco is going to get lucky, and Lula is going to lose a lot more than a toe." He punched the elevator button. "Is that Ranger's Cayenne in your parking lot?"

A small sigh escaped before I could squelch it. "I tried to capture Ernie Dell, but he torched my car and got away. Ranger gave me a loaner."

The elevator doors opened, and Morelli stepped inside.

"How close are you to catching Marco?" I asked him.

"Not close enough."

I returned to the apartment and finished my lunch.

"We should have got dessert," Lula said. "I don't know what we were thinking about, not getting dessert."

"You have to stop obsessing about food," I told her. "You're going to weigh four hundred pounds."

"Are you sayin' I'm fat? Because I think I'm just a big and beautiful woman."

"You're still beautiful," I said. "But I think the *big* is getting a little *bigger*."

"That's a valid point," Lula said. She locked on to Larry. "Do you think I'm fat?"

Larry was deer in headlights. He'd already traveled this road. "Well, you're not *too* fat," he said.

"Not too fat for what?" Lula wanted to know.

"For me. For this dress. I'm sure you look much better in this dress than I do."

"Damn right," Lula said. "Take that dress off and I'll show you. This dress fits me perfect."

Larry stood and reached for the zipper, and I clapped my hands over my eyes.

"It's okay," Larry said to me. "I'm wearing boxers. I didn't have any nice lingerie with me."

"It doesn't matter," I said. "I don't want to see Lula, either. Tell me when it's over."

"Well, what the heck is wrong with this dress?" Lula said a couple minutes later. "I can't get this thing together."

I opened my eyes, and Lula had the dress on, but it wasn't zipped. There was fat bulging out everywhere, and Larry had his knee against

Lula's back and was two-handing the zipper, trying to pull it up.

"Suck it in," Larry said. "I have this problem sometimes, too."

"I'm all sucked," Lula said. "I can't suck no more."

Veins were standing out in Larry's temples and bulging in his neck. "I'm getting it," he said. "I can press two hundred pounds, and there's no reason why I can't get this zipper closed."

The heck there wasn't. The dress wasn't made out of spandex. And even spandex had limits.

"I've almost got it," Larry said, sweat dripping off his flushed face, running in rivers down his chest. "I've got an inch to go. One lousy, motherfucking, cocksucking inch."

Lula was standing tall, not moving a muscle.

"Yeah, baby!" Larry said. "I got it! Woohoo! *Yeah!*" He stepped back and pumped his fist and did a white boy shuffle in his boxers.

Lula still wasn't moving. Her eyes were all wide and bulging, and she was looking not so brown as usual.

"Can't breathe," Lula whispered. "Feel faint."

And then *POW*, the zipper let loose, and Lula flopped onto the floor, gasping for air.

Larry and I peered down at her.

"Maybe I could use to lose a pound or two," Lula said.

We got Lula out of the dress and back into her marigold yellow stretch slacks, matching scoop-neck sweater, and black flak vest. And neither of us mentioned that she looked like a giant bumblebee.

"Are you okay?" Larry asked her.

"Pretty much, but I need a doughnut."

"No doughnuts!" Larry and I said in unison.

"Oh yeah," Lula said. "I forgot."

"I have to get back to work," I said to Lula. "Are you coming with me?"

"I guess," Lula said. "But we gotta stop at your mama's house. Your granny was supposed to cook up a recipe I gave her."

ELEVEN

My mother and Grandma Mazur were in the kitchen. My mother was at the stove, stirring red sauce, and Grandma was at the sink, drying pots stacked in the Rubbermaid dish drainer.

"I made up the recipe just like you said," Grandma told Lula. "And then I put the sauce on some pulled pork. It's in the casserole dish in the refrigerator."

"How does it taste?" Lula asked. "What do you think of it?"

"It tastes okay, but I got the trots as soon as I ate it. I've been in the bathroom ever since. I got hemorrhoids on hemorrhoids."

"Get it out of the refrigerator before your father gets hold of it," my mother said to me. "Bad enough I've got your grandmother running upstairs every ten minutes. I don't want to have to listen to the two of them fighting over who gets in first."

I took the casserole dish out of the refrigerator

and lifted the lid. It looked good, and it smelled great.

"Do you want to try some?" I asked Lula.

"Ordinarily," Lula said. "But I'm on a diet. Maybe you should taste it."

"Not in a hundred years," I told her.

"It could just be a fluke that your granny got the trots," Lula said. "It could be one of them anemones."

"I think you mean anomaly."

"Yeah, that's it."

"We're having ham tonight," my mother said to me. "And pineapple upside-down cake. You should bring Joseph to dinner."

"I'm not seeing him anymore."

"Since when?"

"Since weeks ago."

"Do you have a new boyfriend?"

"No. I'm done with men. I have a hamster. That's all I need."

"That's a shame," my mother said. "It's a big ham."

"I'll come to dinner," I said. "I love ham."

"No Joseph?"

"No Joseph. I'll take his share home and eat it for lunch tomorrow."

"I know what we can do with this casserole," Lula said. "We can take it to the office and feed it to Vinnie. He don't care what he puts in his mouth."

I thought that sounded like a decent idea, so I

carted the pulled pork out to Ranger's Porsche and carefully set it on the floor in the back. Lula and I buckled ourselves in, and I headed for Hamilton Avenue.

"Holy cats," Lula said, half a block away from the office. "You see that car parked on the other side of the street? It's the bushy-headed killer. It's Marco the Maniac. He's sitting there waiting to kill me."

"Don't panic," I said. "Get his license plate. I'm dialing Morelli."

"It's them or me," she said, launching herself over the consul onto the backseat, powering the side window down. "This is war."

"Stay calm! Are you getting the license number?"

"Calm, my ass." And she stuck her Glock out the window and squeezed off about fifteen shots at the two guys in the car. "Eat lead," she yelled, "you sons of bitches!"

Bullets ricocheted off metal wheel covers and bit into fiberglass, but clearly none hit their intended mark because the car took off and was doing about eighty miles an hour before it even got to the corner. I hung a U-turn in front of the bonds office, sending oncoming cars scrambling onto curbs, screeching to a stop.

Lula had discarded the flak vest, rammed herself through the side window, and was half in and half out, still shooting at the car in front of us.

"Stop shooting," I yelled at her. "You're going to kill someone."

The car turned left onto Olden, and I was prevented from following by heavy traffic.

"Get back into the car," I said to Lula. "I've lost them."

"I can't get back," Lula said. "I'm stuck."

I looked over my shoulder at Lula. All I could see was bright yellow ass. The rest of her was out the window.

"Stop fooling around," I told her.

"I'm not fooling. I'm stuck!"

Cars were passing and honking.

"Your ass," Lula said to the cars.

I checked her out in my side mirror and saw that not only was she stuck, but her boobs had fallen out of the scoop-neck sweater and were blowing in the wind. I turned onto a side street and pulled to the curb to take a look. By the time I got out of the car, I was laughing so hard tears were rolling down my cheeks and I could hardly see.

"I don't see where this is so funny," Lula said. "Get me out of the window. I'm about freezing my nipples off. It's not like it's summer or somethin'."

Short of lubing Lula up with goose grease, I didn't know where to begin.

"Do you think it's better if I pull or push?" I asked her.

"I think you should pull. I don't think I'm gonna get my titties and my belly back through the window. I think my ass is smaller. And I don't want no wisecrackin' comment on that, neither."

I latched on to her wrists, planted my feet, and pulled, but she didn't budge.

"I'm losing circulation in my legs," Lula said. "You don't get me out of here soon, I'm gonna need amputation."

I went around to the other side, got into the backseat, and almost fainted at the sight of the big yellow butt in front of me. I broke into a nervous giggle and instantly squashed it. Get it together, I told myself. This is serious stuff. She could lose the use of her legs.

I put my hands on her ass and shoved. Nothing. No progress. I put my shoulder to her and leaned into it. Ditto. Still stuck. I got out of the Porsche and went around to take another look from the front.

"Maybe I should call roadside assistance," I said to Lula. "Or the fire department."

"I don't feel so good," Lula said. And she farted.

"Jeez Louise," I said. "Could you control yourself? This is Ranger's Porsche."

"I can't help it. I'm just a big gasbag. I still got leftover barbecue gas." She squeezed her eyes shut tight and did a full minute-long fart. "Excuse me," she said.

I was horrified and impressed all at the same

time. It was a record-breaking fart. On my best day, I couldn't come near to farting like that.

"I feel a lot better," Lula said. "Look at me. I got room in the window opening." She wriggled a little and eased herself back into the SUV. "I'm not so fat after all," she said. "I was just all swelled up."

My cell phone buzzed, and I saw from the screen that it was Morelli.

"Did I miss a call from you?" he asked.

"Yeah. Marco and his partner were parked in front of the bonds office. They were in a black Lincoln Town Car. I didn't get their license. I followed them to Olden and then lost them."

"I'll put it on the air."

"Thanks."

Ten minutes later, Lula and I trudged into the office with the casserole and came face-to-face with Joyce Barnhardt.

Joyce had been a pudge when she was a kid, but over the years the fat had shifted to all the right places. Plus, she'd had some sucked out and added some here and there. Truth is, most of the original equipment had been altered one way or another, but even I had to admit the end result was annoyingly spectacular. She had a lot of flame-red hair that she did up in waves and curls. Hard to tell which of it was hers and which was bought. Not that it mattered when she swung her ass down the street in spike-heeled boots, skintight low-rider jeans, and a black satin bustier. She wore more eye makeup than Tammy Faye and had lips that were inflated to bursting.

"Hello, Joyce," I said. "Long time no see."

"I guess you could say that to Morelli, too," Joyce said.

Lula cut her eyes to me. "You want me to shoot her? 'Cause I'd really like to do that. I still got a few bullets left in my gun."

"Thanks, but not today," I said to Lula. "Some other time."

"Just let me know when."

"So what are you doing here in the slums?" I asked her.

"Ask Connie."

"Vinnie hired her again," Connie said. "He decided you weren't bringing the skips in fast enough, so he brought Joyce in to take up the slack."

"I don't take up slack," Joyce said. "I take the cream off the top."

From time to time, Joyce had worked for Vinnie, mostly because she was good with a whip and once in a while Vinnie felt like a very bad boy.

"What's in the casserole?" Joyce asked.

I opened the lid. "It's barbecue. Grandma Mazur made it for me for dinner. She knows how I love this recipe."

Joyce spit on the pulled pork. "Just like old times," she said. "Remember when I used to spit on your lunch in school?"

"How about now?" Lula asked. "Can I shoot her now?"

"No!"

Joyce took the casserole dish from me. "Yum," she said. "Dinner." And then she sashayed out of the bonds office, got into her black Mercedes, and roared off down the street with the barbecue.

"I got a dilemma here now," Lula said. "I don't know whether I want her to like my barbecue sauce or get the squirts from it."

Vinnie stuck his head out of his office. "Where is she? Did she leave? Christ, she scares the crap out of me. Still, there's no getting around it. She's a man-eater. She'll clean up the list."

Connie and Lula and I did a collective eye roll because Joyce had tried her hand at bounty hunting before and the only man she ate was Vinnie.

"Am I fired?" I asked Vinnie.

"No. You're the B team."

"You can't have an A team and a B team going after the same skips. It doesn't work."

"Make it work," Vinnie said.

"We should have saved the barbecue for Vinnie," I said to Lula.

"Wasn't me that gave Barnhardt the barbecue," Lula said. "I wanted to shoot her."

I hiked my bag onto my shoulder. "I'm out of here. I'm going to see if Myron Kaplan is home."

"I'm with you," Lula said. "I'm not staying here with this Barnhardt-hiring idiot."

"What about the filing?" Vinnie yelled at Lula. "There's stacks of files everywhere."

"File my ass," Lula said.

According to the information Connie had given me, Myron Kaplan was seventy-eight years old, lived alone, was a retired pharmacist, and two months ago, he robbed his dentist at gunpoint. Myron's booking photo was mostly nose. Several other photos taken when bail was written showed Myron to be slightly stooped, with sparse, wild gray hair.

"There it is," Lula said, checking house numbers while I crept down Carmichael Street. "That's his house with the red door."

Carmichael was a quiet little side street in the center of the city. Residents could walk to shops, restaurants, coffeehouses, corner groceries, and in Myron's case . . . his dentist. The street was entirely residential, with narrow brick-faced two-story row houses.

I parked at the curb, and Lula and I walked to the small front stoop. I rang the bell, and we both stepped aside in case Myron decided to shoot through his door. He was old, but he was known to be armed, and we'd been shot at a lot lately.

The door opened, and Myron looked at me and then focused on Lula in the yellow stretch suit and black flak vest.

"What the heck?" Myron asked.

"Don't mess with me," Lula said. "I'm off doughnuts, and I feel mean as a snake."

"You look like a big bumblebee," Myron said. "I thought I slept through October, and it was Halloween."

I introduced myself and explained to Myron he'd missed his court date.

"I'm not going to court," Myron said. "I already told that to the lady who called on the phone. I got better things to do."

"Like what?" Lula wanted to know.

"Like watch television."

Myron had a cigarette hanging out of his mouth. He was gumming it around, sucking in smoke and blowing it out, all at the same time.

"That's disgustin'," Lula said. "You shouldn't be smoking. Didn't your doctor tell you not to smoke?"

"My doctor's dead," Myron said. "Everybody I know is dead."

"I'm not," Lula said.

Myron considered that. "You're right. You want to do knicky-knacky with me? It's been a while, but I think I can still do it."

"You better be talkin' about some kind of card game," Lula told him.

"We need to go now," I said. "I'm kind of on a schedule."

"Listen, missy," Myron said. "I'm not going. What part of *not going* don't you understand?"

I hated capturing old people. If they didn't cooperate, there was no good way to bring them in. No matter how professional and respectful I tried to act, I always looked like a jerk when I dragged their carcass out the door.

"It's the law," I said. "You're accused of a crime, and you have to go before a judge."

"I didn't commit a crime," Myron said. "I just got a refund. This quack dentist made me false teeth. They didn't fit. I wanted my money back."

"Yes, but you got it back at gunpoint."

"That's because I couldn't get an appointment to see him until January. Couldn't get past his snippy receptionist. When I went in with the gun, I got to see him right away. It's not like I have forever to wait for money. I'm old."

"What about the teeth?" Lula asked him. "Where's the teeth?"

"I left them with the dentist. I got my money back, and he got his teeth back."

"Sounds fair to me," Lula said.

"The court decides what's fair," I said. "You have to go to court."

Myron crossed his arms over his chest and narrowed his eyes. "Make me."

"This is gonna get ugly," Lula said. "We should have left this for Barnhardt."

"I'll make a deal," I said to Myron. "If you come with me, I'll get you a date with my grandmother. She's real cute."

"Does she put out for knicky-knacky?"

"No!"

"Criminy," Lula said to Myron. "What's with you and the knicky-knacky? Do it by yourself and get it over with just like the rest of us."

"He's not real big," I said to Lula. "Probably about a hundred and sixty pounds. If we hog-tie him, we should be able to cart him out to the car."

"Yeah, and he don't have no teeth, so we don't have to worry about him biting us."

"You can't do that to me," Myron said. "I'm old. I'll have a heart attack. I'll pee my pants."

Lula was hands on hips. "I hate when they pee their pants. It's a humiliating experience. And it ruins the upholstery."

I cut my eyes to Myron. "Well? How do you want us to do this?"

"I gotta go to the bathroom before you hog-tie me," Myron said. "Or else I'll pee for sure."

"You've got three minutes," I said to him.

"I can't go in three minutes. I'm old. I've got a prostate the size of a basketball."

"Just *go!*"

Myron trotted off to the bathroom, and Lula and I waited in the front room. Five minutes passed. Ten minutes. I went to the bathroom door and knocked. No answer.

"Myron?"

Nothing. I tried the door. Locked. I called again and rapped louder. *Shit!*

"I need something to pop the lock," I said to Lula. "Do you have a safety pin? Chicken skewer? Knitting needle?"

"I got a bobby pin."

Lula bent the pin open, shoved it in the little hole in the knob, and the door unlocked and we peeked in. No Myron in the bathroom. Open window.

"He gets around, for bein' he's so old," Lula said, looking out the window.

This was the second time today I'd lost a skip through a window. I couldn't even categorize myself as incompetent. I had to go with pathetically stupid.

"Now what are we gonna do?" Lula asked.

Ordinarily, I'd walk the neighborhood and try to ferret out my skip. Problem was, I had Lula in her yellow spandex, and we were way too visible. You could probably see Lula from the space shuttle.

"I'm going to drop you at the office, and I'm going back to work for Ranger," I said. "Morelli told me the crime lab was done with your apartment. Is your landlord replacing your door?"

"I don't know. I gotta call and find out."

I drove past the bonds office twice before pulling to the curb to let Lula out.

"I don't see anything suspicious," I said to her. "I think you're safe."

"This has been another disturbin' day, what with those two assholes lookin' to kill me, and findin' out that I'm fat. I might go back on that bacon diet."

"The bacon diet is unhealthy. And you had packs of dogs chasing you down the street when you were on the bacon diet. All you need to do is control your portions. Stay away from the doughnuts and only eat one piece of chicken or one pork chop or one hamburger at a meal."

"That's ridiculous," Lula said. "Nobody eats just one pork chop. I'd get weak and die."

"Lots of people only eat one pork chop."

"Who?"

"Me."

"Hunh," Lula said. "That's un-American. How am I supposed to stimulate the economy when I'm only eating one plain-ass pork chop? Probably I can't even have gravy on that pork chop."

I made sure Lula got into the office without getting shot or decapitated, and then I pulled my map out of my handbag and started another run through Ranger's accounts.

Morelli called a little after four. "We found the Town Car," he said. "It was parked on a side street near the Bank Center. Easy to spot, since it had a bunch of bullet holes in it. No blood inside. I don't know how she always manages to miss her target. It's uncanny."

"Owner?"

"It was stolen from a car service last night. The lab guys are doing their thing, but that car has been handled by half of New Jersey."

"Thanks. I'll pass this on to Lula."

"Is she with you?"

"No. I dropped her at the bonds office. I'm riding a circuit for Ranger right now."

"Word around town is that he's losing accounts. Having a Rangeman security system has turned into a liability."

"He's working on it."

I was halfway through my account route, and I realized it was almost six o'clock. I took Olden to Hamilton, turned into the Burg, and slid to a stop in front of my parents' house precisely on time.

I could smell the ham the minute I stepped into the foyer. It was an intoxicating aroma of warm, salty goodness and special occasions. My father was already at the table, waiting to stab into the first piece of ham. My grandmother was also seated. And a strange man sat beside Grandma.

"This is Madelyn Mooney's boy, Milton," my mother said to me, setting the green bean casserole on the table. "He just moved back to Trenton."

"Yep," Grandma said. "We thought we'd fix you

up with some hotties since it's kaput with Morelli."

"I'm not interested in getting fixed up," I said.

"You're not getting any younger," Grandma said. "You wait too long, and all the good ones get taken."

I looked over at Milton. He was a sandbag. Overweight, slumped in his chair, pasty white skin, bad complexion, balding orange hair. I was guessing mid-thirties. Not to be judgmental, but he wasn't at the top of the list when God was handing stuff out.

"Milton used to work in the auto industry," Grandma said. "He had a real good job on the line at the factory."

"Yeah," Milton said. "It was sweet until I got fired. And then the bank foreclosed on my house, and my wife left me and took the dog. And now I'm hounded by collection agencies."

"That's awful," I said. "So what are you doing?"

"Nothing."

"He's living with his mother," Grandma said. "Until he gets on his feet."

"I guess it's hard to get a job these days."

"I'm not actually looking for a job," Milton said. "The doctor who treated me after I had the nervous breakdown and set fire to my house said I should take it easy for a while."

"You set fire to your house?"

"Technically, it wasn't my house anymore. It was the bank's house, and between you and me, I think they were happy I burned it down. They were real nice to me while I was in the mental hospital." He speared a piece of ham, studied it, and turned his attention back to me. "My outpatient advisor tells me I need to get out of my mother's house, so that's why I'm considering marrying you. I was told you have your own apartment."

My father picked his head up and paused with his fork halfway to his mouth. "Good God," he said.

"I bet a big, strapping young guy like you has a lot of special talents," Grandma said to Milton.

"I can make French toast," Milton said. "And I can whistle."

"Isn't that something," Grandma said. "Whistling's a lost art. You don't find many whistlers anymore."

Milton whistled "Camptown Races" and "Danny Boy."

"That's pretty good," Grandma said. "I wish I could whistle like that."

My father shot my mother a look like he was in intense pain.

"Pass the potatoes to your father," my mother said to me. "And give him more ham."

I tried to sneak an inconspicuous peek at my watch.

"Don't even think about it," my mother said. "You leave now, and you don't get dessert . . . ever."

TWELVE

Milton left at eight o'clock so he could get home in time to take his meds. I helped my mom with the dishes, had an extra piece of cake, and said good night at nine, pulling away from my parents' house reconsidering my feelings toward Morelli. After two hours of Milton, I was thinking Morelli might be worth a second look.

I drove two blocks down, hooked a left, and turned into his neighborhood. This was blue-collar Trenton at its best. Houses were small, cars were large, green referred to dollars in the bank. At eight o'clock, kids were doing homework and parents were in front of the television. At ten o'clock, the houses were dark. This neighborhood got up early five mornings out of seven and went to work.

Morelli lived in a row house he inherited from his Aunt Rose. He was gradually making it his own, but Rose's curtains still hung in most of the windows. Hard to explain, but I liked the combination of Morelli and his aunt. There was something about the mix of generations and genders that felt right for the house. And I thought it said something good about Morelli that he didn't have to entirely erase the house's history.

I cruised down Morelli's street and had a moment of breathless panic at finding Barnhardt's Mercedes parked in front of Morelli's green SUV. The moment passed, and I continued on to the corner. I made a U-turn and parked on the opposite side three houses down, taking some time to collect myself. In the past, this sort of dilemma would have sent me straight to the nearest 7-Eleven, where I'd clean them out of Reese's Peanut Butter Cups and Snickers bars. Since I'd just had three pieces of my mother's cake, a bag of candy wasn't where I wanted to go.

I did some deep breathing and told myself slashing tires never really solved anything. And besides, here I was sitting in Ranger's car, sleeping in his bed, wearing his stupid uniform, and I was all bent out of shape because Barnhardt was in Morelli's house. I rolled my eyes and thunked my forehead against the steering wheel. Jeez Louise, I was a mess.

Morelli's front door opened, and Barnhardt made a theatrical exit, blowing kisses and smiling. She got into her Mercedes and drove off, rolling past me, never noticing that I was watching.

There were two other vehicles parked by Morelli's house. A red F150 truck and a clunker

Subaru. Now that my breathing was returning to normal and my brain was more or less functioning, I realized I recognized the car and truck. The truck belonged to Morelli's brother, Anthony. And the Subaru belonged to Morelli's cousin Mooch.

I got out of the Cayenne, crossed the street, crept up to Morelli's house, and carefully inserted myself into the azalea bushes planted under his front window. I stood on tiptoe and saw that Morelli, Morelli's dog, Bob, and Mooch, and Anthony were on the couch, watching the game on television. The coffee table in front of them was littered with empty beer cans, opened bags of chips, a cardboard pizza box from Pino's, some plates with forks, and the casserole dish Joyce had taken from me. The casserole dish was empty. Holy crap. Joyce had fed the toxic barbecue to Morelli.

I extricated myself from the bushes and danced around, pumping my fist and thinking, *YEAH! Woohoo! Whoopie!* After about thirty seconds of this, I realized I looked stupid, and it would be beyond embarrassing for Morelli to come out and find me on his lawn. And beyond that, I probably shouldn't have been so happy about three men and a dog getting diarrhea, but the truth is, the only one I felt bad about was Bob. Bob was a big, shaggy-haired, entirely lovable beast. And he didn't deserve diarrhea. I stopped dancing and skulked back to the Cayenne.

I put the Cayenne in gear and drove to my apartment building. I pulled into the lot and found Lula's Firebird parked next to Mr. Macko's Cadillac, and light shining from my apartment windows. I'd been hoping to find my apartment dark and deserted. I loved Ranger's apartment, but it wasn't home. Looking up at my windows, I wasn't sure *that* was home, either. I'm in limbo, I thought. My whole friggin' life is in limbo.

I thought I should go in to see the kitchen progress and verify that Lula was staying the night. Unfortunately, that might involve more of Larry in the blue cocktail dress. Or even worse, Larry in his shorts. I felt like I'd had enough weird for one day, so I maneuvered the Cayenne out of the lot and headed for Rangeman.

I was sound asleep when the bedside phone rang.

"He just hit two accounts," Ranger said. "They phoned in minutes apart. Both of the houses were on your high-risk list. Tank is waiting for you in the garage. I want you to take a look at these houses from the inside."

I looked at the clock. It wasn't quite midnight. I took a moment to come awake, and ten minutes later, the phone woke me up a second time.

"Tank has a key," Ranger said. "And he'll come in and get you if you're not in the garage in five minutes."

I managed to get myself out of bed and vertical, but I wasn't firing on all cylinders. I was wearing Ranger's T-shirt as a nightshirt, and I left the shirt on, tugged on cargo pants, socks, sneakers, and a sweatshirt and grumbled my way to the elevator and down to the garage.

"Whoa!" Tank said when he saw me.

I narrowed my eyes. "What?"

"Nothin'," Tank said. "Guess you were asleep. You just took me by surprise, with the hair and all."

I rolled my eyes up to the top of my head, but I couldn't see my hair.

"I'm feeling grouchy," I said to Tank.

"Do you want to see a picture of my cat?" Tank asked. "That always makes me happy."

I climbed into Tank's Rangeman SUV, buckled my seat belt, and looked at the picture of his cat.

"Cute," I said.

"Do you feel happy?"

"No." Crawling back into bed would make me feel happy.

Both houses were north of town in a high-rent neighborhood by the river. The first house Tank took me to looked like Mount Vernon if Mount Vernon was built in 2008. It was Faux Vernon. Tank drove into a circular driveway and parked behind Ranger's Porsche. A police car and another Rangeman SUV were in front of Ranger. The front door was open and every light was on in the house. We walked in and met Ranger in the foyer.

"Why was this house on your *at risk* list?" he asked me.

"It had some things in common with the houses that were already hit. All houses are single family on large lots. All houses have attached garages that open off a side drive court. All houses have trees and bushes that throw shadows and partially screen the house. None of the houses are on streets with on-street parking."

"Our guy likes to have cover," Ranger said.

"Exactly."

"Look through the house and see if you come up with anything. I'm sending Tank with you so you're not mistaken for a vagrant and arrested."

I flipped Ranger the bird.

Ranger smiled at me. "Cute."

"That's what I said about Tank's cat."

"He made you look at his cat picture?"

"I thought it would make her happy," Tank said.

Ranger's smile widened. "Did it make you happy?" he asked me.

"A little."

I suspected I was to Ranger what Tank's cat was to Tank.

"Take good care of her," Ranger said to Tank.

Ranger left for the second break-in, and Tank and I set off on our exploration. The exploration didn't take long. I was getting to know what to expect. Start with the door leading from the garage and take the shortest route to the master bedroom. Check out the home office, the den, the kids' rooms. Proceed to the front door or possibly back door. Locate the keypads.

I felt like the keypads held the answer to the mystery. There were three keypads in this house. One in the master bedroom, one on a wall by the front door, and one by the door to the garage. None of the keypads were visible from a window.

Tank and I had gone through the house and returned to the door leading to the garage. We were standing in a small hallway behind the kitchen. The laundry room and a half bath opened off the hallway.

"I think this guy is getting the code from the keypad," I said to Tank.

"I've been thinking that, too. It's like when people watch you at the ATM and they get your bank code. It's like someone's looking through walls."

We left Faux Vernon and went to house number two. The second house was only three blocks away in the same neighborhood. It was a huge redbrick box with white columns and a porte cochere.

Ranger met us at the door. "The drill is the same. Cash and jewelry taken from the upstairs master."

"Are the police making any progress on these robberies?"

"Not that I can tell. Not a lot of talent assigned to this desk."

"It's odd that these two houses were hit together."

"Both clients were at the same dinner party," Ranger said. "Somehow, our bandit knew the houses would be empty. Originally, I thought he randomly hit houses that were dark. Now I think he plans ahead. We need to go over the original report taken after each break-in to see if there's a common service provider. Someone who might have talked to the homeowner. And we probably want to go back and reinterview all of the clients who were robbed."

"That still doesn't tell us how he got the codes."

"Trust me, if I catch this guy, he'll tell me how he got the codes."

The first thing I noticed when I woke up was that I wasn't alone. Ranger was in bed with me. And he was asleep. I reviewed the night, and I couldn't remember anything amazing happening. Tank had driven me back to Rangeman around two in the morning. Ranger hadn't come back with us. It was now nine o'clock. I checked around and determined I was wearing all the clothes I was supposed to be wearing. Panties and T-shirt. I slipped out of bed, and Ranger woke up.

"When did you get home?" I asked him.

"A little after five."

"I'm surprised I'm not naked."

"You weren't in the mood," Ranger said. "You told me you'd shoot me with my own gun if I touched you."

"What did you do?"

"I got up and locked my gun in the safe. You were asleep when I came back to bed."

"I was tired."

"Are you tired now?"

"No, but I'm going to work. I have three skips to catch. I need to check in on Lula. And I want to go over the reports from your break-ins."

"The reports are on my desk," Ranger said.

A half hour later, I rolled out of the garage in Ranger's Cayenne and dialed Lula.

"What's going on today?" I asked her. "And where are you?"

"I'm getting ready to leave your apartment. Your kitchen is all clean, and they're putting my new door up this morning. I'm having brunch with Mister Clucky, and then I'm going to your mama's house to cook with your granny. You could have brunch at Cluck-in-a-Bucket with me if you want."

"Cluck-in-a-Bucket has brunch?"

"Only on Sunday. You get orange juice and biscuits and a bucket of nuggets."

"How is that different from every other day?"

"It's the orange juice. Usually, you get a soda."

"Okay," I said. "I'll meet you at Cluck-in-a-Bucket."

I'd grabbed a to-go cup of coffee from the fifth-floor kitchen before I left Rangeman, but I hadn't bothered with breakfast, so biscuits and orange juice sounded good.

I drove through the center of the city and reached Cluck-in-a-Bucket just as Lula was pulling into the lot. Mister Clucky was dancing around in front of the building, and the hideous impaled chicken was spinning overhead.

"Yoohoo, Mister Clucky, honey," Lula called, getting out of her Firebird and waving.

"Boy, you must really like him," I said.

"He's an excellent scrubber, and besides, it's not everybody gets to know Mister Clucky personally. He's one of them minor celebrities."

Mister Clucky was surrounded by kids, so we bypassed him and put our order in.

"I'm going to try my luck with Ernie Dell again," I said to Lula. "Are you in?"

"As long as it don't take too long. Larry gave me his barbecue recipe, and Granny and me are trying it out this afternoon."

I got an orange juice and two biscuits. Lula got an orange juice, a bucket of biscuits, and a bucket of nuggets.

"Crikey," I said, looking at her tray. "I thought you were cutting back on the food."

"You said only have one pork chop and one burger and one steak. So I only got *one* bucket of biscuits and *one* bucket of nuggets. You got a problem with that?"

"You could feed a family of six on that food."

"Not in my neighborhood. I live in a three-pork-chop neighborhood."

Mister Clucky came inside dancing and singing his Mister Clucky song, going table by table.

"I know him personally," Lula said to the woman at the table next to her.

Lula was still wearing the flak vest. She ate half the bucket of nuggets, and she released the Velcro straps to give herself more room.

"Is that a bulletproof vest?" the woman next to Lula asked.

"Yep," Lula said. "And it's hard to make a fashion statement in this on account of it don't come in a lot of colors. I gotta wear it because there's a couple guys tryin' to kill me."

The woman gave a gasp and hustled her two kids out the door.

"Hunh," Lula said. "She just up and left. She didn't even finish her Clucky Burger."

"Next time, say you're wearing a back brace."

We finished eating, Lula said good-bye to Mister Clucky, and we saddled up. We left Lula's Firebird in the lot, and I drove.

"I love this car," Lula said. "My personality don't fit a SUV, but this car is still excellent. It got buttons all over the place. What's this button do?"

"I don't know."

Lula pushed the button and my GPS screen went blank. "Oops," Lula said.

The car phone rang, and I opened the connection.

"This is Hal in the control room," a voice said on the hands-free phone. "Are you all right?"

"Yes."

"You just dropped off my screen. Did you disable your GPS?"

"It was an accident. How do I fix it?"

"Push the button again."

"Where's that voice comin' from?" Lula wanted to know. "It sounds like the voice of God, floatin' around in space."

I disconnected Hal, reconnected the GPS, and turned off Hamilton.

"This time we'll cover all exits," I said. "You take the front door, and I'll take the back door."

"Sounds like a plan. Who's going in first?"

"I'll go in first. You don't go in at all unless I yell for you. You keep your eyes open in case he goes out a front window."

I drove a couple blocks into Ernie's neighborhood, found the alley that ran past the back of his house, and crept along until I reached his driveway. I pulled in and angle-parked behind the garage, blocking his exit.

"I'll give you time to walk around the house, and then I'm going in," I said to Lula. "Just stay put until you hear from me."

Lula checked the Velcro on her vest to make sure everything was secure. "Gotcha."

We left the Cayenne and went our separate ways. I counted off two minutes and knocked on the back door. No answer. I knocked again and tried the door. Unlocked. I stepped into the kitchen and listened. No sound. "Bond enforcement!" I yelled. "Ernie, are you in here?" Nothing. I walked through the house, stood at the bottom of the stairs and called out again. I climbed the stairs and went room by room. No Ernie. I returned to the first floor and opened the door to Lula.

"He's not here," I said. "I'll try again later."

We walked through the house and let ourselves out.

"There's something wrong here," Lula said, standing on the back stoop. "I get the feeling something's not right. What is it?"

A wave of nausea swirled through my stomach. "It's Ranger's Cayenne," I said. "It's gone."

"Yep," Lula said. "That's it, all right. There's a big empty space where the car used to be."

I dialed Rangeman and got Hal. "Is Ranger on the floor yet?"

"No," Hal said. "I haven't seen him. Would you like me to transfer you?"

"No. I don't want to bother him. Is the GPS still working on the Cayenne?"

"Yes."

"Maybe you could send someone after it, since it's been sort of . . . stolen."

There was a beat of silence. "Stolen?" Hal said. "Someone stole Ranger's Cayenne?"

I blew out a sigh. "Yes."

"Uh-oh," Lula said, staring off into the distance. "I don't like the looks of this."

I followed her line of sight and felt my heart skip a couple beats. Black smoke billowed skyward about a quarter mile away.

"Has the car stopped?" I asked Hal.

"Yes."

"No rush," I told him. "It's going to be there for a while."

"Now what?" Lula asked when I got off the phone.

I wanted to get on a plane and leave the country. Get a job in St. Bart's and never come back.

"Hal's sending a car to pick us up," I said.

Ten minutes later, a black SUV rolled into the driveway. Ramon was at the wheel.

"I need to get my car at Cluck-in-a-Bucket," Lula told him. "I gotta go cook up barbecue."

Ramon glanced over at me. "Ranger would like me to take you back to Rangeman."

"Sure," I said. "Drop Lula at the Bucket and take me to the Batcave."

* * *

Ranger was in the shower when I got to the apartment. I flopped onto the couch, pulled a pillow over my head, and hoped when he came out he wouldn't notice me lying there.

Pretend you're in a good place, I told myself. You're on a beach. Hear the waves swooshing in and out. Hear the seagulls.

The pillow got lifted off my face and Ranger looked down at me. "You can run, but you can't hide," he said.

"Just shoot me and get it over with."

"Talk to me."

"Ernie Dell."

Ranger yanked me to my feet, pulled me into the hall and out the door. "He needs to find another hobby."

Ranger is a master of control. He can lower his heart rate at will and walk past a bakery and never be tempted. On the surface, Ranger would appear to have no emotion. It's anyone's guess what rages below the surface. What I do know about Ranger is that he's most dangerous when he's dead calm. And right now he was pretty calm, except for having his hand clamped around my wrist.

Neither of us said a word in the elevator. Ranger guided the Turbo out of the garage, and I gave him directions to Ernie's house. He looked relaxed at the wheel. No angry little lines in his forehead. No tense muscles working in his jaw. He also wasn't talking. He was in his zone.

We drove down the alley behind Ernie's house and parked in his driveway, Ranger still not saying anything, looking at the wreck of a haunted mansion in front of him. We got out of the Porsche and walked to the building's back door. Ranger listened for a moment and knocked. No answer. Ranger knocked again.

There was a sound overhead like a window being raised. I looked up to see and *Splooosh*. I was doused head to foot with red paint.

Ranger was standing inches from me, and he didn't have a drop on him. He was in black Rangeman tactical gear of T-shirt, cargo pants, and windbreaker, and he was pristine. He looked at me and did a small *I can't believe these things always happen to you* gesture with his hands.

"If you so much as crack a smile, that's the end of our friendship," I said to him.

The corners of his mouth twitched a little, and I knew he was smiling inside.

"Babe," he said.

"I'm a mess."

"Yes, but we're going to have fun washing this paint off you when we get back to my apartment." He unholstered his gun and handed it to me. "Stay here and don't move from this spot. If you see Ernie Dell, shoot him."

"What if he isn't armed?"

"He'll be armed by the time the police get here."

Ranger disappeared inside the house, leaving the kitchen door open. A minute later, I heard something crash overhead. The crash was accompanied by a loud grunt, as if the air had been knocked out of someone. I'd seen Ranger in action on other manhunts, and I suspected this was Ernie Dell getting thrown against a wall. There was a moment of silence and then more thumping and crashing. I looked inside, past the kitchen, and saw Ernie sprawled on the floor at the foot of the stairs. Ranger hauled him to his feet and wrangled him to the back door.

"What was all that crashing?" I asked Ranger.

"He slipped on the stairs."

Ernie's hands were cuffed behind his back, and he wasn't looking happy. I was relieved to have captured Ernie, but it was annoying that it was so easy for Ranger to execute a takedown and next to impossible for me.

"You have other talents," Ranger said, reading my thoughts.

"Such as?"

He tucked my hair behind my ear so it wouldn't drip paint on my face. "You're smart. You're intuitive. You're resilient." He thought about it for a beat. "You're stubborn."

"Stubborn is a good thing?"

"Not necessarily. I ran out of good things."

A Rangeman SUV glided into the driveway and parked. Tank and Ramon got out and went pale when they saw me.

"It's paint," Ranger said to them. "Mr. Dell was feeling playful."

Tank clapped a hand to his heart.

"Sweet Mother of God," Ramon said.

Ranger handed Ernie over to Tank. "I'll get the paperwork for you, and you can turn him in for Stephanie. And I need a thermal blanket from the emergency kit for her."

Five minutes later, Ernie was shackled to the floor in the backseat of the Rangeman SUV and trundled off to the police station. This left me with two open files, and as far as I was concerned, Joyce was welcome to both of them. I kicked my shoes off at car-side, wrapped myself in the aluminum blanket from the emergency kit, and eased myself into the Turbo, next to Ranger.

"I'm trying not to drip," I said to him.

"I saw the can in the upstairs bedroom. It's water-based. It should wash off."

"Why don't you have any paint on you? It's always me. Why isn't it ever you?"

"I don't know," Ranger said. "But I like it this way."

Ranger backed out of the driveway and drove toward Olden. I was soaked through with paint and wrapped in an aluminum foil blanket like a baked potato. I'd left my shoes in the driveway, and my feet were getting cold.

"Take me to my apartment," I said to Ranger.

"Isn't Lula there?"

"No. She's cleared out."

THIRTEEN

I let myself into my apartment and went to my kitchen first thing. It was sparkling clean, with only a few pale pink stains in the ceiling paint and a small chunk of the ceiling chipped away from the lid impact. The living room and dining room were nice and neat. No sign of Lula. Yay. Yippee.

The bedroom wasn't nearly so happy. Lula's clothes were still there. Okay, don't panic, I told myself. Maybe she was in a hurry to go to brunch and just hasn't come back to collect her clothes. I was holding a big plastic garbage bag that I'd taken from the kitchen. I stripped down and put everything, including the disposable aluminum blanket, into the garbage bag. There was a limit to how much paint you could wash out of a shirt, and my clothes were way beyond the limit.

I stepped into the shower and, after a lot of scrubbing and shampooing, finally emerged red-free. I fluffed my hair out with the dryer, swiped some mascara on my lashes, and dressed in a ratty T-shirt, washed-out jeans, and a denim jacket. Not a high-fashion day, since my laundry basket with all my clean clothes was still at my mother's house.

I'd promised to test-drive more barbecue sauce tonight at my parents' house. I called Lula for a ride and went down to the parking lot to wait for her.

Mostly seniors on fixed incomes lived in my building. There were a couple Hispanics and a young single mom with two kids, but everyone else had a subscription to *AARP The Magazine*. It was almost five, and half of my building was out taking advantage of the early bird specials at the diner, and the other half was in front of the television, eating a defrosted entrée.

Lula barreled into the lot and came to a sharp stop in front of me. "Hop in," she said. "I gotta get back to help your granny. We're in the middle of saucin' up some chicken."

"Is this Mister Clucky's recipe?"

"Yeah, and I think it's a good one. His secret ingredient is blackberry jelly. Leave it to a cross-dresser to come up with something real creative like that."

Lula was wearing a stretchy orange sweater with a low V-neck and short sleeves, and a matching orange-and-black tiger-striped skirt. No flak vest.

"What happened to the flak vest?" I asked her.

"I was always sweating under it and it gave me a rash. I just gotta be on a more vigilant outlook for those idiot killers. If I get rid of the rash in time, I might wear the vest to the cook-off. Although I hate for it to interfere with my chef outfit."

"Do you still think Chipotle's killers will be at the cook-off?"

"They'll be there," Lula said. "And we'll catch them and be rich. I got a bracelet all picked out at the jewelry store. And I'm going on a cruise down to the Panama Canal. I always wanted to see the Panama Canal."

I agreed with Lula. I thought there was a good chance the killers would be at the cook-off. They were sticking around, and the cook-off seemed to be the logical reason. Although for me, it wouldn't have been reason enough. If I whacked someone's head off and was worried about being recognized, I'd get out of town. These guys didn't seem to be all that smart. They were focused on getting rid of the witness, and in the bargain they were getting more witnesses.

Lula parked at the curb in front of my parents' house and looked around before getting out of the car.

"I guess the coast is clear," she said. "I don't see no killers anywhere."

Everything was business as usual in my parents' house. My dad was in his chair in front of the television. My mom and Grandma Mazur were in the kitchen.

"I got all the chicken soaking in the sauce," Grandma said. "I got batter for biscuits, and we made some coleslaw."

"I got Larry comin' over as soon as he's off his shift," Lula said. "He's gonna show us how to do the grillin'. He should be here any minute."

The doorbell chimed, and Grandma went to open the door.

"Well, lookit you," I heard Grandma say. "You must be Larry. Come on in. We're all in the kitchen waiting for you. And this here's my son-in-law, Frank."

"For the love of everything holy," my father said. "What the hell are you supposed to be?"

"This is from my Julia Child collection," Larry said. "I know she didn't barbecue, but I just love the simplicity of her clothes and the complexity of her dishes."

I stuck my head out the kitchen door and looked beyond the dining room into the living room. Larry was wearing a curly brown wig, a lavender-and-pink flower-print blouse, navy skirt, and navy pumps with very low heels. There actually was a frightening resemblance to Julia Child.

My father muttered something that might have sounded like *flaming fruitcake* and went back to reading his paper.

Larry followed Grandma into the kitchen, and Grandma introduced him to my mother.

"Very nice to meet you," my mother said. And then she made the sign of the cross and reached for the liquor bottle in the cupboard next to the stove.

"We had a mishap with the grill a couple days ago," Lula said to Larry. "But we got it put together again and we're pretty sure it'll work. It's out back."

"And here's the chicken," Grandma said. "We got it sitting in the sauce just like you told us."

"Lookin' good, ladies," Larry said. "Let's barbecue."

Lula grabbed the tray with the chicken. My mother had her hand wrapped around a highball glass. And my grandmother had a broom.

"What's the broom for?" Larry wanted to know.

"Dogs," Grandma said.

We went outside, Larry approached the grill, and the rest of us hung back. Not that we didn't trust Larry's manly ability to ignite a grill; more that we suspected this was the grill from hell.

After a couple minutes of fiddling around, Larry got the grill up and running. He adjusted the flame just so, and he arranged the chicken.

"Good thing you got the night off from being Mister Clucky," Grandma said.

"I never get the Sunday night shift," Larry

said. "Sunday night is dead. All the action takes place for the brunch and the early-dinner crowd. They always give those times to me because I'm the best Mister Clucky."

"You're a pretty good Julia Child, too," Grandma said. "I bet you're fun on Halloween."

At six o'clock, my father took his seat at the table and we all hustled into the dining room with the food. We took our seats and I realized there was an extra plate set.

"You didn't do what I think you did," I said to my mother.

"He seemed like a nice young man," my mother said. "I met him in the supermarket. He helped me pick out a grapefruit. And it turned out he's related to Biddy Gurkin."

The doorbell rang and Grandma jumped out of her chair. "I'll get it. I like when we have a new man at the dinner table."

"You have to stop doing this," I said to my mother. "I don't want a new man."

"I'll be dead someday," my mother said. "And then what? You'll wish you had someone."

"I have a hamster."

"This here is Peter Pecker," Grandma said, leading a tall, bald, red-faced guy into the room.

Lula spewed water out of her nose, and my father choked on a piece of bread.

"Sorry," Lula said. "I never met anyone named Peter Pecker before."

"And he looks just like one, too," Grandma said. "Did anyone else notice that? Isn't that something?"

My mother drained her highball glass and looked to the kitchen.

"Sit here and have a piece of chicken," Grandma said to Peter Pecker. "We made it special."

Pecker sat down and looked across the table at Julia Child. "I thought you died."

"It's not really Julia Child," Grandma said. "It's Larry all dressed up. Earlier today, he was Mister Clucky."

"That's weird," Peter said.

"Not as weird as being named Peter Pecker," Larry said.

"I can't help it if that's what I'm named, asshole."

"Who are you calling an asshole?"

"You, Mister Fruity Tutti."

"You must have heard wrong," Grandma said. "He's not Mister Fruity Tutti. He's Mister Clucky."

"Biscuits," my father said. "Where the hell are the biscuits?"

My mother and grandmother and I snapped to attention and passed the biscuits to my father.

"What do you do at the supermarket?" Grandma asked Pecker.

"I'm assistant manager for produce. I'm the vegetable specialist."

"That sounds like a real good job," Grandma said.

"I know all the vegetables," Pecker said. "And I know all about fruits, too." He looked across the table to Larry. "Nothing personal."

"What's that supposed to mean?" Larry asked. "Are you calling me a fruit?"

"If the high heel fits."

"You're a jerk."

"Hey, pal, I'm not the one wearing ladies' panties."

"This is the United States of America," Larry said. "I can wear whatever kind of pants I want."

"You should stop pickin' on him," Lula said to Peter Pecker. "You don't watch your step, and I'll put my foot up your runty butt."

"Oh, I'm so scared," Pecker said. "Now the fat chick's going to protect the pussy-boy."

Lula was on her feet. "Did someone call me a fat chick? I better not have heard that."

"Fat, fat, fat," Pecker said.

"Pecker head, pecker head, pecker head," Larry said.

"Nobody calls me pecker head and lives," Pecker said. And he launched himself across the table and tackled Julia Child.

The two men went to the floor, punching and grunting, rolling around locked together.

"Look at that," Grandma said, leaning across the table. "He *is* wearing ladies' panties."

My father kept his head down, shoveling in buttered biscuits and barbecued chicken, and my mother went to the kitchen to refill her glass.

Lula hauled her Glock out of her purse and fired off a round at the ceiling. A small chunk of plaster fell down onto the table, and Larry and Pecker stopped gouging each other's eyes out long enough to look around.

"We got chicken on the table," Lula said, pointing the gun at the two men. "And I want some respect for it. What the hell are you thinking, rolling around on the floor like that at dinner hour? You need to get your asses into your chairs and show some manners. It's like you two were born in a barn. Not to mention I got a contest coming up, and I need to know if this is gonna give you all diarrhea on account of everything I've cooked so far has gone through people like goose grease."

Larry righted his chair and sat down, and Pecker went to his side of the table. Pecker's nose was bleeding a little, and Larry had a bruise developing on his cheekbone.

"I hope this chicken's okay," Grandma said, spooning coleslaw onto her plate. "I'm hungry."

Everyone looked to my father. He'd been shoveling food into his face nonstop, including the chicken.

"What do you think of the chicken?" my mother asked him.

"Passable," my father said. "It would be better if it was roasted."

Pecker tested out a leg. "This is pretty good," he said, reaching for another piece.

"It's Larry's recipe," Grandma said.

Pecker looked over at Larry. "No kidding? How do you get that sweet but spicy taste?"

"Blackberry jelly," Larry said. "You add a dab to the hot sauce."

"I would never have thought of that," Pecker said.

I ate a biscuit and nibbled at the chicken. Pecker was right. The chicken was good. *Really good*. I didn't have any delusions about winning the contest, but at least we might not poison anyone.

My father reached for the butter and noticed the chunk of plaster in the middle of the table. "Where'd that come from?" he asked.

No one said anything.

My father looked up to the ceiling and spotted the hole. "I knew when we hired your cousin to do the plastering it wasn't going to hold," my father said to my mother.

"He plastered that ceiling thirty years ago," my mother said.

"Well, some of it fell down. Call him after dinner and tell him he better fix it."

"I heard some interesting news today," Grandma said. "Arline Sweeney called and said they were going to hold the Chipotle funeral here in Trenton."

"Why would they do that?" Lula asked.

"I guess he had three ex-wives who didn't want him in their plot. And his sister didn't want him in her plot. So the barbecue company decided to take charge and bury him here since that's where his head is. And he's gonna be at the funeral home on Hamilton. Right here in the Burg."

"That's weird," Lula said. "Are they going to have a viewing?"

"Arline didn't know anything about that, but I guess they'd have a viewing. There's always a viewing."

"Yeah, but they only got a head," Lula said. "How do they have a viewing with just a head? And what about the casket? Would they put just the head in a whole big casket?"

"Seems like a waste," Grandma said. "You could just put the head in a hatbox."

An hour later, Grandma waved good-bye to Larry and Pecker and closed the front door. "That went well," she said. "We need to have company to dinner more often."

I was holding my laundry basket of clean clothes and the keys to my Uncle Sandor's baby blue and white '53 Buick. He'd bequeathed it to Grandma Mazur when he went into the nursing home, but Grandma Mazur didn't drive it.

Grandma didn't have a license. So I got to borrow the gas-guzzling behemoth when I had a transportation emergency. The car was a lot like my apartment bathroom, not nearly what I would choose but utterly indestructible.

"What's the deal with your apartment?" I asked Lula. "Is your door fixed?"

"Yeah, and I'm moving back in. I just have to stop at your place to get my clothes. I'll be over in a little while. I gotta get some groceries first."

I carted my laundry out to the Buick and slumped a little when confronted with the reality of my life. I would have preferred a new Porsche Turbo, but my car budget was old borrowed Buick. And the truth is, I was lucky to have anything at all. I put the basket in the trunk, slid onto the couch-like bench seat, gripped the wheel, and turned the key in the ignition. The engine rumbled in front of me. Testosterone shot out the exhaust pipe. Big, wide-eyed headlights blinked on.

I slowly backed out of the garage and chugged down the street. Without thinking too much about it, I turned down Adams Street and after a couple blocks found myself in Morelli's neighborhood. On nights like this, after suffering through dinner with a guy dressed up like Julia Child and a guy who looked like an ad for erectile dysfunction remedies, I found myself missing Morelli. He wasn't perfect, but at least he didn't look like a penis.

FOURTEEN

I thought I would quietly cruise by Morelli's house unnoticed, but it turned out Morelli was standing in his small front yard and spotted me half a block away. Hard to miss me in the Buick. I pulled to the curb and he walked over to me.

"What's going on?" I asked. As if I didn't know. Bob was hunched on the lawn, head down, tail up.

"Bob's got problems," Morelli said.

"Must have eaten something that disagreed with him."

"Yeah, I've got the same problem," Morelli said. "Mooch and Anthony came over to watch the game and I think we got some bad food."

"Bummer."

"I thought you were driving Ranger's Cayenne."

"It sort of burned up."

"Sort of?"

"Totally."

Morelli gave a bark of laughter. "That's the

first thing I've had to smile about all day. No one was hurt?"

"No. Ernie Dell stole it and torched it."

"I bet that went over big with Ranger."

"He went after Ernie and rooted him out like a rat in his nest."

"I don't always like Ranger, but I have to admit he gets the job done."

Bob had taken to dragging his butt on the ground, going in circles around the yard.

"Maybe he needs to go to the vet," I said to Morelli.

"This is nothing," Morelli said. "Remember when he ate your red thong? And the time he ate my sock?"

"That was my favorite thong."

"Mine, too," Morelli said. His face broke out in a cold sweat, and he bent at the waist. "Oh man, my intestines are in a knot. I have to go inside and lie down in the bathroom."

"Do you need help? Do you want me to get you Pepto-Bismol or something?"

"No, but thanks for the offer." Morelli waved me away, collected Bob, and they shuffled into the house.

Okay, that was sad. I thought it might be satisfying, but it wasn't at all. I drove on autopilot to my apartment building, surprised when I realized I was parked in the lot. I hauled my laundry basket to the second floor, let myself in, and listened to the silence of my empty apartment. The silence felt lonely. Rex was still with Ranger. I wasn't greeted by rustling pine bedding or the squeak of Rex's wheel. I carted the basket into my bedroom, set it on the floor, and my cell phone rang.

"Bitch," Joyce Barnhardt said when I answered.

"Do you have a problem?"

"You poisoned me."

"I don't know what you're talking about."

"Don't play dumb. You knew exactly what you were doing when you forced that pork on me."

"Gee, I'd really like to talk to you, Joyce, but I have to go do something."

"I'll get you for this . . . as soon as I can leave the bathroom."

I hung up with Joyce, and I heard the front door open.

"I hope you don't mind I let myself in," Lula called from the foyer. "I still got the key you gave me."

"No problem," I said, and I came out to meet her.

There was a *BANG* from the parking lot, followed by the sound of glass breaking.

"That sounded like a window next door," Lula said.

We stuck our heads out the dining room window and looked down at the lot. Two guys were

standing there, and one had some sort of shotgun. They were wearing masks like Zorro, but
they were still recognizable because one of them
was giggling. They were the Chipotle killers.

"Imbecile," the one guy yelled at the other guy.
"You can't even shoot a stupid firebomb into the
right window. You're a total screwup. You never
do anything right."

"You said she lived in the apartment on the
end."

"I said *next* to the end."

"Looks to me like there's smoke comin' from
your neighbor's apartment," Lula said.

The fire alarm went off next door, and I could
hear doors opening and closing in the hall and
people shouting. I turned my attention back to the
lot and saw the smaller of the two men shoulder
the gun.

"Uh-oh," Lula said. "Duck!"

We went flat to the floor, and *BANG!* A small
black ball sailed past us, crashed against the far
wall, and burst into flames. The flames raced
across the carpet and the curtains caught.

"Fire!" Lula yelled. "Fire! Fire! We're gonna
die. We're gonna burn up like we was in hell."

I ran to the kitchen, got the fire extinguisher
from under the sink, and ran back to the dining
room with it. By now, the fire had spread to the
living room, and the couch was on fire. I shot
some foam at the couch and the living room cur-

tains, and then I turned tail and ran for the door. I grabbed my purse on the way out, relieved that Rex was at Rangeman.

Lula was already in the hall, along with Dillon Ruddick, the building super. Dillon had a fire hose working on my neighbor's apartment. Mr. Macko was helping him. Lula and I stumbled down the smoke-filled hall to the stairs.

"I don't know if we should go out," Lula said when we got to the ground floor. "What if they're still there?"

Good point. I opened the door and peeked out into the small lobby. A bunch of tenants were milling around. Red and blue lights from cop cars and fire trucks flashed from the parking lot. A bunch of firemen in boots and gear entered the building and clomped past us, taking the stairs to the second floor. I looked out again and saw that the police were clearing the lobby.

"They're going to make us leave the building," I said to Lula.

"No way," Lula said. "I'm here to stay. There's crazy-ass Marco the Maniac out there."

"I'm sure he's gone by now. The parking lot is crawling with cops."

"Some of those cops aren't real smart."

"Even the dimmest bulb would be suspicious of two guys wearing Zorro masks."

"How'd they find me here anyway?" Lula wanted to know.

"They've probably been following your Fire-bird."

"Well, I'm not drivin' it no more. I'm leaving it here, and I'm calling a cab. And I'm not going home, neither. I'd be sitting there waiting for them to set me on fire."

"Where are you going?"

"I don't know. I haven't figured that out."

We left the stairwell and inserted ourselves into the middle of a clump of displaced tenants. Lula called for a cab, and I called Morelli.

"Are you out of the bathroom yet?" I asked him.

"Yeah, but it's probably temporary."

"How's Bob doing?"

"He's looking better."

"Our two hit men, dumb and dumber, just fire-bombed my apartment. I think they must have been following Lula and figured out that she was living here."

"Was anyone hurt?"

"I don't think so. The firemen are here. And a bunch of cops. Everyone's out of the building, and I don't see the EMTs treating anyone. Marco and his partner are so inept, they shot the first firebomb into my neighbor's window by mistake."

"Were they captured?"

"No. Lula and I heard the shot and went to the window. We saw them in the lot, and they saw us in the window, and next thing, there was a firebomb in my dining room."

"How bad is the fire?"

"I think it was confined to the two apartments. I don't see any more flames coming out the windows, so I'm thinking it's under control. I won't know how much damage was done for a while."

"I'd offer to come rescue you, but I'm not sure I can drag myself to the car."

"Thanks for the thought, but I'm okay. I'll fill you in on the details tomorrow."

I disconnected and Ranger called.

"Babe," Ranger said.

"You heard?"

"The control room picked the call up on the police scanner."

"It was my apartment, but I'm not hurt. I think most of the fire is out, but the firemen are still working in the building."

"Hal is sitting just outside your lot in case you need help."

"Thanks."

The parking lot was clogged with emergency vehicles and fire trucks fighting for space around the parked cars. Fire hoses snaked over the pavement and it was difficult to see past the glare of spotlights and strobe lights.

"The cab's gonna pick me up on the road," Lula said. "It'll never get into the lot."

I walked through the tangle of trucks and gawkers with Lula, keeping alert for the Chipotle killers. Hard to believe they'd still be around, but they were so stupid it was hard to predict what they'd do. We reached the street running parallel to the lot. The Rangeman SUV was parked about twenty feet away. I waved to Hal and he waved back at me. After a couple minutes, the cab arrived.

"I'm gonna have this guy take me to Dunkin' Donuts," Lula said. "I need a bag of doughnuts."

"No! You're supposed to be off doughnuts."

"Oh yeah. I forgot. I'll have him take me to the supermarket, and I'll get a bag of carrots."

"Really?"

"No, not really. You think I'm gonna feel better eatin' a carrot? Get a grip. There's two idiots out there trying to kill me, and you think I'm gonna waste my last breath on a vegetable?"

Lula climbed into the cab, and I returned to the parking lot. Water dripped down the side of the building and pooled on the blacktop. Some of the tenants were being allowed to return to their apartments. Dillon Ruddick was talking to a couple cops and the fire chief. I walked over to join them.

"I knew it would only be a matter of time before we met again," the chief said to me, referring to the fact that this wasn't the first time my apartment had been firebombed. Or maybe he was talking about the two cars that just got toasted.

"Not my fault," I said, thinking that covered all the possibilities.

"What can you tell me about this?" he said to me.

Morelli was the principal on the Chipotle case, and I didn't know how much he wanted divulged, so I didn't say much. I described the firebomb and left it at that.

I looked up at my smoke-stained window. "How bad is it?"

"Some damage in the dining room and living room. Mostly rugs and curtains. The couch is gone. Some water damage and smoke damage. You should be able to get in tomorrow to look around, but you're not going to want to live in it until a cleaning crew goes through."

"What about the bathroom?"

"It didn't reach the bathroom."

I'd been hoping the bathroom was destroyed. I really needed a bathroom remodel.

It was another hour before the fire trucks rumbled out of my lot and I was able to move the Buick. Hal was still at curbside. I rolled my window down and told him he could go back to Rangeman.

"I'm going to spend the night at my parents' house," I said.

"Do you want me to follow?"

"No. I'll be fine on my own."

I drove down Hamilton, cut into the Burg, and parked in front of my parents' house. The house was dark. No lights shining anywhere. Everyone had turned in for the night.

There are three small bedrooms and one bath on the second floor. My parents share a room, Grandma has a room, and the third room was mine when I lived at home. It hasn't changed much over the years. A new bedspread and new curtains that look exactly like the old ones. I quietly crept up the stairs, carefully opened the door to my room, and had a couple beats of utter confusion. Someone was in my bed. Someone huge. Someone snoring! It was like Goldilocks, but reversed. The mountain of quilt-covered flesh turned and faced me. It was Lula!

I was dumbstruck.

When she said she'd find a place to stay, it never occurred to me it would be with my parents, in *my bed*. I was torn between hauling her out of my room and silently skulking away into the night. I debated it for a moment, took a step back, and closed the door. Let's face facts, there was no way I could haul Lula anywhere. I tiptoed out of the house, got into the Buick, and drove to Rangeman.

Ranger was in his apartment when I walked in. He was in the kitchen, standing at the counter and eating a sandwich.

"Sorry," I said. "I didn't mean to barge in on you. I didn't realize you were here."

"I wouldn't have given you a key if I felt I needed privacy," Ranger said. "You can come and go as you please."

"Any more sandwiches?"

"In the refrigerator."

I took a sandwich, unwrapped it, and bit into it. "It's been a long night."

"I can see that," Ranger said. "You look like you've been dragged through a swamp fire."

My sneakers were soaked, my jeans had wicked water up to my knees, and I was head-to-toe soot.

"The Chipotle killers firebombed my apartment. I saw them in the parking lot. I think they were after Lula."

"Is Morelli making any progress?"

"He's got a name for one of them." I went to the fridge and found a beer. "I thought you'd be on patrol."

"My route took me through town, so I decided to take a break and get something to eat." Ranger finished his sandwich and washed it down with a bottle of water. "I'm going back out."

I walked him to the door and watched him take a key from the silver server on the breakfront. Ranger always kept three cars for his personal use. The Porsche Turbo, a Mercedes sedan, and a Porsche Cayenne. He used to have a truck that he loved, but it went to truck heaven and was never replaced. The key he chose tonight was for a Cayenne.

"Replaced already?" I asked him.

"It would have been here sooner, but they had to install the lockbox under the seat."

"I guess you're all about instant gratification."

Ranger grabbed me and kissed me. "If I was all about instant gratification, you'd be naked and in bed."

And he left.

FIFTEEN

I opened my eyes and looked at the bedside clock. Almost six in the morning. I heard keys clink onto the silver server in the hall, and I knew Ranger was home. I vacated the bed and sleep-walked into the dressing room. Not a lot of variety to my clothing choices. Black everything. Life was simple at Rangeman, and this was a good thing at this hour because I wasn't capable of complicated thoughts, such as red shirt or blue shirt.

I grabbed some clothes and hustled into the bathroom. When I came out, Ranger was eating breakfast at the small dining room table.

"It looks like Ella's been here," I said to him.

"She brought you coffee and an omelet."

There was also a breadbasket, plus a fresh fruit platter with raspberries, blackberries, and kiwi. Ranger had a bagel with cream cheese and smoked salmon.

"How was your night?" I asked him.

"Uneventful. And yours?"

"Uneventful once I got here," I said.

Ranger pushed back from the table and stood. "What are your plans for today?"

"I want to take another stab at capturing My-ron Kaplan. I'm hoping to get into my apartment to at least look around. And we have to sign in for the barbecue cook-off this afternoon. Tomorrow is the big day."

"I hate to point out the obvious, but so far as I know, you can't cook."

"It's about barbecue sauce," I said. "You take some ketchup and add pepper, and you've got sauce."

Ranger grinned down at me. "And this is why I love you." He kissed me on the top of my head. "I need to get some sleep. Take whatever car you want."

I finished my omelet, had a second cup of coffee, and headed out, grabbing the keys to the new Cayenne. It would be fun to drive the Turbo, but it wasn't practical for hauling felons back to jail. I stepped into the elevator, pushed the button for garage level, and waved at the little camera in the corner up by the ceiling, knowing someone was manning a monitor, looking at me. And that's when it hit me. The camera.

I got to the garage and hit the button to go back to the seventh floor. I let myself into Ranger's apartment and yelled out to him. "I've got it!"

"I'm in the bedroom," Ranger said.

"Are you naked?"

"Do you want me to be?"

"No." That was a total lie, but I was too chicken to say yes. Even if a woman was sworn off men for life, she'd still want to see Ranger naked. And I was only sworn off men for the time being.

He walked out to see me. "What do you have?"

"Suppose our man gets into the house under some pretext. Like maybe he's checking phone lines or cable lines. And then he plants a small camera in such a way that it gets a video of the owner punching in the code. And then a couple days later, he comes back and gets the camera. Or maybe the camera sends the video out to an exterior location and then he gets the camera when he commits the robbery. Could he do that?"

"I suppose it could be done, but there've been a lot of break-ins, and no one has noticed a camera."

"Yeah, but these cameras are small. And maybe they get placed alongside other devices like smoke detectors or motion sensors."

"I like it," Ranger said. "Run with it."

"Would you mind if I went to some of your accounts and did a fast check of the areas where touch pads have been installed?"

"Make sure you show them your Rangeman ID and tell them you're a tech."

* * *

I rolled out of the garage and realized it was barely seven o'clock. What on earth is a person supposed to do at this hour? I could go to breakfast at the diner, but I'd just eaten. My parents would be getting up around now, and it might be fun to see everyone fighting over the bathroom. But then, maybe not. I drove past the office. No lights on. Connie never came in this early. I cruised past Morelli's house. No one on the front lawn. His SUV parked at curbside. A single light on upstairs. Morelli was most likely moving a little slow this morning. I avoided my apartment building. It was too soon to get in, and I knew the sight of the fire-blackened windows would make me feel sad.

That left me with Myron Kaplan. I returned to the center of the city and parked across the street from Kaplan's house. It was Monday morning and some houses showed signs of life, but not Kaplan's. If I was a television bounty hunter, I'd kick the door down and go in guns drawn to catch Kaplan by surprise. I elected not to do this because it seemed like a mean thing to do to a guy who just wanted to return his teeth, I wasn't any good at kicking doors down, and I didn't have a gun. My gun was home in my cookie jar, and it wasn't loaded, anyway.

So I hung out in Ranger's brand-new Cayenne, watching Kaplan's house, telling myself I was doing surveillance. Truth is, I was snoozing. I had the seat reclined and was feeling very comfy inside the big car with the dark tinted windows.

I woke up a little after nine and saw movement behind Kaplan's front window. I got out of the car and rang Kaplan's bell.

"Oh jeez," Kaplan said when he saw me. "You again."

"I'll make a deal," I said. "I'll take you to breakfast if you go to the police station with me when you're done."

"I don't want to go to breakfast. I haven't got any teeth. I have to gum everything to death. And if I swallow big chunks of stuff, I get indigestion. Can't eat bacon at all."

"You got your money back. Why don't you go to another dentist and get new teeth?"

"I called some other dentists and couldn't get an appointment. I think they're all in cahoots. I'm on a blacklist."

"Dentists don't have blacklists."

"How do you know? Are you *sure* they don't have blacklists?"

"Pretty sure."

"Pretty sure doesn't cut it, chickie."

"Okay, we'll go to plan B. Let's pay a visit to your old dentist."

"The quack?"

"Yeah. Let's talk to him about your teeth."

"Do you have a gun?"

"No."

"Then it's a waste of time," Myron said. "You'll never get in."

"Trust me, I'll get in."

William Duffy, DDS, had an office suite on the fifth floor of the Kreger Building. The waiting room was standard fare. Durable carpet, leatherette chairs, a couple end tables holding artfully arranged stacks of dog-eared magazines. A receptionist desk presided over one wall and guarded the door that led to Duffy.

"That's her," Myron said. "Miss Snippity."

Miss Snippity was in her forties and looked pleasant enough. Short brown hair, minimal makeup, blue dental office smock with the name *Tammy* embroidered on it.

"Don't come any closer," Tammy said. "I'm calling Security."

"That's not necessary," I told her. "We aren't armed." I glanced over at Myron. "We aren't, right?"

"My daughter took my gun away," Myron said.

"We'd like to talk to Dr. Duffy," I said to Tammy.

"Do you have an appointment?"

"No."

"Dr. Duffy only sees by appointment."

"Yes," I said, "but you just opened for the day and there's no one in the waiting room."

"I'm sorry. You'll have to make an appointment."

"Fine," I said. "I'd like an appointment for *now*. Do you have that available?"

"Dr. Duffy doesn't see patients until 10 A.M."

"Okay. Give me an appointment at 10 A.M."

"That's not available," she said, thumbing through her appointment book. "The next available appointment would be three weeks from now."

"Here's the deal," I said to her. "Poor Mr. Kaplan has no teeth. He's getting indigestion, and he can't eat bacon. Can you imagine a life without bacon, Tammy?"

"I thought Mr. Kaplan was Jewish."

"There's all kinds of Jewish," Mr. Kaplan said. "You sound like my daughter. Maybe you want to tell me to get a colonoscopy, too."

"Oh my goodness, you haven't had a colonoscopy?"

"No one's sticking a camera up my rump," Mr. Kaplan said. "I never like the way I look in pictures."

"About Mr. Kaplan's teeth," I said to Tammy.

"I have *no* appointments," Tammy said. "If I break the rule for Mr. Kaplan, I have to break the rule for everyone."

Tammy was starting to annoy me.

"Just this once," I said. "No one will know. I know Dr. Duffy is in. I can hear him talking on the phone. We want five minutes of his time. We just want to talk to him. Five minutes."

"No."

"I told you," Mr. Kaplan said to me. "She's snippity."

I put palms down on Tammy's desk and I leaned in real close to her. Nose to nose. "If you don't let me in, I'm going to picket this building and let everyone know about the shoddy work Dr. Duffy is doing. And then I'm going to run a personal computer check on you and get the names of all your high school classmates and tell them you have relations with ponies and large dogs."

"You don't scare me," Tammy said.

So that was when I went to plan C and broke into my imitation of Julie Andrews, singing, "The hills are alive, with the sound of music. . . ."

Dr. Duffy almost immediately stuck his head out the door. "What the heck?"

"We'd like to talk to you for a moment," I said. "Mr. Kaplan is very sorry he held you up, and he'd like to discuss his teeth."

"I'm not sorry," Mr. Kaplan said. "This office gives me a pain in my behind."

"You aren't armed, are you?" Dr. Duffy asked.

"No."

"Come back to my office. I have a few minutes until my first appointment."

Myron stuck his tongue out at Tammy, and we followed Dr. Duffy down a short corridor, past dental torture rooms.

"What would you like to discuss?" Dr. Duffy said, settling himself behind his desk.

"Do you still have Myron's teeth?"

"The police have them. They're evidence."

"Can they be fixed so they fit him and they're comfortable?"

"They seemed to fit him when he left my office."

"They were fine, and then a week later, they were terrible," Myron said.

"You should have made an appointment to get them rechecked," Dr. Duffy said.

"I couldn't get an appointment," Myron said. "Your snippity secretary wouldn't give me one."

"It would be really great if you could drop the charges against Mr. Kaplan and fix his teeth," I said to Duffy. "He's not a bad guy. He just wants teeth. And for the record, your secretary *is* snippity."

"I know she's snippity," Duffy said. "She's my wife's first cousin, and I can't get rid of her. I'll see what I can do about getting the charges dropped, and I'll call you as soon as the police release your teeth."

"That would be real nice of you," Myron said. "I'm getting tired of oatmeal."

Ten minutes later, we were in front of the courthouse.

"I have to check you in," I said to Myron, "but Connie is on her way to bail you out again. And hopefully, you'll be cleared of charges soon."

"That's okay," Myron said. "I didn't have anything to do today, anyway."

I had my map and a summary of Ranger's accounts in front of me. My plan was to take a look at those accounts I'd tagged as high risk and those accounts that had already been hit. The first two houses were high risk. Each of the houses had a touch pad by the front door and a touch pad by the garage entrance. I couldn't find any evidence of filming devices in the touch-pad areas. The next stop was the only commercial account on my list. It was the insurance company that had been burgled four days ago.

I went directly to the rear-entrance touch pad and looked to find possible lines of sight. Rangeman had installed a motion sensor over the door. This was the spot I'd choose if I wanted to snoop on the touch pad. I'd set the camera above the motion sensor, and it would look like it belonged there. There was no camera there now, but it looked to me like some of the paint above the motion sensor had flaked off.

I asked building maintenance to get me a stepladder. I climbed up, took a closer look, and I was pretty sure something had been taped there. When the tape was removed, the paint had peeled away with it. I took a picture with my cell phone and thanked the maintenance guy for the ladder.

"No problem," he said. "The guy last week needed a ladder, too."

"What guy?"

"The Rangeman guy. What is it that you people keep checking?"

"Do you remember exactly when he was here?"

"Yeah, he was here twice. Monday morning and Wednesday morning."

"Can you describe him?"

"Sure. He was young. Maybe eighteen or nineteen. Slim. About my height. I'm five ten. Brown hair, brown eyes. Sort of dark skin. Nice-looking kid. Is something wrong?"

"No, but I'll check with the office to make sure we're not both doing the same route. Did you get his name?"

"No. He didn't tell me his name. At least, I can't remember."

I had to work hard not to run out of the building. I was so excited, I could barely concentrate on driving. I screeched to a stop in the Rangeman garage and danced in the elevator all the way to the seventh floor. I ran through Ranger's apartment, rushed into his bedroom, and jumped on the bed.

"I've got it! I know how the robberies were done and I know what the guy looks like!"

I was straddling Ranger, who fortunately was under a quilt, because from what I could see, he looked deliciously naked.

Ranger put his hands on my waist. "You've got my attention."

"I noticed the paint was flaked away near a motion sensor that was opposite the touch pad at the insurance company. So I asked for a ladder, and sure enough, you could see where something had been taped to the wall."

"Keep talking."

"Are you sure you're listening? Your hand just moved to my breast."

"You're so soft," Ranger said, his thumb brushing across my nipple.

I got a rush, followed by a lot of desire spread all over the place. "Oh," I heard myself murmur. "That feels good." *No!* Wait a minute. Get a grip. "Jeez," I said. And I scrambled off the bed.

"I almost had you," Ranger said.

"I'm not ready for you. I'm currently off men."

"Taking a hiatus."

"Something like that."

"Tell me more about my break-in expert."

"The maintenance man said a Rangeman employee had been in twice to check on the same motion sensor. I figure, once to install the camera and once to remove it. He said the tech was eighteen or nineteen years old. Around five ten. Brown hair, brown eyes, sort of dark skin. Nice-looking."

"I don't have anyone that young," Ranger said, "but I have several men who would fit the rest of the description and might look younger than they actually are."

"So we're back to someone in-house. That's ugly."

Ranger slipped out of bed. "I'm going to take a shower, and then I'll follow up on this."

I stared at him. He was naked, all right.

"You're staring," he said, smiling.

"I like to look."

"Nice to know," Ranger said, "but we should be able to do better than that for you."

I rummaged through Ranger's refrigerator while he took a shower. Fresh fruit, low-fat cottage cheese, orange juice, nonfat milk, white wine. No leftover pizza. No birthday cake. Ranger was hot, but he didn't know much about food.

I went down to the fifth floor, got an assortment of sandwiches and sides, and brought it all back to Ranger's apartment.

Ranger strolled in and took a turkey club. "Did you get the name of the maintenance guy?"

"Mike. He'll be there until three o'clock today."

"Do you want to ride with me?"

"I can't. I need to check on my fire damage and see if Lula needs help with the cook-off."

"How are you doing with FTAs?"

"I have one open. I saved the worst for last. Cameron Manfred. Armed robbery. Connie has him living in the projects. Works for Barbara Trucking."

"I can go out with you tonight," Ranger said.

I pulled the Cayenne into the parking lot to my building and looked up at my windows. One window was broken. Looked like it was boarded over from the inside. All were ringed with black soot. Grimy water stains streaked down the yellow brick exterior. Water still pooled in the parking lot. What looked like the remains of my couch sat black and sodden alongside the Dumpster. Sometimes it was good not to have a lot of expensive stuff. Less to feel bad about when it got firebombed.

I took the stairs and stepped into the second-floor hall. Dillon had a couple giant fans working at drying the carpet. The door to my apartment was open, and Dillon was inside.

Dillon was around my age, and he'd been the building super for as long as I could remember. He lived in the bowels of the building in a free but tomblike efficiency. He was a nice guy who'd do anything for a six-pack of beer, and he was always mellow, in part from the small cannabis farm in his bathroom. He was a little sloppy in a hip super-casual kind of way, and he tended to show some butt-crack when he came up to fix your plumbing, but you didn't actually mind because his butt-crack was kind of cute.

"I hope it's okay I'm in your apartment," Dillon said. "I wanted to get some of the water-logged stuff out, and I have an insurance agent due any minute."

"Fine by me," I said. "I appreciate the help with the furniture."

"It was a lot worse last time you were fire-bombed," Dillon said. "Most of the damage this time is from water and smoke. It didn't touch your bedroom at all. And it didn't get to your bathroom."

I blew out a sigh.

"Yeah," he said. "I'm sorry it didn't get to your bathroom. I thought about spreading some gasoline around and lighting a match in there, but I was afraid I'd blow myself up. On the bright side, I'm sure this isn't the last time you'll ever get firebombed, so maybe you'll have better luck next time."

"There's a cheery thought."

"Yeah, I'm a glass is half full kind of guy."

"Speaking of glasses. I could use a beer."

"I put some in your fridge. I figured you'd need a cold one."

I cracked open a beer and slogged through my apartment. The curtains were history. The couch I already knew about. The rugs were sort of melted and waterlogged. No biggie on the rugs. They weren't wonderful to begin with, and the building would replace them. My dining room table and chairs were grimy but probably would clean up okay. Everything in my bedroom smelled like smoke. Dillon had another fan working in there.

"How long before I can move in?" I asked him.

"I've got professional cleaners coming in later today. The carpet's been ordered. I'll bring a couple of my buddies in, and we'll do the painting. If all the moons line up right, I'd say a week."

Oh boy. Another week with Ranger. And once he solved his break-in problem, he'd stop working nights, and he'd go to bed early . . . with me. My first thought was *YUM!* My second thought was *Help!*

I stuffed Lula's clothes into a plastic garbage bag, carted it out to the Cayenne, and drove it to the office. Connie was out when I arrived, and Lula was at Connie's desk, answering phones.

"Vincent Plum Bail Bonds," she said. "What do you want?" There was a pause, and Lula said, "Un-hunh, un-hunh, un-hunh." Another pause. "What did you say your name was? Did I hear Louanne Harmon? Because I'm not bailin' out no Louanne Harmon. I suppose there's some good Louanne Harmons out there, but the one I know is a skank 'ho. The Louanne Harmon I know told my customers I was overchargin' for my services when I was workin' my corner. Is this that same Louanne Harmon?" Another pause. "Well, you can kiss my ass," Lula said. And she hung up.

Vinnie stuck his head out of his office. "What was that?"

"Wrong number," Lula said. "They wanted the DMV."

"Where's Connie?" I asked.

"She went to write bond for your Mr. Kaplan, and she didn't come back yet."

"Any word from Joyce?"

"Connie called and told her there was only one open file, and she told Connie you had breast implants and one of them diseases that you get from the toilet seat. I forget what it was."

Terrific. "It looks like you're doing okay."

"Yeah, I'm not dead. Nobody's even shot at me today. I think this is my lucky day. I bet we're gonna win that cook-off tomorrow and catch the Chipotle killers and be on easy street. I even stopped by the travel agency and got a brochure for my Panama Canal cruise. It's one of them boats that had a virus epidemic and everyone got sick and now their rates are real low. I have a chance to get a good deal. Not that I need it anymore."

"So you're still planning on entering the cook-off."

"Damn skippy, I'm gonna enter. We gotta go

to the Gooser Park and sign in this afternoon. And I gotta get my car, too. I was hoping you could give me a ride to your parking lot as soon as Connie gets back."

An hour later, I was back in my parking lot with Lula.

"There's my baby," Lula said. "Good thing I parked way at the end of the lot where nobody else parks. It didn't hardly get any soot on it. And it was out of the water spray. I'm gonna take it to get detailed this afternoon, so it looks fine when I win the contest and capture the bad guys. I'll probably be on television."

I pulled up next to the Firebird, Lula got out, unlocked her car, and slid behind the wheel. I waited for the engine to catch, and then I put the Cayenne in gear and drove out of the lot. I realized Lula was still sitting there, so I returned to the lot, parked next to her, and got out.

"Something wrong?"

"It's making a funny sound. You hear it?"

"Are any of the warning lights on?"

"No. I'm gonna take a look under the hood."

"Do you know anything about cars?"

"Sure I know about cars. I know there's an engine up there. And lots of other shit, too."

Lula popped the hood, and we took a look.

"What are we supposed to be looking for?" I asked her.

"I don't know. Something unusual. Like I once had a neighbor who found a cat in his car. At least, he thought it used to be a cat. It was something with fur. It might have been a raccoon or a big rat or a small beaver. It was hard to tell."

"What's that package wrapped in cellophane with the wires?" I asked her.

"I don't know," Lula said, leaning closer. "I think that might be the problem, though, on account of it's ticking."

"Ticking?"

"Oh shit!" Lula said.

We jumped back and ran for all we were worth and hid behind the Dumpster. Nothing happened.

Lula stuck her head out. "Maybe that was the carburetor, and it was supposed to tick," she said. "Do carburetors tick?"

BABOOOM! Lula's car jumped five feet in the air. The doors and hood flew off into space, and the car burst into flames. There was a second explosion, the Firebird rolled over onto Ranger's Cayenne, and the Cayenne caught. In a matter of minutes, there was nothing left of either car but smoking, twisted, charred metal.

Lula's mouth opened, but no words came out. Her eyes got huge, rolled back into her head, and she keeled over in a dead faint. By the time the fire trucks arrived, the fire had played itself out. Lula was sitting propped against the Dumpster, still not making sense.

"It . . . and . . . my . . . how?" she asked.

I was numb. These idiots were still trying to kill Lula, and I'd just destroyed another Cayenne. I'd been involved in so many fires in the past week, I'd lost count. I had no place to live. I had no idea what I wanted to do about my personal relationships. And I still couldn't get all the red paint out of my hair. I was a disaster magnet.

I suddenly felt warm, and all the little hairs stood up on my arms. I turned and bumped into Ranger.

"This has to be a record," he said. "I've had that car for twenty-four hours."

"I'm sorry," I said. And I burst into tears.

Ranger wrapped his arms around me and cuddled me into him. "Babe. It's just a car."

"It's not just the car. It's me," I wailed. "I'm a mess."

"You're not a mess," Ranger said. "You're just having one of those emotional girl moments."

"Unh," I said. And I punched him in the chest.

"Feel better?"

"Yeah, sort of."

He stepped back and looked at Lula. "What's wrong with her?"

"She's in a state. Her Firebird got blown up."

"She spends all this time with you, and she's not used to cars getting blown up?"

"They aren't usually hers."

"Does she need help?"

"I think she'll come around," I said. "She's breathing now. And her eyes have mostly gone back into their sockets."

I looked past Ranger and saw Morelli come on the scene. He picked me out of the crowd of bystanders and jogged over.

"Are you okay?" he asked me. "What's with Lula?"

"One of those cars used to be her Firebird."

"And the other used to be my Cayenne," Ranger said.

Morelli looked down at Lula. "Does she need a medic?"

"Someone's gonna pay," Lula said. And she farted.

Morelli and Ranger smiled wide, and we all took a step back.

"That should help," I said.

"Yep," Morelli said, still grinning. "Always makes me feel better."

"I have to get back to the office," Ranger said. "Ramon is in a car on the street if you need anything."

Morelli watched him walk away. "It's like he's SpiderMan with Spidey sense. Something happens, and he suddenly appears. And then when the disaster is contained, he vanishes."

"His control room listens to the scanners."

"That was my second guess," Morelli said.

"It was some sort of bomb," I said to Morelli. "It was next to the engine, and it ticked. We were lucky we weren't killed."

"It ticked? Bombs don't tick anymore. Where did they get their material, WWI surplus?"

"Maybe it was something rubbing against a moving part. I don't know anything about this stuff. It was making a noise that sounded like ticking. Anyway, these guys aren't smart."

"I noticed. It makes it all the more annoying that we can't catch them."

"How's Bob?" I asked.

"Bob is fine. His intestines are squeaky clean."

"How are you?"

"I'm clean, too."

And then I couldn't help myself. The bitch part of me sneaked out. "How's Joyce?"

"Joyce is Joyce," Morelli said.

Lula hauled herself to her feet. "I'm in a bad mood," she said. "I'm in a mood to get me some Marco the Maniac. I've had it with this shit. It's one thing to kill me, but blowin' up my Firebird is goin' too far." She looked at her watch. "We gotta get to the park. We gotta sign in."

"We haven't got a car. The Buick is parked at Rangeman."

"I'll call Connie. She can take us."

SIXTEEN

Connie drove a silver Camry with rosary beads hanging from her rearview mirror and a Smith & Wesson stuck under the driver's seat. No matter what went down, Connie was covered.

I was in the backseat with Grandma, and Lula was next to Connie. We were in the parking lot adjacent to the field where the cook-off was to be held, and we were watching competitors pull in, dragging everything from mobile professional kitchens to U-hauls carrying grills and worktables.

"I didn't expect this," Grandma said. "I figured we come with a jar of sauce, and they'd have some chicken for us."

"We got a grill," Lula said, getting out of the Camry. "We just didn't bring it yet."

"Did you get a set of rules when you registered?" Connie asked Lula.

"No. I did the express register, bein' that the organizer was under some duress. And on top of that, I didn't have to pay no registration fee, so he might have been trying to save on paper."

A registration table had been set up at the edge of the lot. Competitors were signing in, taking a set of instructions, and leaving with a tray.

"What's with the tray?" Lula asked the guy in line in front of us.

"It's the official competition tray. You put the food that's going to be judged on the tray."

"Imagine that," Grandma said. "Isn't that something?"

We got our tray and our rules, and we stepped aside to read through the instructions.

"It says here that we can't use a gas grill," Connie said. "We need to cook on wood or charcoal. And we have to pick a category. Ribs, chicken, or brisket."

"I'm thinking ribs," Lula said. "Seems to me it's harder to poison someone with ribs. I guess there's always that trichinosis thing, but you don't know about that for years. And I'm gonna have to get a different grill."

"All these people got tents and tables and signs with their name on it," Grandma said. "We need some of that stuff. We need a name."

"How about Vincent Plum Bail Bondettes," Connie said.

"I'm not being nothin' associating me with Vincent Plum," Lula said. "Bad enough I gotta work for the little pervert."

"I want a sexy name," Grandma said. "Like Hot Vagina."

"Flamin' Assholes would be better," Lula said. "That's what happens when you eat our sauce. Can you say Flamin' Assholes on television?"

"This is big," I said, looking out over the field. "There are flags with numbers on them all over the place. Every team is assigned a number."

"We're number twenty-seven," Lula said. "That don't sound like a good number to me."

"What's wrong with it?"

"It's not memorable," Lula said. "I want to be number nine."

My eye was starting to twitch, and I had a dull throb at the base of my skull. "Probably, they gave us Chipotle's number," I said.

"Do you think?"

"Absolutely. He got decapitated, and you registered late, so you got his number."

I hoped she bought this baloney, because I didn't want to hang out while Lula pulled a gun on the registration lady.

"That makes sense," Lula said. "I guess it's okay then. Let's find our spot."

We walked down rows of flags and finally found twenty-seven. It was a little patch of grass between the red-and-white-striped canopy of Bert's BBQ and the brown canopy of The Bull Stops Here. Our neighbors had set up shop and taken off. From what I could see, that was the routine. Stake out your territory, get your canopy and table ready to go. Hang your sign. Leave for the day.

"The instructions say we can get back in here at eight o'clock tomorrow morning," Connie said. "We can start cooking anytime we want after that. The judging is at six in the evening."

"We got a lot of stuff to get together," Lula said. "To start, we gotta find one of them canopies and a grill."

"Not everybody has a canopy," Grandma said.

"Yeah, but the canopy is classy, and it keeps the sun off the top of your head, so you don't get a sunburn," Lula said.

We all looked at the top of Lula's head. Not much chance of sunburn there. Not a lot of sunlight reached Lula's scalp.

"I've got a couple hours free this afternoon," I said to Lula. "We can go around and try to collect some of the essentials. We just have to stop by Rangeman, so I can get the Buick."

"I'll go with you," Grandma said.

The first thing we gotta do is get us a truck," Lula said. "This Buick isn't gonna hold a grill and all. I bet we could borrow a truck from Pookey Brown. He owns that junkyard and used-car lot at the end of Stark Street. He used to be a steady customer of mine when I was a 'ho."

"Boy," Grandma said. "You had lots of customers. You know people everywhere."

"I had a real good corner. And I never had a business manager, so I was able to keep my prices down."

I didn't want to drive the length of Stark, so I cut across on Olden and only had to go two blocks down to the junkyard. The name on the street sign read C.J. SCRAP METAL, but Pookey Brown ran it, and scrap metal was too lofty a description for Pookey's business. Pookey was a junk collector. He ran a private dump. Pookey had almost two acres of broken, rusted, unwanted crapola. Even Pookey himself looked like he was expired. He was thin as a reed, frizzy haired, gaunt featured, and his skin tone was gray. I had no clue to his age. He could be forty. He could be a hundred and ten. And I couldn't imagine what Pookey would do with a 'ho.

"There's my girl," Pookey said when he saw Lula. "I never get to see you anymore."

"I keep busy working at the bond office," Lula told him. "I need a favor. I need to borrow a truck until tomorrow night."

"Sure," Pookey said. "Just take yourself over to the truck section and pick one out."

If you had a junker car or truck, and somehow you could manage to get it to C.J. Scrap, you could park it there and walk away. Some of them even had license plates attached. And every now and then, one got parked with a body in the trunk. There were thirteen cars and three pickup trucks in Pookey's "used car" lot today.

"Any of these trucks run?" Lula asked.

"The red one got a couple miles left," Pookey said. "I could put a plate on for you. You need anything else?"

"Yeah," Lula said. "I need a grill. Not one of them gas grills, either."

"I got a good selection of grills," Pookey said. "Do you need to cook in it?"

"I'm entered in the barbecue contest at the park tomorrow," Lula said.

"So then you need a *barbecuing* grill. That narrows the field. How about eating? Are you gonna personally eat any of the barbecue?"

"I don't think so. I think the judges are eating the barbecue."

"That gives us more selection," Pookey said.

By the time Lula was done shopping at C.J. Scrap, she had a grill and a card table loaded into her truck. The plate on the truck was expired, but you could hardly tell for the mud and rust. I followed her down Stark and parked behind her when she stopped at Maynard's Funeral Home.

"I gotta make a pickup here, too. You stay and guard the truck," Lula said, sticking her head in the Buick's window. "Bad as it is, if I leave it alone for ten minutes in this part of town, it'll be missing wheels when I get back." She looked at Grandma, sitting next to me. "Do you have your gun?"

"You betcha," Grandma said. "I got it right here in my purse. Just like always."

"Shoot whoever comes near," Lula said to Grandma. "I won't be long."

I looked over at Grandma. "If you shoot *any-one*, I'm telling my mother on you."

"How about those three guys coming down the street? Can I shoot them?"

"No! They're just walking down the street."

"I don't like the looks of them," Grandma said. "They look shifty."

"Everyone looks like that on Stark Street."

The three guys were in their early- to mid-twenties, doing the ghetto strut in their ridiculous oversize pants. They were wearing a lot of gold chains, and one of them had a bottle in a brown paper bag. Always a sign of a classy dude.

I rolled my window up and locked my door, and Grandma did the same.

They got even with the Buick and looked in at me.

"Nice wheels," one of them said. "Maybe you should get out and let me drive."

"Ignore them," I said to Grandma. "They'll go away."

The guy with the bottle took a pull on it and tried the door handle. Locked.

"Are you sure you don't want me to shoot him?" Grandma asked.

"No. No shooting."

They tried to rock the car, but the Buick was a tank. It would take more than three scrawny homies to rock the Buick. One of them dropped his pants and pressed his bare ass against the driver's side window.

"You're gonna have to Windex that window when we get home," Grandma said.

I was looking at the funeral home, sending mental telepathy to Lula to get herself out to her truck, so we could leave, and I heard the back door to the Buick get wrenched open. I hadn't thought to lock the back door.

One of the men climbed onto the backseat, and another reached around and unlocked the driver's door. I reached for the ignition key, but my door was already open, and I was getting pulled out of the car. I hooked my arm through the steering wheel and kicked one of the guys in the face. The guy in the back was grabbing at me, and the third guy had hold of my foot.

"We're gonna have fun with you and the old lady," the guy in the backseat said. "We're gonna do you like you've never been done before."

"Shoot!" I said to Grandma.

"But you said . . ."

"Just fucking *shoot* someone!"

Grandma carried a gun like Dirty Harry's. I caught sight of the massive barrel in my peripheral vision and *BANG*.

The guy holding my foot jumped back and grabbed the side of his head, blood spurting through his fingers. "Son of a bitch!" he yelled. "Son of a fuckin' bitch! She shot off my ear."

I knew what he was saying because it was easy to read his lips, but I wasn't hearing anything but a high-pitched ringing in my head.

The guy in the backseat scrambled out of the Buick and helped drag the guy with one ear down the street.

"Do you think he'll be all right?" Grandma asked.

"Don't know. Don't care."

The door to the funeral home opened, and Lula and a mountain of a guy came out carrying a bundle of what looked like aluminum poles partially wrapped in faded green canvas. They threw the bundle into the back of the truck, and the guy returned to the funeral home. Lula said something to Grandma and me, but I couldn't hear.

"What?" I said.

"HOME!" Grandma yelled.

I followed Lula to my parents' house and dropped Grandma off. I think Grandma said they were going to put the truck in the garage, so no one would steal the grill. Personally, I didn't think she had to worry about anyone wanting the grill.

I drove through town to Rangeman and went straight to Ranger's apartment. I kicked my shoes off and flopped onto his bed. When I woke up, I was covered with a light blanket, and I could see Ranger at his desk in the den. The ringing wasn't nearly so loud in my head. It was down to mosquito level.

I rolled out of bed and went into the den.

"Tough day?" Ranger asked.

"You don't even want to know. How was your day?"

"Interesting. I showed your maintenance man Mike file pictures of all Rangeman employees remotely fitting his description, and he couldn't identify any of them. Our bad guy wears a Rangeman uniform but doesn't work here."

"Could he be a former employee?"

"There were only two possibilities, and I got a negative on them."

"Now what?"

"I have someone checking all the accounts for evidence of touch-pad surveillance. He's also cataloging Rangeman visits on those accounts."

"It wouldn't be difficult to duplicate a Rangeman uniform. Black cargo pants and a black T-shirt with *Rangeman* embroidered on it."

"My men all know to show their ID when entering a house, but the accounts are lax at asking. Most people see the uniform and are satisfied."

I was suddenly starving, and there was a wonderful smell drifting in from the kitchen. "What's that smell?"

Ella brought dinner up a half hour ago, but I didn't want to wake you. I think we've got some kind of stew."

We went to the kitchen and dished out the stew.

"I've got a fix on Cameron Manfred," Ranger said. "During the day, he works for a trucking company that's a front for a hijacking operation. It would be awkward to make an apprehension there. Lots of paranoid people with guns. Manfred leaves the trucking company at five, goes to a neighborhood strip bar with his fellow workers until around seven, and then heads for his girl's apartment. He gives his address as the projects, but he's never there. It's actually his mother's address. We're going to have to hit him at the girl's place tonight. If there isn't enough cover to tag him on the street, we'll have to let him settle and then go in after him. I have to take a shift at eleven, but we should have this wrapped up by then."

We were in a Rangeman-issue black Explorer. Ranger was behind the wheel, and we were parked across from a slum apartment building one block over from Stark Street, where Cameron Manfred was holed up with his girlfriend. It was a little after nine at night, and the street was dark. Businesses were closed, steel grates rolled down over entrances and plate-glass windows. There was a streetlight overhead, but the bulb had been shot out.

We'd been sitting at the curb for ten minutes, not saying anything, Ranger in hunt mode. He was watching the building and the street, taking the pulse of the area, his own heart rate probably somewhere around reptilian.

He punched a number into his phone. A man answered, and Ranger disconnected. "He's there," Ranger said. "Let's go."

We crossed the street, entered the building, and silently climbed to the third floor. The air was stale. The walls were covered with graffiti. The light was dim. A small rat scuttled across Ranger's foot and disappeared into the shadows. I shuddered and grabbed the back of his shirt.

"Babe," Ranger said, his voice barely audible.

There were two apartments on the third floor. Maureen Gonzales, Manfred's girlfriend, lived in 3A. I stood flat to the wall on one side of her door. Ranger stood on the other side and knocked. His other hand was on his holstered gun.

A pretty Hispanic woman opened the door and smiled at Ranger. She was wearing a man's shirt, unbuttoned, and nothing else. "Yes?" she said.

Ranger smiled back at the woman and looked

beyond her, into the room. "I'd like to speak to Cameron."

"Cameron isn't here."

"You don't mind if I look around?"

She held the shirt wide open. "Look all you want."

"Nice," Ranger said, "but I'm looking for Cameron."

"I told you he's not here."

"Bond enforcement," Ranger said. "Step aside."

"Do you have a search warrant?"

There was the sound of a window getting shoved up in the back room. Ranger pushed past Gonzales and ran for the window. I turned and raced down the stairs and out the front door. I saw Manfred burst out of the alley between the buildings and cross the street. I took off after him, having no idea what I'd do if I caught him. My self-defense skills relied heavily on eye-gouging and testicle rearrangement. Beyond that, I was at a loss.

I chased Manfred to Stark and saw him turn the corner. I turned a couple beats behind him, and the sidewalk was empty in front of me. No Manfred.

The only possibility was the building on the corner. There was a pizza place on the ground floor and what looked like two floors of apartments above it. The pizza place was closed for the night. The door leading to the apartments was open, the hallway was dark. No light in the stairwell. I stood in the entry and listened for movement.

Ranger came in behind me. "Is he up there?"

"I don't know. I lost him when he turned the corner. I wasn't that far away. I don't think he had time to go farther than this building. Where were you? I thought you'd be on top of him."

"The fire escape rusted out underneath me at the second floor. It took me a minute to regroup." He looked up the stairs. "Do you want to come with me, or do you want to keep watch here?"

"I'll stay here."

Ranger was immediately swallowed up by the dark. He had a flashlight, but he didn't use it. He moved almost without sound, creeping up the stairs, pausing at the second-floor landing to listen before moving on.

I hid in the shadows, not wanting to be seen from the street. God knows who was walking the street. Probably, I should carry a gun, but guns scared the heck out of me. I had pepper spray in my purse. And a large can of hair spray, which in my experience is almost as effective as the pepper spray.

I was concentrating on listening for Ranger and keeping watch on the street, and was completely taken by surprise when a door to the rear of the ground-floor hallway opened and Manfred stepped out. He froze when he saw me, obviously just as shocked to find me standing there as I was to see him. He whirled around and retreated through the door. I yelled for Ranger and ran after Manfred.

The door opened to a flight of stairs that led to the cellar. I got to the bottom of the stairs and realized this was a storeroom for the pizza place. Stainless-steel rolling shelves marched in rows across the room. Bags of flour, cans of tomato sauce, and gallon cans of olive oil were stacked on the shelves. A dim bulb burned overhead. I didn't see Manfred. Fine by me. Probably the only reason I wasn't already dead was that he'd left his girl's house in such a rush, he'd gone out unarmed.

I cautiously approached one of the shelves, and Manfred stepped out and grabbed me.

"Give me your gun," he said.

My heart skipped a beat and went into terror tempo. *Bang, bang, bang, bang*, knocking against my rib cage.

"I don't have a gun," I said.

And then, without any help from my brain, my knee suddenly connected with Manfred's gonads.

Manfred doubled over, and I hit him on the head with a bag of flour. He staggered forward a little, but he didn't go down, so I hit him again. The bag broke, and flour went everywhere. I was momentarily blinded, but I reached back to the shelf, grabbed a gallon can of oil, and swung blind. I connected with something that got a grunt out of Manfred.

"Fuckin' bitch," Manfred said.

I hauled back to swing again, and Ranger lifted the can from my hand.

"I'm on it," Ranger said, cuffing Manfred.

"Jail's better than another three minutes with her," Manfred said. "She's a fuckin' animal. I'm lucky if I can ever use my nuts again. Keep her away from me."

"I didn't see you come down the stairs," I said to Ranger. "It was a whiteout."

"Any special reason you grabbed the flour?"

"I wasn't thinking."

Manfred and I were head-to-toe flour. The flour sifted off us when we moved and floated in the air like pixie dust. Ranger hadn't so much as a smudge. By the time we got to the Rangeman SUV, some of the flour had been left behind as ghostly white footprints, but a lot of it remained.

"I honestly don't know how you manage to do this," Ranger said. "Paint, barbecue sauce, flour. It boggles the mind."

"This was all your fault," I said.

Ranger glanced over at me and his eyebrows raised a fraction of an inch.

"You could have taken him down in the apartment if you hadn't spent so much time staring at his naked girlfriend."

Ranger grinned. "She wasn't naked. She was wearing a shirt."

"You deserved to fall off that fire escape."

"That's harsh," Ranger said.

"Did you hurt yourself?" I asked him.

"Do you care?"

"No," I said.

"Liar," Ranger said. He ruffled my hair and flour sprang out in all directions.

Manfred said something to Ranger in Spanish. Ranger answered him as he assisted him into the backseat of the Explorer.

"What did he say?" I asked Ranger.

"He said if I let him go, I could have his girl."

"And your answer?"

"I declined."

"You'll probably regret that as the night goes on," I said to him.

"No doubt," Ranger said.

Ranger and I had Manfred in front of the docket lieutenant. It was a little after ten, and things were heating up. Drunk drivers, abusive drunk husbands, and a couple drug busts were making their way through the system. I was waiting for my body receipt when Morelli walked in. He nodded to Ranger and grinned at me in my whiteness.

"I was at my desk, and Mickey told me I had to come out to take a look," Morelli said.

"It's flour," I told him.

"I can see that. If we add some milk and eggs, we can turn you into a cake."

"What are you doing here? I thought you were off nights."

"I came in to cover a shooting. Fred was supposed to be on, but he got overexcited at his kid's ball game and pulled a groin muscle. I was just finishing up some paperwork."

Mickey Bolan joined us. Bolan worked Crimes Against Persons with Morelli. He was ten years older than Morelli and counting down to his pension.

"I wasn't exaggerating, right?" Bolan said to Morelli. "They're both covered with flour."

"I'd tell you about it," I said to Bolan, "but it's not as good as it looks."

"That's okay," Bolan said. "I got something better, anyway. The rest of Stanley Chipotle just turned up at the funeral home on Hamilton."

We all stood there for a couple beats, trying to process what we'd just heard.

"He turned up?" Morelli finally said.

"Yeah," Bolan said. "Someone apparently dumped him on the doorstep. So I guess someone should talk to the funeral guy."

"I guess that someone would be me," Morelli said. He looked at his watch. "What the hell, the game's over now, anyway."

"I need to get back to Rangeman," Ranger

said to me. "If you have an interest in Chipotle, I can send someone with a car for you."

"Thanks. I don't usually get excited about seeing headless dead men, but I wouldn't mind knowing more."

"I can give her a ride," Morelli said. "I don't imagine this will take long."

SEVENTEEN

Eddie Gazarra was standing in the funeral home parking lot, waiting for Morelli. Eddie is married to my cousin Shirley-the-Whiner. Eddie is a patrolman by choice. He could have moved up, but he likes being on the street. He says it's the uniform. No choices to make in the morning. I think it's the free doughnuts at Tasty Pastry.

"I was the first on the scene," Gazarra said when we got out of Morelli's SUV. "The drop was made right after viewing hours. Morton shut the lights off, and ten minutes later, someone rang the doorbell. When Morton came to the door, he found Chipotle stretched out and frozen solid."

Eli Morton is the current owner of the funeral home. For years, Constantine Stiva owned the place. The business has changed hands a couple times since Stiva left, but everyone still thinks of this as Stiva's Funeral Home.

"Where is he now?" Morelli asked.

"On the porch. We didn't move him."

"Are you sure it's Chipotle?"

"He didn't have a head," Gazarra said. "We sort of put two and two together."

"No ID?"

"None we could find. Hard to get into his pockets, what with him being a big Popsicle."

We'd been walking while we were talking, and we'd gotten to the stairs that led to the funeral home's wide front porch. I recognized Eli Morton at the top of the stairs. He was talking to a couple uniformed cops and an older man in slacks and a dress shirt. A couple guys from the EMT truck were up there, too. The body wasn't visible.

"Maybe I'll wait here," I said.

"It's not so bad," Gazarra told me. "He's frozen stiff as a board. All the blood's frozen, too. And the head was cut off nice and clean."

I sat down on the bottom step. "I'll *definitely* wait here."

"I'll get back to you," Morelli said, walking the rest of the way with Gazarra.

The medical examiner's truck rolled past and pulled into the lot. It was followed by a TV news truck with a dish. I saw Morelli glance over at the news truck and move a couple of the uniformed guys from the porch to the lot to contain the media.

I sat on the step for about a half hour, watching people come and go. Finally, Morelli came back and sat alongside me.

"How's it going?" I asked him.

"The forensic photographer just finished, and the ME is doing his thing, and then we're moving the body inside to a meat locker. He's starting to defrost."

"Is he staying here for the funeral?"

"Eventually. The body will have to go to the morgue for an autopsy first, and then it'll get released for burial. Right now, I need someone to identify the body."

"Do you think it might not be Chipotle?"

"This is a high-profile case, and there was no identification on the body."

"Aren't there tests for that sort of thing?"

"Yeah, and they'll do them when they do the autopsy. I just need someone to eyeball this guy for a preliminary ID."

"His sister?"

"We haven't been able to reach her."

"One of his ex-wives? His agent?"

"They're all over the place. Aspen, New York, L.A., Sante Fe."

"So who are you going to get?"

"Lula."

"You're kidding."

"She saw him get murdered," Morelli said. "I'm hoping she remembers his clothes and enough of his build to give me an ID. I've got two television trucks and a bunch of reporters sitting in the lot. If I don't give them something, they'll make something up, so I'm going to have to talk to them. Before I do that, my chief wants an ID."

"Have you called Lula?"

"Yeah. She's on her way over."

There was activity at the top of the porch, and Morelli stood.

"Looks like they're getting ready to move the body," he said. "I'm keeping it on ice here for Lula. I thought it was easier than trying to get her to go to the morgue. I'd appreciate it if you could wait here for her and bring her in when she arrives."

"Sure."

Twenty minutes later, I saw my father's cab drive into the lot. The cab parked, and Lula got out and waved to the knot of newsmen standing by one of the trucks.

"Yoohoo, I'm Lula," she said to them. "I got called in to identify the body."

I jumped up and sprinted to the lot, intercepting the horde that rushed at her.

"Lula will talk to you later," I told them, herding Lula out of the lot. "She has to talk to the police first."

"Do I look okay?" Lula asked me. "I didn't have a lot of time to fix my hair. And I didn't have my full wardrobe at my disposal."

"You look fine," I said. "The silver sequined

top and matching skirt is just right for an evening decapitation identification."

"You don't think it's too dressy?"

On everyone but Lula and Tina Turner, yes.
On Lula and Tina Turner, no. It was perfect.

"I thought there might be television here," Lula
said. "You know how television always likes a
little bling."

"Does my father know you have his cab?"

"Everyone was asleep, and I didn't want to
bother no one, so I helped myself to the cab. I
would have rather taken your mother's car, but I
couldn't find the key."

We went up the stairs and into the foyer. No
problem for me now. I was real brave once the
body was removed.

Morelli ambled over. "Thanks for coming out
to do this," he said to Lula.

"Anything to help the police," Lula said. "Are
the television cameras in here? Is that a tabloid
photographer over there?"

"No television cameras," Morelli said. "And
the photographer is the department's forensics
guy."

"Hunh," Lula said. "Let's get this over with
then. It's not like I was sitting around thinking
I'd like to go look at a dead guy with no head. I
got sensibilities, you know. The thing is, I hate
dead guys."

"It's just a fast look," Morelli said. "And then you can go home."

"After I talk to the television people."

"Yeah," Morelli said. "Whatever. Follow me. We have the body in one of the freezers downstairs."

"Say what? I'm not going downstairs to no freezer compartments. That's too creepy. How many bodies does this guy have in his freezer?"

"I don't know," Morelli said. "I didn't ask, and I didn't look. Would you rather see this body in the morgue?"

"Hell no. Only way you're getting me in a morgue is toes up."

"Can we get on with it?" Morelli said. "I've had a long day and my intestines are a mess."

"I hear you," Lula said. "I got issues, too. I think there must be something going around."

"I'll wait here," I said. "No reason for me to tag along."

"The hell," Lula said. "I'm needing moral support. I wasn't even gonna come until Morelli told me you'd do this with me."

I cut a look at Morelli. "You said that?"

"More or less."

"You're scum."

"I know," Morelli said. "Can we *please* go downstairs now?"

The funeral home had originally been a large Victorian house. It had been renovated, and rooms and garages had been added, but it still had the bones of the original structure. We followed Eli Morton down a hallway off the lobby. To our right was the kitchen. To our left was the door to the basement.

A couple years ago, the basement had been destroyed in a fire. It had all been rebuilt and was now nicely finished off and divided into rooms that opened off a center hall. Morton led us to the room farthest from the stairs.

"I have three cold-storage drawers and three freezer drawers in here," Morton said. "I almost never use the freezer drawers. They were put in by the previous owner."

The floor was white tile, and the walls were painted white. The fronts to the freezer drawers were stainless steel. Gazarra pulled a freezer drawer out, and it was filled with tubs of ice cream.

"Costco had a sale," Morton said. "Your guy is in drawer number three."

He rolled number three out, Lula gaped at the body without the head, and Lula fainted. *Crash.* Onto the white tile floor. I didn't faint because I didn't look. I walked in staring at my feet, and I never raised my eyes.

"Crap," Morelli said. "Get her out of here. Someone take her feet. I've got the top half."

Gazarra and Morelli lugged Lula into the hall and stepped back. Lula's eyes snapped open, and we all stared down at her.

"You fainted," I told her.

"Did not."

"You're on the floor."

"Well, anybody would have fainted. That was disgusting. People aren't supposed to be going around without their head," Lula said. "It's not right."

"Was that Chipotle?" Morelli asked.

"Might have been," Lula said. "Hard to tell with the frost on him, but it looked like the same clothes. I don't know where they been keeping him, but he got freezer burn."

Morelli and Gazarra helped Lula to her feet.

"Are you going to be okay?" Morelli asked her.

"I could use a drink," Lula said. "A big one."

"I have some whiskey," Morton said, leading the way up the stairs and into the kitchen.

Morton poured out a tumbler of whiskey for Lula and took a shot for himself. The rest of us settled for a rain check.

"Does that count as an ID?" I asked Morelli.

"Good enough for me."

"Where do you suppose Marco the Maniac has been keeping the body? It was frozen straight out. That means it was kept in a commercial freezer."

"There are commercial freezers all over the place."

"Still, it's not like Marco and his partner are just hanging out around the house here. They know someone well enough to let them store a dead guy in the freezer."

"There are probably dead guys in half the commercial freezers in Trenton," Morelli said.

Lula chugged the whiskey. "This is good stuff," she said. "I'm feeling much better. Maybe I need just a teensy bit more."

Morelli got the bottle off the counter and poured out more for Lula. He draped an arm across my shoulders and brought me into the hallway.

"She's going to be in no shape to talk to the reporters," he said. "You're going to have to drive her directly home."

"Gotcha."

He leaned in to me. "I could have whispered that in your ear in the kitchen, but I thought this was more romantic."

"You think this is romantic?"

"No, but it's all I've got," Morelli said. "This is the highlight of my week."

"I thought you were dating Joyce."

"If I was dating Joyce, I'd have fang marks in my neck and I'd be down a couple quarts of blood."

"Not to change the subject, but why would Marco take a chance by coming out and dropping the body off on the porch? Why not throw it in the river, or bury it, or make it into hamburger? He's a butcher, right?"

"Good question. Of course, he's known as Marco the Maniac, so this might not have been a rational act." Morelli kissed me just above the collar of my T-shirt. "Do you think we can overlook the fact that we're in a funeral home for a moment?"

"No. For one thing, Gazarra is trying to get your attention."

Gazarra was waving from the front door. "Can the ME take over?" Gazarra hollered.

"Yes," Morelli said. "I'm done with Chipotle for now."

"I'm going to get the cab," I told Morelli. "I'll bring it around to the front door, and you can hustle Lula into it."

I got the key from Lula's purse and jogged to the lot. My father's cab was white with CAB printed in red all over it. CAB was an acronym for a small company named Capitol Area Buslettes.

I got into the cab, cranked it over, and drove out of the lot. I stopped in front of the funeral home, and an elderly man got in the backseat.

"Excuse me," I said. "I'm off duty."

"Two Hundred Eldridge Road," he said. "It's one of the new high-rises down by the river."

"This is a private cab. You have to get out."

"But I called for a cab. And now here you are."

"You didn't call for *my* cab."

Morelli and Gazarra had their arms locked across Lula's back. They whisked her down the stairs and across the sidewalk without her feet touching once. They came up to the cab parked at the curb and looked inside.

"What's going on?" Morelli wanted to know.

"He thinks I'm driving a cab."

"Cupcake," Morelli said, "you *are* driving a cab."

"Yes, but . . . oh hell, just dump Lula in with him."

Morelli stuffed Lula into the backseat with the man, leaned through the driver's side window and kissed me, and waved me away.

"Who's this?" Lula asked.

"I'm Wesley," the man said. "You can call me Wesley."

"How come I'm in a cab with you?"

"I don't know," Wesley said. "This is a very strange cab company."

"Hunh," Lula said.

She slumped in her seat, put her head on Wesley's shoulder, and fell asleep. Fifteen minutes later, I dropped Wesley at 200 Eldridge Road.

"How much do I owe you?" he asked.

"I don't know," I said. "It's free."

"Thanks," he said, giving me a dollar. "Here's a tip."

I turned around and drove Lula to my parents' house. I made sure she got in the house and up the stairs, and then I drove to Rangeman. I parked the cab next to the Buick and took the elevator to the seventh floor. I looked in at Rex and said hello. Someone had given him fresh water and filled his food dish with nuts and vegetables and what looked like a tiny piece of pizza. I went to the bedroom, dropped my clothes on the floor, and crawled into bed.

I was just coming awake when a warm body slipped into bed next to me.

"What time is it?" I asked him.

"A little after seven A.M."

He threw an arm and a leg over me and nuzzled my neck.

"I have just enough energy left to make both of us happy," he said.

He kissed my shoulder and the pulse point in my neck. He got to my mouth and my cell phone rang.

"Ignore it," he said.

It kept ringing.

"I can't ignore it," I told him. "I can't concentrate."

"Babe, I'm going to be so good to you, you won't need to concentrate."

I snatched at the phone. "What?"

It was my father. "You've got the cab, and I'm supposed to pick up Melvin Miklowski at seven-thirty."

"Use Mom's car."

"I can't use her car. I have to have the cab. And anyway, she's at Mass."

"Have the company send another cab."

"There are no other cabs. Everyone has morning pickups. That's what we do. We take people to the train station. For three years, I've taken Melvin Miklowski to the train station precisely at seven-thirty, every Tuesday. He has a Tuesday meeting in New York, and he catches the train at eight A.M. He counts on me. He's a regular."

"I'm all the way across town at Rangeman."

"Then you can pick him up. He's downtown at 365 Front Street."

"Okay. Fine."

I hung up and blew out a sigh.

"That doesn't sound good," Ranger said.

"It was my dad."

"Heart attack?"

"Cab pickup."

EIGHTEEN

I got to 365 Front Street with five minutes to spare. At 7:30, Melvin exited his house and quickly walked to the cab.

"I'm Frank's daughter," I told him. "My father couldn't make it."

"Do you drive a cab for a living, too?"

"No. I'm a bounty hunter."

"Like on television."

"Yeah." It wasn't at all like on television, but it was easier to go with it. Besides, people were always disappointed when I told them what I did every day.

"Are you packin'?" Melvin asked.

"No. Are you?"

"It would be cool if you were packin'. It would make a better story."

"You could pretend," I said. "Who would know?"

"Do you at least own a gun?"

"Yeah. I have a Smith & Wesson."

"Have you ever shot anyone?"

"No." That was a fib, too, but shooting someone isn't something you brag about.

"What do I owe you?" Melvin said when I dropped him at the train station.

"I don't know," I told him. "I don't know how to work the meter. You can settle with my father next week."

I'd rushed out of Rangeman without breakfast, and now I had some choices. I could return to Rangeman, I could go to Cluck-in-a-Bucket, or I could get my mom to make pancakes. My mom won by a mile.

I drove to Hamilton and cut into the Burg. I reached my parents' house and had lots of parking choices. The Buick wasn't there. Lula's Firebird wasn't there. And I was in the cab.

Lula was at my mother's small kitchen table when I walked in. She was drinking coffee, and she looked like she was at death's door.

"That was an upsetting experience last night," she said. "Police identifications give me a headache."

"Maybe you should take more pills," Grandma said. "You gotta cook barbecue today."

"I'll be okay," Lula said. "I'm feeling better now that I've got coffee."

"Have you had breakfast?" my mom asked me.

"No."

"What would you like?"

"Pancakes!"

My mom has a special pancake bowl. It has a handle on one side and a pour spout on the other. And it makes the world's best pancakes. I helped myself to a mug of coffee and sat across from Lula while my mom whipped up the batter.

"We've got lots of things to do this morning," Lula said. "Grandma and me are taking the truck to the park to get our mobile kitchen going. Connie said she'd get the ribs. And I thought you could go to the grocery store and get all the odds and ends."

"Sure."

"I even got a special surprise coming. I had this brainstorm yesterday on making sure we got on television. Larry's delivering it to the park later this morning."

My mother brought butter and pancake syrup to the table and set out knives and forks for everyone.

"Where's Dad?" I asked my mother. "I thought he'd be waiting for me to bring his cab back."

"He took my car to get serviced. He went early, since he didn't have to pick Mr. Miklowski up."

Terrific. That meant I was stuck with the cab until I got back to Rangeman and swapped it for the Buick. And truth is, I couldn't say which of them I hated more.

My first stop was the supermarket. Not bad this early in the morning because it takes the seniors

time to get up and running. By ten, they'd start
to roll in, clogging up the lot with their handicap-
tagged cars. Being a senior citizen in Jersey is a
lot like belonging to the Mob. A certain attitude
is expected. If you don't respect a Mob member
in Jersey, you could get shot. If you don't respect
a senior, they'll ram a shopping cart into your
car, rear-end you at a light, and deliberately block
you from going down the nonprescription meds
aisle by idling in the middle of it in their motor-
ized basketed bumper cars while they pretend to
read the label on the Advil box.

I worked my way through the list Lula had
given me. A giant-size ketchup, Tabasco sauce,
molasses, cider vinegar, orange juice, a bunch of
spices, some hot sauce, M&Ms, aluminum foil,
a couple disposable baking pans, Pepto-Bismol,
nonstick spray oil.

"Looks to me like you're making barbecue,"
the lady at the checkout said to me.

"Yep."

"Did you hear about that barbecue cook? The
one who got his head cut off? It's on the news
that they found his body. It's all everyone's talking about. I heard the *Today* show is sending
Al Roker and a film crew to the cook-off in the
park today."

I loaded everything into the trunk and drove to
Tasty Pastry to get doughnuts for Larry. I parked

at the curb, ran inside, and got a dozen doughnuts. When I came out, there was a woman sitting in the backseat of the cab.

"I'm off duty," I told her.

"I'm only going a couple blocks."

"I'm late, and I still have to go to the hardware store. You have to get out."

"What kind of a cab is this that doesn't want
to make money?"

"It's an off-duty cab!"

The woman got out and slammed the door.
"I'm going to report you to the cab authority,"
she said. "And I know who you are, too. And I'm
telling your mother."

The hardware store was on Broad. I took a
shortcut through the Burg, hit Broad, went one
block, and parked in the small lot attached to the
hardware store. I ran inside and gathered together
a bag of charcoal, fire starter, and one of those
mechanical match things.

"Is this to barbecue?" the checkout kid asked.

"Yeah."

"You should get a couple bundles of the special wood we've got. You put it in the grill, and it
makes everything taste great."

"Sure," I said. "Give me a couple bundles."

He swiped my credit card, and I started to
sweat. Barbecuing was expensive. Thank goodness I had the extra job with Rangeman.

I threw everything into the trunk alongside the groceries and peeled out of the lot. I stopped for a light, and an old guy got into the backseat.

"Out!" I said. "I'm off duty."

"What?"

"Off duty."

"I'm going to the senior center on Market."

"Not in this cab you're not."

"What?"

"I'm off duty!" I yelled at him.

"I don't hear so good," he said.

"Read my lips. *Get out*."

"I got rights," he said.

The light turned, and the woman behind me gave me the finger. I stepped on the gas, raced the half mile to the senior center, and came to a screeching stop at the wheelchair ramp. I jumped out of the cab and yanked the old guy out of the backseat. I got back behind the wheel, made sure all the doors were locked, and took off. I looked in the rearview mirror and saw the old guy was standing there, waving money at me. I hooked a U-turn, drove up to him, snatched the money out of his hand, and kept going. Three dollars. Good deal. I'd put it toward my credit card.

I had everything on the list, so I pointed the cab toward Gooser Park. The sun was struggling to shine through scattered clouds, and the air was crisp. Perfect weather for a barbecue.

* * *

I turned into the park and cruised the lot, looking for a space close to the cook-off area. If the event had been held on a weekend, the lot would have been packed to overflowing by now. As it was, it was only half full. I'd been told they scheduled the event for a Tuesday to obtain better television coverage. Fine by me. I was happy not to have to battle a couple thousand people for a parking place and private time in a portable potty.

I did the best I could with the parking, loaded myself up with the groceries, and set off for our assigned space. All over the field, teams were working at marinating meat and chopping vegetables. The air smelled smoky from applewood and hickory fires, and the barbecue kitchens were colorful with striped awnings and checkered tablecloths. Except for our kitchen. Our kitchen looked like the Beverly Hillbillies were getting ready to barbecue possum.

The green awning over our area advertised Maynard's Funeral Home. The grill was rusted. The table was rickety. A handwritten sign with our team name was taped to the table. FLAMIN'. The rest of the name had been ripped off. I assume this was done by a horrified cook-off organizer. Grandma and Lula were at the ready, spatula and tongs in hand, all dressed in their white chef's jackets and puffy white chef's hats.

I dumped my stuff on the rickety table. "I'll be right back," I said. "I have to go back for the charcoal. I couldn't carry it all at once. Where's Connie?"

"She should be here any minute," Lula said. "She got a late start on account of she had to write bail for some drunken loser who pissed on the mayor's limo."

I walked back to the cab, got the rest of the stuff out of the trunk, and my cell phone rang.

"We got lucky," Ranger said. "We found a camera watching a touch pad in one of the houses you targeted. I had Hector install a video system of the area, and we can monitor it from Rangeman."

"It's going to be interesting to see who's doing this. There's a good chance it's someone you know."

"I just want the break-ins stopped. It's bad for business, and I'm tired of riding surveillance every night. I assume you're at the park?"

"Yes. I'll be here all afternoon. The cook-off ends at six tonight with the judging."

"You're driving a vehicle that isn't monitored. We don't have a blip for you on the screen."

"I'm still in my father's cab."

"Be careful." And he was gone.

I lugged the charcoal and wood and fire starter stuff across the field to Lula and Grandma. Lula filled the bottom of the grill with charcoal and piled the wood on top. She poured accelerant on and used the gizmo to light it. *WHOOOSH!* The accelerant caught, flames shot up, and the canopy caught fire. One of the guys in the kitchen next to us rushed over with a fire extinguisher and put the canopy fire out.

"Thanks," Grandma said to him. "That was quick thinking. Last time that happened, it burned up Lula's chef hat and cremated our maple tree."

"You might want to move the canopy so it's not over the grill," the guy said. "Just a suggestion."

Connie hurried to the table and set two bags on it. "I saw the flames from the parking lot," she said. "What happened?"

"The usual," Grandma said. "No biggie."

Connie, Lula, Grandma, and I each took a pole and moved the canopy back a few feet. There was a large black-rimmed, smoking hole in the top and a smaller one in the front flap where the funeral home name was written. It now said MAYNARD FUN HOME. I thought it was an improvement. God works in mysterious ways.

We all set to work mixing the sauce and getting the ribs into the marinade.

"I was talking to some people in the parking lot," Connie said. "One of them was on the barbecue committee, and they said Al Roker and his crew were going to be walking around all afternoon. They were waiting for the van to show up."

"Al Roker is a big star," Grandma said. "He might be about the most famous person we've had in Trenton."

"There was that singer last year," Lula said. "Whatshername. She was pretty famous. And Cher came through once. I didn't see her, but I heard she rode a elephant."

"We're not as fancy as some of these people," Grandma said. "I don't know if Al Roker is gonna want to film us."

"I got it covered," Lula said. "You'll see soon as Larry gets here, we'll have it locked in."

Connie looked up at the sign. "It just says Flamin'."

"One of the committee people got a stick up her butt about cussing," Grandma said. "We tried to explain Assholes wasn't being used as a cuss, that it was the part of the body effected by our sauce, but she wasn't having any of it."

"Bein' that we burned a hole in our roof, it turns out Flamin' isn't such a bad name for us, anyway," Lula said.

Weekday or not, there were a lot of people at the cook-off. Swarms of them were milling around in front of the kitchens and strolling the grounds. I could see Larry's head bobbing above the crowd as they all made their way along the path. He reached us and handed a big box to Lula.

"I can't stay," he said. "I have to work today."

"Thanks," Lula said. "This is gonna make celebrities out of us. This could get me my big break."

"I couldn't get exactly what you wanted," Larry said. "So I got you the next best thing."

Larry left, and Lula tore the box open. "I got the idea from Mister Clucky," she said. "Cluck-in-a-Bucket got Mister Clucky the dancin' chicken, and we're going to have the dancing barbecue sparerib."

No one said anything for a full thirty seconds. I mean, what was there to say? A dancing sparerib. As if the funeral home canopy and the massacred sign wasn't enough humiliation for one day.

Grandma was the first to find her voice. "Who's gonna be the sparerib?" she asked.

"I don't know," Lula said. "I didn't decide. Probably everyone wants to be. I guess I could do eenie meenie minic mo."

"There's no way in hell you're getting me in a sparerib suit," Connie said.

"Let's see what we got," Lula said, pulling the suit out of the box. "What the heck? This isn't no sparerib. This isn't even a pork chop."

"It looks like a hot dog," Grandma said. "I guess it was all Larry could get on short notice."

"This don't work," Lula said. "How can someone be the Flamin' dancing hot dog when we're cooking ribs?"

"It could be a pork hot dog," Grandma said.

"That's true," Lula said. "A pork hot dog's pretty close to a rib. It's sort of like a ground-up rib."

She held the suit up. It looked to be about six feet from top to bottom. The hot dog was in a padded bun and was enhanced with a stripe of yellow mustard.

"It's a real colorful costume," Grandma said. "I wouldn't mind wearing it, but then no one would know who I was when I was on television."

That sounded like a good deal to me. "I'll wear it," I said.

There were holes in the bottom where my legs could stick out, armholes in the sides of the bun, and part of the hot dog was made of mesh, so I could sort of see. I got the thing on, and Grandma zipped me up.

"This is disappointing," Lula said. "It's not as good as Mister Clucky."

"She's got a saggy bun," Grandma said.

Connie squished my bun. "It's foam. It needs reshaping."

Everyone worked on the bun while I stood there.

"It's hot in this thing," I said. "And I can't see through the hot dog skin. Everything's brown. And there's only a little window to look through."

"I can't hardly hear what you're saying

through all that padding," Grandma said. "But don't worry, we got you looking pretty good."

"Yeah," Lula said. "Dance around. Let's see what you got."

"What kind of dance?" I asked her.

"I don't know. Any kind of dance."

I jumped around a little and fell over.

"This is top-heavy," I said.

"It don't look top-heavy," Lula said. "It's all one size top to bottom. Imagine if we got a pork chop instead of a hot dog."

I was on my back, and all I saw was brown sky. I rolled side to side, trying to flip over. No luck. I was stuck in the stupid bun. I flopped around, flailing my arms and kicking my feet. I got some decent momentum going rocking back and forth in my bun, but in the end, it didn't get me anywhere.

Lula looked down at me. "Stop clownin' around. You're scarin' the kids. You're even creepin' out the big people. It's like someone threw away a giant twitching hot dog."

"I can't get up!"

"What?"

"*I can't fucking get up*. What part of that don't you understand?"

"Well, you should have said so instead of just layin' there thrashin' around."

Connie and Lula grabbed my arms and hauled me to my feet.

"This might not be a good idea," I told them. "This suit is unwieldy."

"You just gotta get used to it," Lula said. "I bet Al Roker will be here any minute. Anybody seen Al Roker?"

Some people stopped to look at me.

"What is it?" a man asked.

"It's a dancing hot dog," Lula said.

"It's not dancing," the man said.

There was a kid with the man. "I want to see the hot dog dance," the kid said.

I did a couple moves and fell over. "Shit!"

The kid looked up at the man. "The hot dog said *shit*."

Everyone hurried away.

"Dancing hot dogs don't say *shit*," Lula said to me, pulling me upright.

"What do they friggin' say?"

"They say *oops*."

"I'll try to remember."

"And that's a cranky tone I'm hearing," Lula said. "Hot dogs are happy food. If you was a brussels sprout, you could be cranky. Or maybe a lima bean."

"I don't feel happy. I'm sweating like a pig in this thing."

"Hey," Lula said. "You were the one who wanted to be the hot dog. Nobody *made* you be the hot dog. And you better learn how to dance before Al gets here, or you're going to miss your chance at having a national television debut."

My stomach got queasy, and I felt my skin crawl at the back of my neck. "What's out there that I can't see?" I asked. "Spiders? Snakes?"

"It's Joyce Barnhardt," Grandma said.

I turned around, and sure enough, it was Barnhardt. Her red hair was piled high on her head, her mouth was high-gloss vermilion. Her breasts were barely contained in a red leather bustier that matched skintight red leather pants and spike-heeled red leather boots.

"Who's the hot dog?" Joyce wanted to know.

"It's Stephanie," Grandma said.

"Figures. I suppose you wanted her to be the hot dog so it would have a nice straight line. Nothing worse than a hot dog with boobs, right?"

I gave Joyce the finger. "Boobs this, Joyce."

"What are you doing here?" Grandma asked Joyce. "Are you in the barbecue competition?"

"I put a couple things together," Joyce said, and she turned to face Lula. "I listen to the police bands. I know all about the Chipotle killers stalking you. And I figure those guys are here looking to put a bullet in you. Or maybe carve you up for barbecuing."

"So you're here to protect me?" Lula said.

"No, Dumbo. I'm here to capture the idiots and get the reward."

Joyce sashayed away, and we all made the sign of the cross.

"I always smell sulfur burning when she's around," Connie said.

"I want to do some walking and look at the other kitchens," Grandma said. "We got an hour before we have to start cooking the ribs."

"That's a good idea," Lula said. "We should be looking for the killers, anyway. I'm all ready for a takedown. I got my gun and my stun gun and some pepper spray. And I got body armor on under this white jacket."

NINETEEN

Connie, Lula, Grandma, and I eased into the crowd that was slowly making its way past the cook-off teams.

"Look at this group," Grandma said. "They've got one of them drums for cookin' a pig."

I couldn't see the drum. The drum was lost behind my hot dog skin. I turned to look and bumped into a kid.

"The hot dog stepped on me," the kid said.

"Sorry," I said. "Excuse me." I stepped to the side and knocked a woman over.

Connie picked the woman up. "It's her first time as a hot dog," Connie told the woman. "Cut her some slack."

Lula had me by my bun, steering me forward. "Watch out for the hot dog," she was telling people. "Make way for the hot dog."

"I think I'm getting the hang of this," I said to Lula. "I'm okay as long as I only go forward."

Lula's grip tightened on my arm. "It's him."

"Who?"

"The Chipotle killer. Marco the Maniac."

"Where?"

"Up there in front of us. The guy who's all dressed up in a cheap suit."

I squinted through the hot dog skin. I couldn't see a guy in a suit. "Does he have a cleaver?"

"No. He's got an ice-cream cone."

Lula hauled her gun out of her purse. "Hey! Marco the Maniac!" she yelled at him. "Hold it right there. I'm making a citizen's arrest."

Marco looked around, spotted Lula, and froze.

"Guess it's not so funny when he don't have his cleaver," Lula said.

A family walked between us and Marco, and Marco threw his ice-cream cone down and took off.

"He's running away," Lula said. "After him!"

After him? Was she kidding?

Lula had one side of my costume, Connie had the other, and I could feel Grandma pushing from behind.

"Wait," I said. "I can't run. I can't . . ." *CRASH*. I knocked over a prep table. "Sorry!"

Lula kept dragging me. "He's going for the parking lot," Lula said.

"I see him," Connie said. "He's getting into that silver BMW. Who's got a car here?"

"What about *your* car?" Grandma asked.

"It's way on the other side of the lot."

I wriggled my arm out of the armhole and pulled the keys to the cab out of my pants pocket. "I've got the keys to the cab."

Connie got behind the wheel, Lula sat next to her, and Grandma got into the backseat. I tried to sit next to Grandma, but I couldn't get all of me in. Everyone jumped out and ran around to my side and pushed and shoved.

"She's too fat," Grandma said. "She don't fit in the door."

"Bend the bun," Connie said. "There's too much bun."

"Stand back," Lula said. And she put her butt to me and rammed me in.

Everyone rushed back into the car, Connie rocketed out of the parking place and whipped around the lot. "I see him," she said. "He turned left out of the park."

"If you get close enough to him, I can shoot out his tires," Lula said.

"Yeah, me, too," Grandma said. "You take the right-side tires," she said to Lula, "and I'll take the left-side tires."

We were on a two-lane road that ran for almost a mile before hooking up with a four-lane highway.

"I can't catch him in this cab," Connie said

after a half mile. "I've got it floored, and we're losing him." Her eyes flicked to her side mirror. "Crap," she said. "It's a cop."

Lula and Grandma stuffed their guns back into their purses, and Connie popped the button on her shirt so she showed more cleavage. She pulled over, and the cop stopped behind her, lights flashing. We'd crossed the line, and we were in Hamilton Township. I didn't know any of the Hamilton Township police.

"Do you know why I pulled you over?" the cop asked Connie.

Connie leaned back to give him a good look at the girls. "Because you couldn't catch the guy in front of me?"

"We were trying to run down a killer," Grandma said. "And the hot dog is a personal friend of Joe Morelli."

"Morelli is the reason my bowling team lost the trophy," the cop said. "I hate Morelli."

Morelli was waiting for us when we rolled into the cook-off lot. Lula had called him and told him about Marco the Maniac, and now Morelli was leaning against his SUV, watching Connie park the cab. Lula and Connie and Grandma got out, but I was stuck.

"What are you, some superhero?" Lula asked Morelli. "How'd you get here so fast?"

"I was already here. We have some men on-site." Morelli looked into the cab. "There's a hot dog in the backseat."

"It's Stephanie," Grandma said. "She's stuck. Her bun's too big."

"Gotta cut back on the dessert," Morelli said.

"Very funny," I said to him. "Just get me out of here."

Morelli pulled me out of the cab and gave me the once-over. "What are you doing in a hot dog suit?"

"It was supposed to be a sparerib, but the costume shop was all out, so the best we could get was a hot dog."

"Yeah, that makes sense," Morelli said. "What have you got in your hand?"

"We got stopped by Officer Hardass. Connie got a speeding ticket, and I got a ticket for not wearing a seat belt. I was in the backseat. Do you have to wear a seat belt in the backseat?"

Morelli took the ticket from me and put it in his pocket. "Not if you're a hot dog."

"I hope we didn't miss Al Roker," Grandma said.

Morelli looked over at her. "Al Roker?"

"He's bringing a whole crew with him, and he's going to film the cook-off, and we're going to be on television," Grandma said.

"It's not Al Roker," Morelli said. "It's Al Rochere. He's got a cooking show on some cable channel."

"How do you know that?" Lula said. "They could both be coming."

"I have a list of media and celebrities present," Morelli said. "There's extra security for this event because of the Chipotle murder."

"Look at the time," Grandma said. "We gotta get the ribs going."

Connie, Lula, and Grandma set off power-walking across the field. I tried to follow, but I walked into a trash can and fell over.

"Oops," I said.

Morelli looked down at me. "Are you okay?"

"I can't see in this stupid suit."

Morelli picked me up. "Would you like me to get you out of this thing?"

"Yes!"

He worked at the zipper in the back and finally peeled me out of the hot dog suit. "You're soaking wet," he said.

"It was hot in the suit."

Morelli wrapped an arm around me and shuffled me off to a booth selling cook-off gear. He bought me a T-shirt, a hat, and a sweatshirt, stuffed the hot dog suit into a bag, and sent me to the ladies' room to change.

"This feels much better," I said to him when I came out. "Thanks."

"You look better, too."

"Out of Rangeman black?"

"Yeah." Morelli wrapped his arms around me.

"I miss you. Bob misses you. My grandmother misses you."

"Your grandmother hates me."

"True. She misses hating you." Morelli straightened the hat on my head. "Maybe I could learn to like peanut butter."

"You don't have to like peanut butter. Just stop yelling at me."

"That's the way my family communicates."

"Find another way to communicate. And why are we arguing all the time? We argue over everything."

"I think it's because we aren't having enough sex."

"And that's another thing. Why are you so obsessed with sex?"

"Because I don't get any?"

I tried not to laugh, but I couldn't help myself. "I guess that could do it."

I saw flames shoot into the sky and then black smoke.

"It looks like Lula fired up the grill," I said to Morelli. "I should get back to them."

We made our way through the crowd, back to the Flamin' kitchen. The guy from the kitchen next to us was standing with the fire extinguisher in his hand, shaking his head.

"Unbelievable," he said. "You moved the canopy back, and then you set your ribs on fire and torched your hat."

Lula still had the hat on her head, but the top was all black and smoking, and foam dripped off the hat onto Lula's white chef coat.

"Looks to me like the ribs are done," Grandma said, peering over the grill at the charred bones. "You think they need more sauce?"

"I think they need a decent burial," Connie said.

The rusted bottom of the grill gave way, and everything fell out onto the ground.

"Don't that beat all," Grandma said.

Morelli's cell phone buzzed. He walked away to talk, and when he returned he was smiling.

"They caught Marco," he said. "He was trying to get to the airport in Philly. He's being brought back to Trenton."

"Do we get the reward?" Lula wanted to know. "We gave information that got him captured."

"I don't know," Morelli said. "That's up to the company offering the reward."

"The barbecue sauce company," Lula said. "The one with the picture of Chipotle on the jar. Fire in the Hole sauce."

"Yep."

"What about the other moron?" Lula said. "What about the guy who was always shooting at me?"

"Marco fingered him the minute he was caught. Zito Dudley. Marco said as far as he knew, Dudley was still on the cook-off grounds."

"We gotta find Dudley before anyone else," Lula said. "Or we might have to split the reward, bein' that there were two killers and only one million dollars. We should spread out, and if you see him, shoot him."

"I wouldn't mind shooting him, but I don't know what he looks like," Grandma said.

"He looks sort of like the Maniac," Lula said. "Only shorter."

"Dudley sounds familiar," Connie said. "I just saw that name somewhere. Zito Dudley. Zito Dudley."

The fire-extinguisher guy was basting the ribs on his grill. He looked over when Connie said Zito Dudley.

"Zito Dudley is presenting the check to the winner of the cook-off," he said. "He's associated with Chipotle's barbecue sauce."

Lula's eyes went wide. "Get out. That wiener is part of Chipotle's company?"

"It's not actually Chipotle's company," the guy said. "Chipotle got money for putting his name on the jar. The company is owned by someone else." He reached behind him to his prep table, grabbed the cook-off program, and handed it to Lula. "His picture is in here. It's on the last page. He's standing with the cook-off committee."

We all looked at the picture of Dudley.

"That's him, all right," Lula said. "Nasty little bastard."

Morelli was on his phone talking to his partner, feeding him the information, asking for more men.

Something was causing a disturbance on the opposite side of the field. We all craned our necks and stood tall to see what the noise and movement was about. People were parting in front of us, and suddenly a man burst out of the crowd. He was running for all he was worth, and Joyce was chasing him in her high-heeled boots.

"It's him," Lula said. "It's Dudley!"

They got even with our booth, and Joyce launched herself into the air and tackled Zito Dudley. Lula rushed in, pulled Joyce off Dudley, and grabbed his foot.

"He's mine," Lula said.

Joyce kicked Lula in the leg and wrestled Dudley away from her. Lula put a neck lock on Joyce, and they went down to the ground, kicking and clawing and cussing, taking Dudley with them. There was a gunshot, and Joyce yelped and flopped onto the ground, blood oozing from her red leather bustier.

Morelli had his gun drawn, but Dudley was on his feet, holding a gun to Lula's head.

"Drop your gun," Dudley said.

Connie, Grandma, Morelli, the guys next to us, and several passersby all dropped their guns.

"You won't get anywhere," Morelli said to Dudley. "There are police all over this park."

"I've got a hostage. And I'd be real happy to have one more excuse to shoot her. I've been trying to shoot her all week. And I would have done it, if I wasn't saddled with Marco the Moron."

"I thought he was a Maniac," Grandma said.

"I want a helicopter brought in," Dudley said. "And I want one unarmed pilot flying it."

"That only happens in the movies," Morelli said. "Trenton can't afford helicopters. We're lucky we're not all riding bicycles."

"Get the traffic report helicopter then. Get one from the beach patrol. Get one from NASCAR. You don't get me out of here in a helicopter, and I swear I'll kill my hostage."

Morelli went back to his cell phone. "I'll make some calls," he said to Dudley. "Maybe I can come up with something. Would National Guard be okay?"

Dudley looked at Joyce on the ground, bleeding.

"Get a medevac. I know you've got one of those."

"You got it," Morelli said. "I've got two paramedics here. I want you to allow them to treat her."

"Sure. Get her out of the way."

"This is confusing," Lula said. "What happens to the reward? How am I gonna get the reward from you if you're the one I caught?"

"It's my brother-in-law's reward. He's the owner of the company. I'm just a token vice president.

He's the one who was the big Chipotle fan. Put his picture on all the sauce jars. I told him not to do it, but would he listen to me? Hell, no. Now see where that got us."

"Where'd it get you?" Grandma wanted to know.

"It got us nowhere. Chipotle refused to sign a new contract. He was screwing my brother-in-law's bimbo gold-digger wife. They were going to start their own company as soon as the divorce went through." Dudley looked over at Morelli. "Where's the helicopter?"

"It's on its way. You should hear it any minute."

"Some brother-in-law you've got," Connie said. "What did he do, go to the Chicago Mob and hire someone to whack Chipotle? And then send you along to babysit and make sure the job got done?"

"He would have been better to let me do it myself. He had this idea to get rid of Chipotle and turn it into a media frenzy. Get free publicity by chopping his head off. Chipotle never saw it coming. He was still drunk from the night before. Unfortunately, we had a witness who would have been safe, except she entered the contest."

Al Rochere ran over with his film crew and went in for an interview.

"Get him out of here," Dudley said. "I'll shoot her. Swear to God."

"Wait a minute," Lula said. "This could be my big break."

There was the unmistakable *wup wup wup* of a helicopter, and the medevac chopper flew low over us and landed in an empty area of the field.

Dudley still had the gun to Lula's head. "I'm taking her with me. I'll release her when we land."

"I don't like this," Lula said. "I don't like helicopters. I'm gonna get the runs."

"Shut up, and get walking."

"I don't feel so good," Lula said. And she farted.

Dudley stepped back and fanned the air with his gun. "Jeez, lady, what have you been eating?"

"Barbecue," Lula said. And she sucker punched him in the throat.

Dudley gagged and dropped his gun. And Morelli was on him.

"Is there still a reward?" Lula asked. "Does anybody know the ruling on that?"

A bunch of cops and security guards swarmed in, keeping the curious back. Morelli's partner cuffed Dudley and a couple uniforms moved in to help.

"My hero," I said to Morelli.

Morelli grinned. "Lula's the hero. She sucker punched him."

"And it was a pip of a fart, too," Grandma said.

I looked over at Joyce. The paramedics had her stable and ready to medevac out.

"How is she?" I asked one of them.

"Lost some blood, but I don't think anything critical was hit."

"I need to go downtown with Dudley," Morelli said to me. "Call me when you get things figured out."

I walked to our kitchen, where Grandma, Lula, and Connie were standing, staring at the blackened ribs and ashes spread across the ground.

"I don't suppose we're gonna win the contest, what with the grill falling apart and the ribs burning up," Grandma said.

"I'm tired of this whole barbecue thing, anyway," Connie said. "I could use a calzone."

"I'm in for a meatball sub," Lula said.

"And spaghetti," Grandma said. "Do you think we should stick around to see who wins the contest?"

"I don't care who wins the contest, since it's not me," Lula said.

Connie had her bag hiked up on her shoulder. "We can read about it in the paper tomorrow."

TWENTY

It was a little after six when I pulled into the Rangeman garage. Marco the Maniac and Zito Dudley were in jail. Joyce was being treated. Lula, Grandma, and Connie were at Pino's. I parked the cab next to the Buick and took the elevator to the seventh floor.

Ranger had called shortly after four o'clock and asked that I come in when the dust settled on the barbecue fiasco. I entered his apartment and found him in his office, at his computer.

"Come here," he said. "I want you to see something. This came in at four o'clock."

I looked over his shoulder at a grainy picture of a wall. A motion detector was fixed at the top of the wall, and alongside the motion detector was a small square box, the same size as the detector. A slim young man dressed in khakis and a white collared shirt came into the picture, looked around, fixed on the Rangeman camera for a moment, and left.

"Is that your break-in guy?" I asked Ranger.

"He fits the description, other than the uniform. I have Hal and Ramon watching the house, and they missed him. He drove up in a van from the client's pest control company."

"Was anyone home when he went in?"

"Mrs. Lazar, the homeowner. Her husband was still at work. She said she let someone in from pest control. We called the company, and they said he didn't belong to them. He was in and out before we could get the information to Hal and Ramon."

"So for some reason, he changed his routine. Maybe he saw Hector go into the house to install your camera."

"Or maybe he just decided it was time for a change."

"Now what?"

Ranger pushed back in his chair. "More of the same."

"I'm still driving my father's cab. Unless you have something for me to do, I'm going to run to the Starbucks on the corner, get him a couple of his favorite cookies as a thank-you, and return the cab."

"Sounds like a plan," Ranger said.

I took the elevator to the first floor and walked the half block to Starbucks. I ordered a coffee for myself and three cookies for my father. There were several people in line, buying a caffeine fix to get them through the night after a day in the office. Several people were hunkered down in the big leather armchairs, making use of the Internet connection. A guy sat alone at one of the small tables. He had a cup of coffee, and he was absorbed in a handheld electronic game. He was wearing loose-fitting jeans, a Cowboy Bebop T-shirt, and a baggy sweatshirt.

It was the guy in Ranger's surveillance video. I hadn't recognized him at first. He looked like everyone else at Starbucks. Except for the game. The game caught my attention.

I pulled my phone out of my pocket and dialed Ranger. "I think I've got him," I said. "You know how the break-in guy always took those little electronic games kids play? Well, I'm in Starbucks, and there's a guy who looks like the guy in your video, and he's sitting here playing with one of those games."

"Sit tight," Ranger said. And he disconnected.

The break-in guy stood and pocketed his game. He stretched and left the coffee shop, walking north on Myrtle Street. I left the pickup line and followed at a distance. I called Ranger and gave him the new directions. The break-in guy went into an ugly 1970s-style office building. Five floors of tinted glass and aquamarine panels interspersed with yellow brick.

I was able to see him through the revolving glass door. He crossed the small lobby and stepped into an elevator. I ran into the lobby and read through the list of tenants. Fourth floor: GOT GAME SECURITY. Bingo.

I was on the phone with Ranger again, and an instant later, three black Rangeman SUVs rolled to a stop outside the building.

I took the elevator with Ranger and Tank, Ramon and his partner took the stairs, Hal and his partner stayed in the lobby. We reached the fourth floor, and Ranger tried the door to Got Game Security. Locked. He rapped on the door. The door buzzed unlocked, and Ranger pushed the door open.

The break-in guy was at a ratty wooden desk. He looked at Ranger standing in his doorway and went pale.

"What?" he said. And then he jumped up and tried to make a run for an adjoining suite.

Ranger reached him in two strides, grabbed him by the shirt, and threw him against the wall. He hit with a *SPLAT* and slid down the wall like a sack of sand.

"Get him out of here," Ranger said to Tank.

There was nothing in the office other than the desk and a desk chair. No phone. No computer. Ranger pulled the top drawer open, and it was filled with handheld games.

The door to the adjoining suite opened, and a scrawny guy with a mop of curly red hair and freckled skin peeked out. "Oh shit!" he said. And he slammed the door shut.

Ranger opened the door, and we walked into a room crammed with all the stuff that had been stolen. The red-haired guy was pressed against the far wall, and I swear I could see his heart beating against his Final Fantasy T-shirt.

"Talk to me," Ranger said.

The red-haired guy opened his mouth and nodded his head, but no words came out. His eyes got glassy, and he slid down the wall and sat down hard on the floor. He looked to be about eighteen years old.

"Do we need medical?" Ramon asked, entering the room.

"Give him some time," Ranger said.

We stood around for a couple minutes, waiting for the kid's eyes to focus. When he looked like he had a thought in his head, Ranger pulled him to his feet.

"We wanted to be security guys," the kid said. "We wanted a job at Rangeman, but you wouldn't even talk to us. You wouldn't even take our applications. The guy at the desk said we were too young. So we figured we'd start our own security company."

"And?"

"And Toby thought it would be cool if we financed our company by robbing your accounts.

Like we could make a game out of it. Toby is all into games. He had it all figured out. He had all these rules to keep it interesting. Toby's probably the smartest guy I know."

Ranger looked around. "Why have you got all the stolen property stacked up here?"

"We didn't know what to do with it. We figured we'd fence it, but we don't know anybody who does that. So we used the money to rent these offices while we looked for a fence."

"Turn them in," Ranger said to Ramon. "Let me know if there are problems."

Ramon took the kid out of the office, and his partner followed.

"You should be happy," I said to Ranger. "You solved your mystery."

"I was almost ruined by two goofy kids. I'm embarrassed."

"Whoa," I said. "That's an emotion."

"You think I don't have emotions?"

"I don't think you very often get embarrassed."

"It takes a lot," Ranger said.

"You brought me in to snoop around. Now that you've found your bad guys, does this mean I'm being terminated?"

Ranger looked at me. "That's your decision."

"I think I'll keep the job for a while longer, but I'll move out of your bed."

"That's the safe way to go," Ranger said. "But not the most satisfying. The job will get boring."

"But not your bed?"

"Not if we're in it together."

There was no doubt in my mind.

An hour later, I was in my father's cab with Rex on the seat next to me and a small stash of Rangeman uniforms in a bag on the backseat. I was on my way to my parents' house, but I took a detour and drove past Morelli's house just for the heck of it. Lights were on in his downstairs windows, and his SUV was parked curbside. I pulled in behind the SUV, went to Morelli's door, and knocked.

Morelli grinned when he saw me. "Couldn't resist my charms?"

"Couldn't resist your television. My father's going to be watching baseball, and the Rangers are playing the Devils tonight."

"I'm all set," Morelli said. "I've got chips and dip and beer."

I ran back to the cab and got Rex's cage. Rex wouldn't want to miss the Rangers playing, and he loved chips.

I put Rex on the coffee table, and I settled in on the couch, next to Bob.

"Have you heard anything about Joyce?"

"She's going to be okay."

"And what about the guy who owns the sauce company and hired Marco to whack Chipotle?"

Morelli scooped some dip onto a chip and fed it to me. He had to reach over Bob to do it. "They're looking for him, but haven't found him so far. He's probably in Venezuela."

"That was pretty scary at the cook-off. It took a lot of guts for Lula to punch that guy."

"I'm more impressed with the fart."

"Men."

"Hey, what can I say, men like farts."

I told him about finding the break-in guy and his friend, Morelli fed me another chip, and I drank some of his beer.

"Look at us," I said to Morelli. "We aren't arguing."

"That's because the game hasn't started," Morelli said. "Maybe we shouldn't watch the game. Maybe we should do something else. Are you still off men?"

"I think I'm off and on."

Morelli grinned at me. "Which night is this? Off or on?"

I smiled back at him. "There are some things a man should find out for himself."

My Uncle Pip died and left me his lucky magic bottle. I suppose I'm lucky because he left my Grandma Mazur his false teeth. So, I've got this bottle now, and I don't exactly know what to do with it. It's not like I have a mantel. My name is Stephanie Plum, and I live in a bare-bones apartment on the outer edge of Trenton, New Jersey. I share the apartment with my hamster Rex, and he doesn't know what to do with the bottle either. The magic bottle is the size and shape of a beer bottle. The glass is red, and it looks hand-blown. It's not entirely ugly, especially if you like beer, but it's also not exotically pretty. And so far it hasn't been lucky or magical. I have the bottle sitting on my kitchen counter, between Rex's hamster cage and the brown bear cookie jar that holds my gun.

It was Monday morning, and Lula was in my apartment doing a pity pick-up because my hunk of junk car was dead, and I needed a ride to work.

"Hunh," Lula said. "What's that red bottle on your counter?"

"It's my magic bottle."

"Oh yeah, what's so magic about it? It don't look like magic to me. Looks like one of them designer beer bottles only it's got a fancy glass stopper in it."

"It's my inheritance from Uncle Pip."

"I remember Uncle Pip," Lula said. "He was older than dirt, right? Had a big carbuncle on his forehead. He was the one wandered out of the senior complex a couple weeks ago during that thunderstorm, pissed on a downed electric wire, and electrocuted himself."

"Yep. That was Uncle Pip."

I'm a bond enforcement agent, working for my cousin Vinnie, and Lula is the office file clerk, wheelman, and fashion maven. Lula likes the challenge of fitting her plus-size body into a size-8 poison-green spandex miniskirt and leopard-print top, and somehow it all comes together for Lula. Lula's skin is milk chocolate, her hair this week is fire engine red, and her attitude is pure Jersey.

I'm a couple inches taller than Lula, and where her body is overly voluptuous, mine is more 34B. My idea of fashion is a girl-cut stretchy t-shirt, jeans, and sneakers. My skin is nowhere near chocolate, my shoulder-length, naturally curly hair is plain ol' brown, my eyes are blue, and I'm still trying to find my attitude.

I hung my purse on my shoulder and pushed Lula to the door. "We need to move. Connie called ten minutes ago, and she sounded frantic."

"What's with that?" Lula said. "Last time Connie was frantic was never."

Connie Rizzoli is the bail bonds office manager. My heritage is half Italian and half Hungarian. Connie is Italian through and through. Connie is a couple years older than I am, has more hair than I do, and a consistently better manicure. Her desk is strategically placed in front of Vinnie's door, the better to slow down stiffed bookies, process servers, hookers with obviously active herpes, and a stream of perverted degenerates with quick-rich schemes hatched while under the influence of who-knows-what.

I live ten minutes from the office on a day without traffic. This wasn't one of those days, and it took Lula twenty minutes to get her red Firebird down Hamilton Avenue. Vinnie's bail bonds business is located on Hamilton, just up from the hospital, and between a dry cleaner and a used bookstore. There's a front room with large plate glass windows, an inner office where Vinnie hides, a row of file cabinets, and behind the file cabinets is storage for everything from guns and ammo to George Foreman grills held hostage until some poor burger-loving slob comes up to trial.

Lula parked at the curb, and we pushed through the door into the front room. Lula plunked herself down on the brown, fake-leather couch against the wall, and I settled into an orange plastic chair in front of Connie's desk. The door to Vinnie's office was open, but there was no Vinnie.

"What's up?" I asked Connie.

"Mickey Gritch snatched Vinnie. Last night he caught Vinnie in a compromising position, pants down on Stark Street, on the corner of Stark and 13th. And from what I've pieced together, Gritch and two of his boys dragged Vinnie at gunpoint into the back of a Cadillac Escalade and took off."

"I know that corner," Lula said. "That's Maureen Brown's corner. Maureen and me used to hang out back when I was a 'ho. She wasn't as good a 'ho as me, but she wasn't no skank 'ho either."

Lula worked Stark Street prior to her job as a file clerk. She had a rocky beginning, but she's getting herself together, and I suspect someday she'll be the governor of New Jersey.

"Anyway, I guess Vinnie had a run of bad luck at the track, and now he owes Mickey $786,000," Connie said.

"Whoa," Lula said. "That's a lot of money."

"Some of it's vig," Connie told her. "The vig might be negotiable."

Mickey Gritch has been Vinnie's bookie for as long as I can remember, and this isn't the first time Vinnie's owed money, but I couldn't ever remember him owing this much money.

"Mickey Gritch works for Bobby Sunflower now," Lula said. "You don't want to mess with Bobby."

"Is this serious?" I asked Connie.

"Times are tough, and Mickey wants his money," Connie said. "Too many people stiffing him, so they're going to make an example of Vinnie. If Vinnie doesn't come up with the money by the end of the week, they're going to kill him."

"Bobby Sunflower would do it," Lula said. "He made Jimmie Sanches disappear . . . permanently. Lots of other people too from what I hear."

"Have you gone to the police?" I asked Connie.

"The police aren't my first choice. Vinnie owes this guy for illegal gambling. Knowing Vinnie, it's possible some of the money came out of the business. We used to be owned by Vinnie's father-in-law, but last year it was sold to an insurance company. The insurance company isn't going to tolerate Vinnie's gambling with their money. If this gets out, we could all be out of a job."

"What about the father-in-law?" Lula asked. "Everyone knows he's got a lot of money. Plus he could squeeze Bobby Sunflower."

Vinnie's father-in-law is Harry the Hammer. As long as Vinnie does right by Harry's daughter Lucille, it's all good, but I suspect Harry wouldn't be happy to hear Vinnie got snatched while he was boffing a Stark Street 'ho.

"Gritch already went to Harry. Not only won't Harry fork up the money to spring Vinnie, if Vinnie gets out of this alive, Harry will bludgeon him to death," Connie said.

"Well, that settles it then," Lula said. "I guess it's *adios*, Vinnie. Personally I could use one of them breakfast sandwiches from Cluck in a Bucket. Anyone interested in a Cluck in a Bucket run?"

"If there's no Vinnie, there's no bail bonds office," Connie said. "No bail bonds office means we don't get paid. We don't get paid and there's no Cluck in a Bucket for anyone."

"That's not good," Lula said. "I'm used to a certain standard of living. Cluck in a Bucket is one of my first food choices. Not to mention I got bills. I charged a fabulous pair of Via Spigas last week. I only wore them once so I guess I could take them back, but then I don't have shoes to wear with my new red dress, and I got a date Friday worked around the dress."

"We don't have a lot of options," Connie said. "We're going to have to do this ourselves."

"I'd like to help," I said, "but I don't have that kind of money."

That was a gross understatement. I didn't have *any* kind of money. I was a month behind on my rent, my car was trash, and my boyfriend's dog ate my sneaker. Actually I use the term "boyfriend" loosely. His name is Joe Morelli, and I'm not sure how I'd categorize our relationship. Sometimes we're pretty sure it's love, and other times we suspect it's insanity. He's a Trenton plainclothes cop with a house of his own, a grandmother from hell, a lean muscled body, and brown eyes that can make my heart skip beats. We grew up together in lots of ways, and the truth is, he's probably more grown-up than I am.

"I wasn't thinking of money," Connie said. "You're a bounty hunter. You find people. All you have to do is find Vinnie and bring him in."

"Oh, no. No, no, no. Not a good idea. This is Bobby Sunflower we're talking about. He's mean! He wouldn't like it if I stole his hostage."

"Hey, girl," Lula said. "They're gonna ventilate Vinnie if you don't do something. And you know what that would amount to?"

"No Via Spigas?"

"You bet your ass."

"I wouldn't know where to begin," I said.

"You could begin with Ranger," Lula said. "He knows everything, and he's got a thing for you."

Ranger is the other man in my life, and if I described my relationship with Morelli as confused, there would be no words for my relationship with Ranger. He's former Special Forces, currently runs and partially owns a security firm, is drop-dead handsome in a dark Latino kind of way, and is sex walking. He drives expensive black cars, wears only black clothes, and he sleeps naked. I know all this first-hand. I also know prolonged Ranger exposure is dangerous. Ranger can be addicting, and it's a bad addiction for a traditionally raised woman like me, since his life plan doesn't include marriage. For that matter, considering the number of enemies Ranger's made, his life plan might not even include living.

"Do you have any suggestions other than Ranger?" I asked Lula.

"Sure. I got lots of suggestions. Mickey Gritch is easy to find. Vinnie's got him in his Rolodex. Hell, Gritch probably has a website, and a Facebook page."

"Do you know where he lives? Where he conducts business? Where he might have Vinnie stashed?"

"No. I don't know none of those things," Lula said. "Hey, wait a minute, I know one of them. I know where he does business. He does it from his car. He drives a black Mercedes. It's got purple pimp lights running around the license plate. Sometimes I see him parking in the lot next to the 7-Eleven on Marble Street. It's a good spot since it's close to the government buildings. You work all day in government, and you want to either blow your brains out or buy a lottery ticket."

"What about Bobby Sunflower?" I asked her.

"Nobody knows where he hangs. He's like the phantom. He comes and goes and disappears like he's smoke."

"I guess we could sit at 7-Eleven and watch for Gritch," I said.

"Hold on," Connie said. "Let me run him through the system. If he owns a car, I can give you a home address."

People have a television idea about bounty hunters chasing felons down back alleys and kicking in doors in the middle of the night. I've chased a few guys down back alleys, but I've never mastered the art of door kicking. Mostly real bounty hunters track people on the computer and make sneaky phone calls pretending to be conducting a survey or delivering a pizza. The age of electronic information is pretty amazing. Connie has computer programs that will help you access your next-door neighbor's third-grade report card.

"I have a couple addresses for Gritch," Connie said. "One is his home address and the other is his sister's. Her name is Jean. Looks like she's a single mom. Works at the DMV. I have six business properties for Bobby Sunflower. A pawnshop, a garage, a car wash, a residential slum on Stark, a titty bar, and a mortuary."

The translation was that Sunflower was into fencing stolen goods, chopping up stolen cars, laundering money, pimping women, and probably the mortuary had a crematorium.

"So I guess we gotta keep Vinnie from visiting Bobby Sunflower's mortuary," Lula said.

"What about all my open bonds cases?" I asked Connie. "Last week you gave me six guys who failed to appear for court. And that was on top of a stack of older files. I can't look for Vinnie and find felons at the same time."

"Sure we can," Lula said. "Probably half of those idiots you're looking for will be at Sunflower's titty bar. I say we go do some surveillance, and first thing we stop at the bakery. I changed my mind on the breakfast sandwich. I'm in a doughnut mood now."

I followed Lula out of the office, and three minutes later we were parked at the curb in front of Tasty Pastry.

"I'm only getting one doughnut," Lula said, getting out of the Firebird. "I'm on a new diet where I only have one of anything. Like I can have one pea. And I can have one piece of asparagus. And I can have one loaf of bread."

We walked into the bakery and conversation stopped while we sucked in the smell of sweet dough and powdered sugar, and we gaped at the cases of cakes and pies, cookies, cinnamon rolls, doughnuts, and cream-filled pastries.

"I don't know what I want," Lula said. "How can I choose? There's too much, and I only got one doughnut. I can't be making a mistake on this. This is critical. I could ruin the whole rest of the day if I pick the wrong doughnut."

I had my doughnuts bagged and paid for, and

Lula was still undecided, so I went outside to wait in the morning sunshine. I was debating which of the two doughnuts I'd eat first, and before I reached a decision, Morelli's green SUV rolled to a stop in front of me.

Morelli got out and walked over. His black hair was curling along his neck and over his ears, not by design but by neglect. He was wearing jeans and running shoes and a blue button-down shirt with the sleeves rolled. At six feet he was half a head taller than me, which meant if he stood close enough, he could look down my tank top.

"Are you working?" I asked him.

"Yeah. I'm riding up and down the street doing cop things." He leaned forward, hooked his finger into my scoop neckline, and looked in.

"Jeez," I said.

"It's been a while. I wanted to make sure everything was still there. If I guess what's in the bakery bag, do I get one of the doughnuts?"

"No."

"You got a Boston cream and a jelly doughnut."

I narrowed my eyes at him. "How do you know that?"

"It's what you always get."

The door to the bakery was shoved open, and Lula barreled out. "Okay," she said. "I'm ready to go rescue Vinnie." She realized Morelli was standing next to me, and she did a fast stop. "Oops."

"Rescue Vinnie?" Morelli asked.

"He's sort of missing," I told him.

Morelli took the Boston cream out of the bag and ate half. "Word on the street is that a bunch of people are very unhappy with Vinnie. Word is he owes a lot of money. Do you need help?"

"Would I have to file a police report?"

"No, but you'd have to give me the rest of the doughnut."

"Thanks for the offer, but I have some leads. I'll stumble along on my own this morning and see what turns up."

Morelli gave me the leftover half of my Boston cream and jogged back to his car.

I looked at the two bags Lula was holding. "I thought you were getting just one doughnut."

"And that's exactly what I did. I got one of everything. I'm telling you this is a beauty of a diet."

We sat at the small table in front of the bakery and ate our doughnuts while I read through the files on Mickey Gritch and Bobby Sunflower.

"We have home addresses for Gritch and his sister, but I can't see Gritch stashing Vinnie in either of those places," I said to Lula. "That leaves Bobby Sunflower's businesses. The pawn shop is on Market Street, the car wash is in Hamilton Township, and the rest are on Stark Street. Let's do drive-bys and see if anything jumps out at us."

"Might as well do the car wash first," Lula said. "If I like the looks of it, I might let them wash my Firebird."

Janet Evanovich continues her *New York Times* best-selling Barnaby series with her first graphic novel, *Troublemaker.*

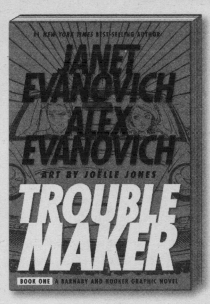

978-1-59582-488-2
$17.99
ON SALE JULY 20

Rosa is missing, and **ALEX BARNABY** and **SAM HOOKER** have only twenty-four hours to find her. Their search will take them out of the palm-tree-lined, sun-filled streets of one of the hottest cities in the world, Miami, and deep into its seedy underbelly. In order to rescue their friend, they will have to survive the Florida swamps, gift-wrapped body parts, a cult of voodoo worshipers, and their greatest challenge to date . . . Hooker's mom.

Written by **JANET** and **ALEX EVANOVICH** and illustrated by **JOËLLE JONES!**